NIGHT TRAIN TO BERLIN

By the same author:

Ages 9-12:

Celia and Granny Meg go to Paris

Celia and Granny Meg Return to Paris

Young Adult:

Chief Inspector Maigret Visits London

Max Survives Paris

NIGHT TRAIN TO BERLIN

MARGARET DE ROHAN

Copyright © 2016 Margaret de Rohan
The moral right of the author has been asserted.

Apart from any fair dealing for the purposes of research or private study, or criticism or review, as permitted under the Copyright, Designs and Patents Act 1988, this publication may only be reproduced, stored or transmitted, in any form or by any means, with the prior permission in writing of the publishers, or in the case of reprographic reproduction in accordance with the terms of licences issued by the Copyright Licensing Agency. Enquiries concerning reproduction outside those terms should be sent to the publishers.

Matador
9 Priory Business Park,
Wistow Road, Kibworth Beauchamp,
Leicestershire. LE8 0RX
Tel: (+44) 116 279 2299
Fax: (+44) 116 279 2277
Email: books@troubador.co.uk
Web: www.troubador.co.uk/matador

ISBN 978 1785892 240

British Library Cataloguing in Publication Data.
A catalogue record for this book is available from the British Library.

Printed and bound by CPI Group (UK) Ltd, Croydon, CR0 4YY
Typeset in 11pt Aldine by Troubador Publishing Ltd, Leicester, UK

Matador is an imprint of Troubador Publishing Ltd

Agnus Dei, qui tollis peccata mundi,
miserere nobis

Agnus Dei, qui tollis peccata mundi,
miserere nobis

Agnus Dei, qui tollis peccata mundi
dona nobis pacem

Amen

AUTHOR'S NOTE

I had a completely different topic in mind for my first adult book, and a different location. I'd even done some research in Wymondham, Norfolk in preparation for writing it.

But every time I discussed this with 'Nathaniel from Norfolk' his response was 'why not Berlin?' So eventually I thought *Yes, why not Berlin indeed.* And this book is the result.

I also had the first line of *Scarborough Fair* playing in my head. But how to reconcile an English folk song with Berlin? That is the question I've tried to answer in *Night Train to Berlin*. I hope my readers will find the book enjoyable, and sometimes also confronting.

Nat came with me on the Night Train in October 2014 – it was the least he could do! It was then that I saw for myself the egregious folly which is the European Union's Schengen Agreement. Having open borders between European countries was a lovely idea, but did the EU never consider *The Law of Unintended Consequences* in the quest for ever greater integration?

As one of my characters says in *Night Train* 'you could take a surface to air missile on that damn train and no one would be any the wiser.' Nor would they – until, of course, a terrorist attack happened! *But hand-wringing after the event does not restore the dead to life.*

The EU has form for ignoring *The Law of Unintended Consequences*. For example the common European currency: how could countries as different in national character and work ethic as Germany and Greece ever cope with the 'one size fits all' Euro?

And what did the German Chancellor think would happen when she issued her 'come one, come all' invitation which plunged Europe into crisis in the summer of 2015?

And, more importantly, why hasn't she already resigned?

Finally, grateful thanks to the always helpful and patient Matador/Troubador people. You know who you are and how much you have done for me. God bless.

London, December 2015.

ONE

Tuesday 7th March. Paris

The seven men sat huddled around a wooden table near the centre of the shabby room. The curtains were drawn against what remained of the day and the windows were fastened. The atmosphere in the room was heavy, airless; bordering on fetid, but none of them seemed to notice. An old-fashioned ceiling light hung low over the table: a channel of grace in a crude space.

A casual observer, chancing upon the scene, might have thought someone had died, or alternatively, that a séance was about to be held. That observer's appraisal would not have been too far off the mark; only the tense would have been wrong. The death, or rather deaths, were yet to come.

'Do you see what I see?' the thick-set man near the centre of the group said. 'Four days he was in Paris – four long days – and what did he do? He played the innocent tourist, that's what. He went here, there, and everywhere, but never once did he go near the police, or the security services. Not once.'

He picked up the pile of photographs on the table

and began to deal them out to each man as though they were playing cards.

'Now look at the photos again and this time examine each one of them carefully. Use one of the magnifying glasses if you need to – but tell me what you've finally noticed! And what you should have noticed before. Call yourselves agents do you? Hah! A boy scout would have done better than you!'

He spoke in English, but that was not his mother tongue, so he spoke with a middle-eastern overlay. He was the boss. A tough, battle-hardened man of around sixty years of age. His face was heavily tanned and lined by the sun, a long scar visible on his right cheek. None of the other men would have dared to cross him, or even contradict him. He had killed before and would not hesitate to kill again, and all of them were well aware of that fact. And, as if that were not enough, his temper was quick and sometimes ruthless.

A much younger man, perhaps in his mid-twenties and with a lighter complexion, cleared his throat nervously, and then spoke. 'He only made *real* contact with two people twice. The woman and the lad – that's right, Ammi – isn't it? Just those two: once at the Eiffel Tower and again at Napoleon's Tomb.' The boss was the brother of the younger man's mother, which permitted his use of 'Ammi', the Arabic word for uncle.

'Well done, Jamal,' his uncle said. 'Yes, just those two people – the woman and the lad, out of all the other Parisians with whom he came in touch. Now why was that do you think? Why them and why twice?'

The question hung in the air for what seemed like forever. No one wanted to be the first to speak; the first to get it wrong. Finally, Jamal, educated, precise, English faultless, cleared his throat again and said, 'They were his contacts in Paris, Ammi – isn't that right?'

'Yes, my bright boy,' the older man said, breaking into what looked suspiciously like a smile as he regarded his sister's son, 'they were his contacts. And so the next question is…'

'Where are they now?'

His uncle nodded, 'Yes indeed; where are they now? Now – all of you – get out there on the streets and find them. That's our number one priority. If we can't find *him*, surely, Allah willing, we can find *them*, and they will lead us to *him*.'

'Did he speak to the woman and the lad?' Jamal asked. 'Or did he give them anything?'

'Yes, and also no,' his uncle replied. 'At Les Invalides he spoke but we can't decipher what he said, and she replied but we can't fathom what she said either. At the Eiffel Tower he spoke only to say what, from the footage I've seen, looks like *thank you* after the woman picked up something he'd dropped.'

'Let me see, Ammi,' Jamal said.

'Okay,' his uncle scrolled back on his tablet. 'Here. See if you can work out who said what to whom and why.'

Jamal studied the film for five minutes or more, running it back and forth and sometimes freezing it. Finally, he shook his head.

'No luck?' Ibrahim asked.

'Some luck, Ammi, but I fear nothing that can really help us. I can't understand what he said at Les Invalides because he was looking straight at her, but I can – at least I *think* I can – see what she replied. But it doesn't make sense.'

'Tell me, anyway,' Ibrahim said quietly.

'She said *parsley, sage, rosemary and thyme.*'

'Some kind of shopping list for him?' his uncle asked. 'Was someone making soup?'

'Who knows? What did he drop at the Eiffel Tower?'

'A newspaper. A *Berlin* newspaper, *Die Welt,* which he arranged to land almost at the woman's feet. She looked at it for a few moments then smiled and gave it back to him. Then he thanked her and walked away without even a backwards glance. Two days later he meets her again at Les Invalides.'

'Why didn't whoever was doing the filming stop him right there and then, sir?' Yusuf, another man, asked.

'Because he was following orders as a true worker for the cause should. And those orders were to shadow him and film – that's all,' his boss, replied. 'But somewhere, in or around Les Invalides, he lost him. Then there was a commotion in the street and the police came, and now we can't find him. He's gone to ground somewhere.'

'We must find him, and stop him,' Jamal said passionately. 'If we don't we'll get the blame for whatever he's planning to do.'

His uncle frowned. 'Yes, we'll get the blame: our people *always* get the blame, one way or another.' As he spoke he suddenly looked old. Old and war-weary. *I want done with all of this,* he thought. *Let someone else take up the cause now. I feel Allah's calling me home soon. And it can't come too soon for me.*

★

'I don't want you to go, Megan,' Philippe Maigret said. 'Not you and Nat on your own. If you wait a week or so I'll go with you. I've already said I will.'

'And I've told *you* that this is Nat's half-term and Monday 13th is the only date that will work for us. And that *particular* train, on that *particular* day, is a one-off celebration of some *Deutsche Bahn* milestone and it's the only time there will be a dining car.'

'It's nothing like the Orient Express, if that's how you're imagining it,' her husband said with one of his legendary sighs.

'I know that, but it might be a scaled down version if we're lucky. And at least it will be an *adventure* for us. What could possibly go wrong? The train is non-stop. Paris to Berlin and that's it. We leave Gare de l'Est at just after eight at night and arrive at Berlin Hauptbahnhof at eight-thirty the next morning. I'll spend all that day in Berlin then fly back to Paris the next afternoon, and Nat will return to Norfolk a few days after – simple.'

Oh my love – if only you knew even a fraction of the possibilities there are for what could go wrong! The sights I've seen and the anguish I've witnessed. Yes, witnessed – and experienced too. But you can't imagine those things and I can't tell you. Not without damaging your faith and destroying your peace of mind. And I can't do that to you because I love you, Philippe Maigret thought. *Love you – and need you.*

'But still…'

'Besides, I need you to take care of the cat and…'

'And that's another thing. Why do we even have a cat? Was there any discussion about it? No – you arrived home one day with a cat and it seems it was a *fait accompli.*'

'She followed me home. She's a rescue cat, love.'

'I don't even like cats…'

'Miss Tibbs, our cat, is a rescue cat, too,' Nat said, looking up from his tablet on which he was devising a crossword puzzle. 'But she came from an animal shelter, not a park.'

'She loves you, Philippe – I can tell she does.'

'She loves whoever feeds her.'

'Stop sulking. You only have to feed her for two days, and be sure to walk her twice a day in the park. She likes the feel of the grass under her paws. And she's quite used to her little harness now; you'll have no trouble putting it on her.'

'I'm not walking her and that's final.'

'Then she'll shred our expensive sofas and curtains and I'll have to replace them when I get back.'

'Do you know how many times I've been wounded in the performance of my duty?' Philippe said to no one in particular.

Nat, his step-grandson, was very interested. 'How many times?'

'Once that I know about,' Megan said before Philippe

could answer. 'That was at Gare du Nord when you were shot in the shoulder and carelessly bled all over me.'

'*Four times,*' the chief inspector said. 'Four times, and the time I was shot at Gare du Nord was probably the least serious wound I've had. And now,' he paused for effect, 'and now I'm to be relegated to the role of cat-walker. Not even a dog... but a damn cat!'

'Careful,' Megan warned, glancing at Nat as she suspected an outburst of bad language might be imminent. 'And don't say what you're thinking.'

'What am I supposed to be thinking?'

'You're about to spout Shakespeare again, aren't you?'

'Maybe...'

'I hate to disillusion you, Chief Inspector Maigret, but although you are an exemplary police officer you are definitely not *the triple pillar of the world*, nor am I a *strumpet...*'

'What's a strumpet?' Nat asked, looking up again.

'It's a medieval form of musical instrument similar to a trumpet,' Megan said, thinking quickly.

'Oh,' Nat said, returning to his tablet, satisfied.

'It is not!'

'Well... it might be. It certainly *could* be. And what would you know about the matter anyway?'

'Only that it now appears I've arrested a good number of... *medieval instruments* during the course of my career,' he said, winking at her. 'And I must admit that I enjoyed every single moment of those er... impromptu musical performances!'

Later that night, as they were preparing for bed, Megan said, 'People can be very strange sometimes – don't you think? I mean the way they'll do odd things for no reason. Total strangers; people who might otherwise seem normal and... well, *sane*. And then out of the blue they'll do the most surprising thing.'

'Oh dear,' Philippe said, with another of his sighs as the police officer took over from the husband. 'Who said what to you today – and where? Sometimes, Madame Maigret, I could swear you have a flashing sign above your head that reads loonies and misfits apply here!'

'Loonies is not a politically correct word for a police officer to use. I'm not saying another word without my lawyer present.'

'If only that were true….'

Megan picked up the nearest pillow and threw it at him: she scored a direct hit.

'Ouch!'

'Sorry!'

'So what happened today? Tell me.'

'Okay. It was nothing *sinister*, just a little weird, that's all,' she said. 'And the man who….'

'Just the facts please, ma'am. The who, the where, and the what.'

'Okay. An attractive, fair-haired man, maybe thirty or thirty-five, at Les Invalides when I was there with Nat this afternoon.'

'And the what?'

'He said, *Are you going to Scarborough Fair?*'

'*Comment?*'

'That's what he said, Philippe. *Are you going to Scarborough Fair?*'

'And that's *all* he said?'

'Yes.'

Her husband frowned. 'That doesn't make sense. I hope you ignored him – that's what I would have done.'

'And yet you wonder why some people think the French are arrogant!'

'You're not telling me you actually replied to his nonsense?'

'Of course I replied! I said *parsley, sage, rosemary and thyme.*'

'Dear God, why would you say something like that?'

'Because it's the next line of the folk song.'

'A folk song? An *English* folk song?'

'Yes. It's a very *old* English folk song –
Are you going to Scarborough Fair
Parsley, sage, rosemary and thyme
Remember me to one who lives there
She once was a true love of mine.

And then he just walked off and we didn't see him again. Although we had actually seen him before. A day or so earlier. Nat will probably remember exactly when.'

'Where?'

'At the Eiffel Tower.'

TWO

Wednesday 8th March

Chief Inspector Maigret tossed and turned that night. The words of the folk song kept spinning around in his head together with images of the Eiffel Tower and busts of Napoleon Bonaparte. *Are you going to Scarborough Fair – that sounds like a classic way of establishing contact with someone working undercover*, he thought. *Make the approach, say the line then wait for the response. If the wrong response is given walk away: the person is not your contact after all, but no harm's been done: your cover has not been compromised.*

But Megan had made the correct response, yet the man had still walked away. He knew that because at 3am he reluctantly left his warm bed and his sleeping wife to make an Internet search on his laptop. And there he read the entire folk song in a number of different versions. *So why had the man walked away?*

The next morning, as soon as he arrived at police HQ – 36, quai des Orfévres, not far from Notre Dame, he tapped on the glass of his office to summon Inspector Georges Martin.

'Close the door, Georges,' he said. 'And pull up a pew. Want a coffee?'

'Yes, sir – thanks.'

'Now then,' his chief said, 'I'm about to say something to you and I want you to say the first thing that comes into your head as I speak. Got that?'

'Yes, Chief.'

'The very *first* thing – no questions, no preamble. Yes?'

'Yes.'

'*Are you going to Scarborough Fair?*'

'*Parsley, sage, rosemary and thyme,*' Georges Martin replied without hesitation.

His chief was astonished. 'You *know* the folk song? The *English* folk song?'

'Yes, Chief,' Georges Martin replied looking a little sheepish, 'I am, or rather *was,* a big Simon and Garfunkel fan. *Scarborough Fair* is on their *Greatest Hits* CD, although they didn't actually write the song, even if many people think they did. It's been known for hundreds of years in England, and other singers had recorded *Scarborough Fair* long before Simon and Garfunkel discovered it.'

'*Mon Dieu,*' his boss said, easing the tension in his forehead with the tips of his fingers.

'You look tired,' Georges said without thinking.

'Of course I'm tired, man! I've been awake half the night.'

'Oh.'

'Sorry, Georges; it's not your fault I didn't sleep well

last night. The blame for that can be laid at the feet of Madame Maigret, as usual.'

'Another one of her… er…adventures?'

'Looks like it.'

'What's happened now, sir? You know I'm a good and… er, *discreet* listener.'

'Yes you are, *mon ami*. So let me tell you what happened to Madame when she went on what should have been an innocent outing to Les Invalides yesterday afternoon with young Nat. This man…'

'I'd have thought she'd be safe there, sir – the place is usually *infested* by the *Gendarmerie*,' Georges interrupted.

His boss chuckled. 'Indeed, the dreaded *Gendarmerie*! However, as your senior officer, I feel obliged to remind you that they are *usually* on *our* side! Now not another word until I've finished my story.'

A few minutes later, as the chief inspector ended his tale, he leant back in his chair, massaged his aching forehead again, and asked, 'So – what do you make of all that, Georges?'

For a few moments Georges sat quite still and said nothing. Then he abruptly left the room without so much as a word to his boss, returning seconds later with a piece of paper which he passed to Chief Inspector Maigret.

'What's this?' he asked suspiciously.

'It's a report of a hit-and-run outside Les Invalides at 3.45pm yesterday. Look at the description of the victim, sir – it could be… *might* be… the same man.'

'Medium build, fair-haired male, aged between

thirty and forty,' his chief inspector said, reading from the accident report. 'Is he dead?'

'Not yet, but he's in a pretty bad way.'

'Where?'

'Intensive care at the Pitié-Salpêtrière Hospital.'

The chief inspector stood up, walked around his desk, opened the door and called, 'Jacques! Get the car, we're going to the P-S Hospital, and at top speed with heavy-duty siren please!'

Twenty minutes later the three of them – the chief inspector, Inspector Georges Martin, and Sergeant Jacques Laurent – arrived at the hospital where an immediate turf war ensued, with a great deal of shouting and waving of hands, between the over-wrought senior registrar and the under-slept Chief Inspector Maigret. Georges and Jacques stood well back and awaited the inevitable verbal explosion from their boss.

'Twenty euros says the boss will have to pull his revolver stunt again,' Georges whispered to Jacques, 'before the doctor gives in.'

'The boss wouldn't do that – not in a hospital! Is he even wearing it?'

'Don't know. Might be, could be.'

'Nah, not taking the bet, Georges; not enough info to go on. Anyway I hope to God he's not wearing it.'

'Why?'

'Because I *loaded* it a couple of days ago and he might not remember that!'

'Why'd he want it loaded? That revolver's hardly ever loaded and I'm almost certain it's never been fired.'

'He said we live in dangerous times now and that he felt it... er, *prudent* to take all precautions.'

'If that's the case I think we'd better get involved now,' Georges Martin said quickly. 'Not a good look for the boss to gun down a doctor in his own hospital!'

So they did.

'If I might suggest a small compromise, sirs,' Inspector Martin said gingerly, glancing sideways at his boss.

'What!' the registrar and the chief inspector shouted in unison.

'I thought that, perhaps, we might be permitted to examine the *clothes* that the injured man was wearing yesterday, and perhaps even take a couple of photographs of him. Without disturbing him, of course.'

'Well, yes, I see no reason why that can't be done,' the registrar said, calming down a little although his face remained the colour of a squashed plum.

'And perhaps just a question or two? Certainly no more than three,' Georges Martin said, chancing his luck.

'No, no, no – no questions! The man is in no fit state for questions! And that's the end of this discussion.'

'I give you my word, Doctor,' Philippe Maigret said. 'One question and one question only. Agreed?'

'Very well, Chief Inspector,' the doctor said after some hesitation. 'One question only and entirely against my better judgement.'

When the chief inspector saw the patient he understood the doctor's reluctance: his face was a mishmash of cuts and there was considerable swelling. *No point taking any photos,* Philippe Maigret thought, *I doubt his own mother would recognise him in this state.*

'Wait outside please, Georges and Jacques. See if you can find this poor man's clothes. I'm not sure he's even conscious.'

Maigret sat down by the side of the man's bed and took hold of his hand. Without fully knowing why he began stroking it. *The human touch,* he thought. *Maybe it will do some good.*

After a while the man's eyelids fluttered but he did not open his eyes.

'You are safe now, *mon ami*,' the chief inspector said softly in French. 'You are in a hospital and we will take good care of you. Would you like some water?'

There was a miniscule movement of the man's head. Maigret poured a small amount of water into the glass and held it to the man's lips. He clutched at it, took a couple of slurps through the straw, then slumped back again on his pillows, exhausted. Maigret removed the handkerchief from his top pocket, wrapped it around the glass, emptied the remaining water back into the jug and carefully dropped the glass into his pocket. Then he began stroking the patient's hand again. Suddenly, in a move that made him jump, the man, still with eyes closed, grabbed at his hand and whispered, 'Beware the Ides of March.'

'*Comment?*'

'Beware the Ides of March… The Ides…'

'That's enough now, Chief Inspector,' the doctor said, standing in the doorway.

'But I haven't asked him my one question yet!'

'No, but he spoke to you and that's more than enough intervention for now.'

Ignoring what the doctor had said, Philippe Maigret touched the man's hand, and once more his eyes fluttered. 'Are... you... going... to... Scarborough... Fair,' Maigret said distinctly.

An almost imperceptible movement of the man's head.

'Where is Scarborough Fair, *mon ami*?'

'Berlin.'

THREE

'Out!' The doctor ordered, as he pressed the emergency bell. 'Get out *now*, Chief Inspector – this man needs medical attention.'

'When can I see him again?'

'God knows,' the doctor replied wearily. 'I'm going to recommend that he be placed in an induced coma to relieve the pressure on his brain. Now get out and let me do my job!'

Chief Inspector Maigret made a hasty exit out of the room to find Georges and Jacques lurking further down the corridor.

'Did you find his clothes?' he asked.

'Yes, Chief, they're in a small storage room at the end of this section,' Georges Martin said.

'And? You've examined them?'

'Yes, sir – well at least we've given them a quick look. And…'

'I don't want any quick looks from members of my team,' the chief inspector said testily. 'What I asked for was a thorough examination.'

'Sir, his clothes; jeans, shirt and light jacket, are torn

and heavily bloodstained,' Jacques said, 'but we did what we could…'

'And?'

'The labels have been cut out of his clothes, his wallet had money but no ID, and there was no passport. There were no credit cards either.'

'How much money, and in what currency?'

'Euros, and a lot of them, we haven't counted it but it looks like over 1000, maybe even 2000. Oh and this,' Georges Martin said, handing a coin to his boss.

'What is it?'

'It's English; a fifty pence coin.'

'And this, sir,' Jacques said, giving his chief another coin.

Chief Inspector Maigret examined the coin carefully. 'It seems that it's a new shekel. It appears that our mystery man has been in both England and Israel recently. And now he's landed on our doorstep. And he's a very troubled man, that much I know.'

'He's a terrorist, isn't he, boss?' Georges said. 'Or a spy – everything points to something like that.'

'Hmm, maybe.' *Or something worse,* the chief inspector thought, *a mercenary, a soldier of fortune.* 'Now foot down and siren on please Jacques, we need to get back to HQ and take a good look at what we have here. Oh, and before I forget, put this in the glovebox and have the Lab see if we have anyone on file who matches the fingerprints,' he said, removing the glass from his coat pocket. 'And tell them to be quick about it. But be careful how you handle the glass; I didn't have any evidence bags on me.'

'You swiped the glass from the hospital, sir?' an impressed Jacques asked.

'I don't care for the use of the word 'swiped'. I merely... er *borrowed* it for the purpose of obtaining evidence. We will return it as soon as we're finished with it.'

As the three detectives drove back to police HQ, Georges Martin asked, 'Did you get anything out of the man, sir? I mean anything useful.'

His boss sighed. 'Yes, I did. He was agitated about something that's supposed to be happening on the Ides of March...'

'The Ides of March, sir? Do you mean the fortune-teller warning Caesar that he if he went to the Senate that day he was likely to be topped?' Inspector Martin interrupted.

His boss winced at his officer's use of foreign slang. 'I fear you've been watching too much gangster television again, *mon ami*. In France we do not "top" people,' he said.

'Well exterminate then.'

'And we don't do that, either! Nor was it a fortune-teller who warned Caesar. It was a soothsayer.'

'Which is pretty much the same thing, isn't it, boss?' Jacques said.

'I suppose so,' Philippe Maigret admitted with another sigh. 'At any event, Caesar *was* warned about the Ides of March which we know as 15th March.'

'Strange name, the Ides,' Jacques mused. 'Why didn't the Romans just say 15th March, like we do?'

'The Romans did not number days of the month from the first through to the last. Instead they counted back from three fixed points of the month,' Philippe Maigret said. 'The Nones, which were the 5th or 7th day, depending on the length of the month, the Ides, which were the 13th or the 15th, and the Kalends, the first of the *following* month. The Ides usually occurred *near* the middle of most months, but on the 15th for March, May, July and October. The Ides were supposed to be determined by the full moon because the Roman calendar was lunar based. On their earliest calendar, the Ides of March would have been the first full moon of the new year. The Ides of each month was sacred to Jupiter, the Roman's supreme deity, so the high priest would lead the Ides sheep in a procession to the place of sacrifice.'

'Sounds like a big deal, Chief, but this is all ancient history,' Georges said. 'What has it got to do with the man in the hospital?'

'Yes, *very* ancient history since Julius Caesar was assassinated on 15th March 44BC!'

'But whatever the injured man was plotting to do on the 15th is beyond him now because he'll probably still be in hospital then, or dead.' Jacques said. 'So, in a way, that's good news, isn't it?'

'Yes, or it *would* be good news if the man in the hospital was the one doing the plotting!'

'He's not?'

'No, I don't think so. I believe he's trying to *stop* whatever it is that's supposed to be happening in Berlin on the Ides.'

'Berlin?'

'Yes, that's what he said – Berlin.'

'So what's that got to do with Scarborough Fair?' Georges Martin asked.

'A good question. Do either of you actually *know* where Scarborough is?' their chief inspector asked.

'England somewhere,' Georges guessed.

'Yes. It's on the north-east coast of England, in the county of Yorkshire, to be precise.'

'So a long way from Berlin.'

'Yes, but it might interest you to know that on weekdays there are usually eight trains from Scarborough to Berlin Hauptbahnhof. Of course it can take between thirteen and eighteen hours to get there and four, sometimes even seven, changes to do it. But it can be done.'

'How do you know all that, Chief?' Jacques asked.

'I know it because I spent half the damn night searching the Internet while the rest of Paris was sleeping!'

When they arrived back at HQ, Jacques rushed straight off to the Lab to get the fingerprints on the glass examined, while the chief inspector took Georges into his office. Once they were inside, he closed the door behind them with a definite thud: the do not disturb sign had been emphatically posted!

'Now,' he said, 'leaving aside the man in the hospital, Scarborough and Berlin for a while, there's another line of enquiry that we should be following which, until now, we've overlooked. And that is…?'

'Who was the man's *real* contact at Les Invalides?'

'Precisely.'

'Unless the man is just an idiot, who makes a habit of saying ridiculous things to women,' Georges said almost to himself. 'For all we know it might even be his standard pick-up line.'

'I don't believe that,' his boss said.

'Hmm. And, by all accounts, the hit and run was quite deliberate.'

'Has the car been found?'

'Not yet; it was reported stolen the day before and the owner seems like an ordinary respectable citizen.'

'Which leads to a further question: how many *grand-mères* do you think might visit historic sites with their grandchildren during half-term?'

'Hundreds, sir. Thousands even. It's impossible to say.'

'And probably equally impossible to find the *real* contact.'

'Seems like our only lead is the man in the hospital, Chief.'

'Who is probably already in an induced coma.'

'So where do we go from here, sir?'

'I'm not sure. I suppose we'll have to hope for a match on his fingerprints, although that's a long shot too.'

Chief Inspector Maigret's phone rang.

'*Bonjour,* Philippe,' the breezy voice boomed down the line, 'how goes it on your side of the ditch this bonnie new day?' It was Chief Inspector Clive Scott of the Met Police in London.

'So-so, Clive.'

'Just so-so? Trouble in marital Paradise?'

Philippe Maigret laughed. 'You've got it in one, *mon ami,*' he said.

Georges Martin decided to make a tactical withdrawal, quietly closing the door behind him.

'What's Madame Maigret been up to now?' Clive Scott asked.

'Just the usual thing; still finding problems for me wherever she goes.'

'Ah well, I did warn you that you were taking on a force of nature before you married her…'

'Yes, you did,' Philippe said. 'And you were right – she is! But I've no regrets.'

'Pleased to hear it. Tell me what's happened.'

He did. As he finished his story, he thought *I spoke to the man in hospital in French and he answered me in excellent French. But he spoke to Megan in English. Why? How did he know to do that? Can it really be the same man? Maybe it's just a coincidence. You don't believe in coincidences,* his subconscious reminded him. *No, I don't,* he admitted. *So is it the same man, or not?*

He would not have to wait long for his answer.

'Let me put you in the picture about wives, Philippe,' Clive Scott said, interrupting his train of thought.

'Please don't. I'm probably depressed already!'

'Okay, but try not to fret. I'm with Georges Martin on this one. The guy in the hospital was probably just having a laugh. Or else he's a nutter, or even a pervert. Same sort of thing happened to my wife when we were in New York a few years ago. But that man had some kind of *foot fetish*.'

'Foot fetish, Clive?'

'Yeah. Mrs Scott decided to do some shopping uptown. Naturally, since I loathe shopping, I ducked out of that one pretty damn quick and went to the Witney instead.'

'And…?'

'She was strolling along Madison Avenue when some cushions in a shop window attracted her attention. One of the cushions had the words *Angels can fly because they take themselves lightly,* stitched on it. Not bad advice, eh? Then suddenly this young man, well dressed, behaviour and appearance quite normal, appeared next to her and said, "I like your shoes, Miss. Did you buy them in New York?" To which Mrs S replied, "No, I bought them in London". 'So of course, he immediately realised that she had an English accent. Next thing he bends down to take a closer look at the shoes. So far, so good, my wife thinks he's still innocently admiring her footwear. Then a little five foot whirlwind – in the shape of a middle-aged lady who has been watching from the other side of the window – flies out of the store screeching, "Pervert – Pervert – get away from her you pervert before I call the cops!" And with that he takes off PDQ and that's the last my wife sees of him. At which point the whirlwind calmly returns to her shop without a further word: job done, you might say, leaving my wife to wonder what the hell just happened.'

'And the moral of this story, Clive, is what exactly?'

'Well, if you want a moral, *mon ami,* I guess it would be *don't judge a book by its cover,* because when my wife went into the store to ask the whys and wherefores of everything, the shop owner told her that she'd seen this creep before and that he always began his antics by drawing attention to a woman's foot in some way. Then he'd find an excuse to touch her ankle, then her leg, gradually working his way... er... *north* towards the er...'

'Temple of heavenly delights?' volunteered a now laughing Philippe Maigret.

'Or, as I like to say, *the garden of good and evil.* But you get the picture, *mon ami.*'

'Oh yes, I definitely get the picture, Clive,' he said, dabbing at his eyes with a tissue.

'Good. And think about it; what possible connection could there be between Scarborough and Berlin? My wife's gran used to live in Scarborough; it's a perfectly nice, respectable place.'

'I'm sure it is, *mon ami.* Oh, wait a moment, I think Jacques has some news about the man's fingerprints.'

'You're not going to like the results, boss,' Jacques whispered as he passed the photograph to Maigret.

'*Merde,*' Maigret said quietly. 'Clive, the man in the hospital is one of yours.'

'One of my what? You have a trace of him on your database?'

'Oh, yes, we have a trace alright.'

'Who is he?'

'He's David Quinn.'

'Never heard of him!'

'Then I suggest you contact your MI5 or MI6, because I'm sure they'll have heard of him!'

'What?'

'In fact, I think they probably both know him!'

'He's an agent?'

'Was, maybe. Now it appears he's seen the light. What is that expression you use? Oh, yes – *poacher turned game-keeper*? Although it could be the reverse in David Quinn's case. We're sending his file to you now so you can decide for yourself after you've read what we have on him.'

'How does the *Police Nationale know* of this... David Quinn, Philippe? How'd you come by his fingerprints?'

'You don't seriously expect me to answer questions like *that* do you, Clive?' Chief Inspector Maigret said as he abruptly ended the connection.

'Georges,' he shouted, 'get on to Security at the hospital – tell them the hospital's to be totally lockeddown until further notice. No one in or out unless it's a medical emergency. And they're to put a guard on David Quinn immediately: you take charge when you get there. See if the registrar can move him to a different room. Jacques can drive: take Masson and Garnier with you and trust no one. I want a twenty-four hour guard on Quinn and make sure you're all armed. Seal off his floor: no one, not even medical staff, allowed in without their credentials thoroughly checked by one of you. Got the picture?'

'On it, sir – got the *full* picture!'

But they were very nearly too late.

FOUR

Jacques screeched the car to an abrupt stop outside the hospital and his three colleagues jumped out.

'Wait here, Jacques,' Georges Martin said, 'and keep your eyes open for anything that looks unusual. Masson – you come with me. Garnier, enforce the lockdown with the security guard at the main entrance. If anyone objects or causes trouble stay calm, but discreetly – as if by accident – let them see that you're armed. I'll give you a shout if we need you upstairs.'

Georges and Henri Masson raced into the hospital flashing their *Police Nationale* ID as they did.

'Your turn to take the stairs, Henri,' Georges said, pumping the elevator button impatiently. 'Intensive care is on the fourth floor.'

'Thanks a lot, Georges,' Masson replied, wincing at the thought.

When Georges Martin reached the fourth floor everything looked like business as usual. The corridors were bustling with nursing staff and other hospital personnel: it was obvious that the floor had not been sealed off as he had instructed while en route. Resisting the urge to fire a couple of shots into the ceiling Georges shouted, 'Armed police officer – everyone stay exactly where you are, nobody move until I say so.'

There was instant silence: all movement stopped as though someone had devised a freeze-frame moment in a movie.

'Where are the security officers for this floor?' Georges demanded.

'There… there's er… just me, *monsieur*,' a thin, balding man said nervously, holding his hand in the air but otherwise remaining perfectly still.

'Credentials? Show me!'

The man lowered his hand, and indicated the ID he wore on a chain around his neck which had been obscured by his jacket.

'Here, sir,' he said.

'Join me, *mon ami*,' Georges replied in a more friendly tone, while still inwardly fuming at the way his orders had been ignored.

'Now look here,' a white-coated man said as the security guard walked towards Georges, 'this is a hospital, not a prison, you have no right…'

'Shut up,' Georges said angrily. 'I have *every* right. This is a security matter, and this hospital is now on lockdown.'

Instant silence again.

Meanwhile, Detective Sergeant Henri Masson was still trudging his way up the four flights of stairs, cursing Georges Martin at every step. Sometimes he put on a spurt and ran up half a flight. Then he reverted to trudging again; but the cursing never stopped! As he put his hand on the handle of the door leading to the fourth floor he heard Georges shouting. He lifted his hand carefully off the handle, stood very still and listened.

'You there – skulking half-way down the corridor! Stop moving,' Georges shouted again. Silence but movement from the man in question.

'I said stop! Armed police! I'll fire if you don't stop!'

Next the sound of someone running, and the door to the stairs was flung open, nearly knocking Henri Masson off his feet.

'What the…' he exclaimed. Then the butt of the weapon hit his temple with considerable force and he fell backwards down the stairs. Although barely conscious he was aware that the man who had hit him was now standing directly above him. *He's going to finish me off,* Masson thought.

His assailant raised his arm and took aim. Masson held his breath. *This is it*, he thought, waiting for the impact. Then two shots – *Bang! Bang!* – and the man who had been poised above him was now falling on top of him with nothing more than a long, drawn-out sigh. Masson managed to push him sideways and looked up. Georges Martin was standing at the top of the stairs, his Sig Sauer SP 2022 still in his out-stretched hand.

'But you didn't warn him, Georges. You should have *warned* him, that's standard procedure,' Masson said, as delirium began to take custody of his senses.

'I warned him *twice* upstairs, you prat,' Georges growled running down the stairs. He gently lifted his colleague's head into his lap to make him more comfortable. And that was the last lucid moment Masson experienced before he finally lost consciousness.

★

'It's a pity you had to kill him, Georges,' his chief said when he heard the news. 'How's Masson doing?'

'I had no choice, sir, it was him or Masson. He was going for a head shot at close range when I fired.'

'I know, I know. But I'd have preferred him alive and there will still need to be an internal enquiry. And Masson?'

'He'll live. He's being treated for concussion and shock, but he's okay. The nurses are fussing over him like you wouldn't believe and he's milking it for all it's worth.'

'Well, half his luck – he's a good-looking chap and I'm sure the nurses are enjoying themselves too,' his boss replied. 'Any ID on the assailant?'

'No, same deal as the man he was after; no labels in his clothes, no passport and this time no money either. Nothing at all.'

'Hold the fort for a while, Georges, I'll be with you in an hour. Meanwhile, reinforcements are on their way; six of our top lads, deploy them where you think best.'

'Will do, sir. Oh, the registrar's asked if you want the hospital to do the pathology and post-mortem on the dead man?'

'No, we'll do it at HQ so we know it's been done

right. Dr Lambert is the best pathologist I've ever known; nothing gets past him. Oh, hold on Georges – or rather I'll call you when I'm on my way, my other phone's ringing.'

It was Chief Inspector Scott of the Met Police.

'They want him back, Philippe,' he said without preamble. 'Back in London, I mean. And the sooner the better.'

'I hope you're joking, Clive. Because if…'

'No joke, *mon ami*…'

'And no *chance*, my friend. This is an *entirely* French matter.'

'And I'm not the one doing the asking – you do understand that, don't you? I'm not the organ-grinder, just the poor over-worked monkey.'

'Then tell your political masters that two attempts have now been made on David Quinn's life – both in Paris – and both times French nationals have saved him.'

'Twice?'

'Yes. Twenty minutes ago Georges Martin had to despatch an armed assailant who was at the hospital, obviously looking to finally get rid of your Mr Quinn.'

'He's dead?'

'Assailant, yes. Quinn no; in an induced coma and likely to remain that way for the next couple of days.'

'Any ID or useful info on the would-be assassin?'

'Nothing obvious at first glance. We'll take his fingerprints when we have him in Pathology. And now that's all you'll get out of me, Clive,' Philippe Maigret said, preparing to end the call.

'Philippe – wait!' Clive Scott shouted down the phone.

'What?'

'I think,' he said, choosing his words with care, 'that as David Quinn is a British national... then er... in a spirit of cross-border co-operation and er... *entente cordiale* as it were...'

'Get on with it, man. I haven't got all day!'

'It would be er... *helpful* to your... *cause*... if you invited me to Paris to er *assist* in this matter.'

'What? No chance, Clive.'

'We invited you to do some policing in London...'

'Yes, but against my will and only because it suited Scotland Yard's purposes!'

'True enough, Philippe. But this time it's... *different* er *political. Very political.*'

'Are you saying *threats* have been made? Has someone pulled rank?'

'You're a clever chap, my friend,' Clive Scott said, still choosing his words cautiously. 'Always very *astute* and quick on the uptake.'

'Who? Tell me!'

'Who'd you think? Rank has been pulled in a massive way! I'd say that before long a certain person in Paris will be getting a phone call from a certain person in Whitehall. And what an interesting conversation that would be to overhear!'

'Well, two can play at that game, Clive. I'll make a quick phone call to my friend Christophe Saint-Valéry and that will be the end of this intimidation.'

'So in France the Minister for Police out-ranks the President or Prime Minister, does he? Now that's a surprise!'

'You bastard, Clive!'

'Needs must when the devil drives, *mon ami*. But I'm a capable bastard: a *German-speaking* bastard, to be precise and…'

'What? You've never mentioned that before.'

'You've never asked! But I think you might just find my German very useful before too much longer.'

'But you're English.'

'No, I'm *British*. I'm also an army brat; my father served in the BAOR…

'What?'

'The British Army on the Rhine, surely you've heard of it, Philippe.'

'Yes, of course, Britain was part of the Allied Occupation of Germany at the end of the Second World War.'

'I was born in the British Army Hospital in Hanover. Probably the first words I spoke were in German because our au pair was German. My sister and younger brother were born there too; we're all German speakers, although my sister's the best. But then she has the advantage of being married to a German; a genial professor by the name of Wilhelm, and living in Freiburg in the southwest of the country. Do you know it, Philippe? It's a famous old university town right in the middle of the Baden wine growing area. You should see their wine cellar! And it's also the warmest and sunniest place in the whole of Germany which is why we spend our summer holidays there.'

'Well, well, well – you're full of surprises this morning,' Philippe Maigret said, although the rapidly delivered information had made his head throb. 'But David Quinn spoke to my wife in English and to me in French, and very good French at that, so where's the need for a German speaker?'

'It's the language mostly spoken in Berlin! And I'll bet you that's where you and I will be heading before very much longer – certainly before 15th March.'

'You know what's happening in Berlin then?'

'Might do, but not on the phone. I'll tell you more when I'm in Paris. Now, are you willing to extend me an invitation to come, matey? And I mean a *very* nice, cordial, *official* invitation – one without *too* many impossible strings attached to it.'

'I'll call you back in precisely one hour, Clive,' Chief Inspector Maigret replied.

'Make it thirty minutes, if you don't mind, Chief Inspector Maigret.'

'Very well, thirty minutes it is.'

Then he terminated the call.

★

Meanwhile, in the sittingroom of the luxurious Avenue Foch apartment of Louise Maigret, Philippe Maigret's mother, Megan was relating the encounter with the mysterious man at Les Invalides over several cups of coffee. Rosa, Louise Maigret's young Colombian housekeeper, was agog with excitement.

'Do you want to see a photo of him?' Nat said, eager to impress the pretty girl. 'I'm fairly sure I've got a couple of him on my phone.'

'You didn't tell me that, Nat,' his granny complained.

'You didn't ask me, Megs.'

'Well of course I didn't ask you! How could I when I didn't know you'd taken any?'

'Why does Nathaniel call you Megs, instead of *grand-mère*?' Louise Maigret whispered to Megan.

'Oh that's simple, Louise. My darling grandkids ganged up on me some time ago. They said that now they're all in their teens they're much too old to call me Granny. So they chose Megs instead.'

'And you don't mind?'

'Not a bit. I'm sure there were far worse names they could have chosen.'

'Here he is!' Nat said triumphantly. 'Want a look, Rosa?'

'Hmm,' said Rosa, carefully examining the photograph. 'He's a handsome man – *non*?'

Nat shrugged. 'Maybe, I wouldn't know about that!'

'Let me see,' Megan said.

'Okay.'

'No, wait!' Rosa said, unwilling to surrender the phone because something had caught her eye. 'Who's this, Nat?'

They all gathered around the phone, trying to see what Rosa had noticed.

'What are we actually looking at?' Louise Maigret asked.

'This, Madame. See here in the background? While the handsome man is talking to the er... other Madame Maigret...'

'Madame Megan,' her employer said.

'Yes. He's talking to Madame Megan while Nat's taking the photo but there's someone else in the picture too. See the man in the background? I think he's taking a photograph of *all* of them.'

'I see him. How very strange. Strange, and a little sinister too, perhaps.'

'I'm not sure I agree, Louise. Les Invalides was full of tourists yesterday, and every one of them was taking photographs. This man is probably just an innocent tourist.'

'An *innocent tourist* who took a photo of you and Nat standing in front of the little souvenir shop. Why would he do that?'

'Well, er... when you put it that way it does seem slightly odd,' Megan conceded. 'Perhaps we need to mention it to Philippe. But first have a good look through all of your photos, Nat. See if you can find any others of the man taking the photograph.'

'I've taken hundreds since I've been in Paris – it will take ages to go through all of them.'

'I'll help you,' the obliging Rosa said. 'Come into the kitchen and I'll make us another hot chocolate while we look.'

'Okay.'

Ten minutes later they were back in the sittingroom again.

'We've found two more,' they said together.

'Show me.'

'Wait a minute,' Louise Maigret said, 'I need my magnifying glass.' She hurried out of the room and returned a few minutes later. 'Now, let me take a better look.'

She took the mobile from Megan and studied the photograph carefully.

'Good heavens,' she said, 'I think that's lovely Akram from the little *boulangerie* near the park where we walk Brodie!'

'The man who gives us a little taste of everything new that they bake, Madame?'

'Yes, Rosa. I'm sure it's Akram. See for yourself.'

Rosa took another long look using the magnifying glass.

'It's Akram,' she said.

And it was.

★

Exactly thirty minutes after their phone conversation had ended, Chief Inspector Maigret phoned Chief Inspector Scott in London.

'The First Secretary of our embassy in London will be delivering the letter to Scotland Yard very soon,' he said. 'The envelope will be addressed to you.'

'It's a good letter, Philippe? I mean a *very good* letter that ticks all the right boxes?'

'Not a single box left unticked; I dictated it myself. And now there's a small something you could do for me, Clive, but it has to be off the books. And by that I mean way, way, off the books: *outside of the actual library in fact.*'

'A little favour between you and me that no one else needs to know about?'

'Precisely.'

'What is it, *mon ami*? Chocolates from Harrods or some Scottish smoked salmon or some special marmalade, perhaps?'

'No food. Patrick Evremond: I need him in Paris before the weekend. I have an undercover job for him.'

'What, exactly?'

'I want him to follow my wife.'

FIVE

'You must be mad,' Clive Scott said. 'If your missus discovers you have a minder trailing after her she'll *kill* you!'

'No, first she will divorce me, *and then* she'll kill me just to make her displeasure quite clear!'

'Then why risk it?'

'Because, as you said in our earlier conversation, *needs must.* I have no choice. As things stand at present my wife and grandson will leave Gare de l'Est on the night train at 20.05 hours on Monday and arrive in Berlin at 08.30 hours the next morning which will be…'

'Tuesday 14th March – so where's the problem?'

'The problem is that they will spend *all* of the next day in Berlin too which will be…'

'Wednesday 15th March, or the Ides of March as the Romans knew it.'

'Exactement.'

'In that case I'd say you are currently somewhere between Gibraltar and the Inland Revenue, mate.'

'What?'

'A rock and a hard place.'

'Oh – yes, precisely. The thought of Megan, with

her talent for finding trouble wherever she goes, on the loose in Berlin on the Ides… and then the Scarborough Fair question… well… it's killing me.'

'And I haven't told you everything I know yet…'

'Tell me now, Clive.'

'Can't – this is not a secure line. You'll have to make her change her mind.'

'Don't you think I've tried that already? I have more chance of being hit by a meteor than getting my wife to change her mind about almost anything. You said it yourself; she's a force of nature.'

'Okay, I'll contact young Patrick for you.'

'Thanks, Clive. If he can help me out ask him to text his passport details to my phone, he has the number, and I'll get him on the Berlin train on Monday night no matter how many strings I have to pull to do it. But tell him he'll have to sit up in one of the couchettes they have because all the sleeping compartments have long since been taken. Ask him to book a hotel wherever he likes in Paris as long as it is not too close to our apartment; I can't risk him bumping into Megan before Monday night. And he's to do the same in Berlin. Oh, and he can stay there for three nights then fly back to London, all at my expense, of course.'

'And what's his brief, exactly?'

'Simple. He's to follow Megan and keep her out of trouble.'

'Not so simple, as we both know! And he's still only in his early twenties so really not much more than a lad. Are you sure he's up to the job?'

'He was definitely up to the job the last time he was in Paris: he's smart, resourceful, and certainly not lacking in courage. Oh, and before I forget – do you want me to arrange accommodation for you, Clive?'

'Er, no. Thanks for the offer, but I'll er… take care of that myself. I'll be fine…'

'Of course you will! How stupid of me. You'll be staying at 35 Rue du Faubourg Saint-Honoré won't you?' Philippe chuckled. 'Your masters really do want to keep you on a very short leash, don't they? I'm sure you'll find the British Embassy very comfortable.'

'You've been there?'

'Yes, once or twice they've even let me in through the front door! But let me make one thing very, very clear, Clive. *No spooks.* When David Quinn is conscious again I will extend you the courtesy of questioning him at the same time as I do. But if I see so much as one spook anywhere near the Pitié-Salpêtrière Hospital I will shoot him myself. And I'll be looking to do as much damage as I can. Do I make myself clear?'

'Positively crystal-like, mate.'

'Good.'

'So – tell me – just out of interest, Philippe. Do you know what *all* of our spooks look like then?'

'Of course not! Don't be ridiculous.'

'Oh,' Clive said, relaxing a little.

'I wouldn't know a MI5 agent if I passed him in the street. There's no need since they only operate within the UK, but the MI6 lot – well, that's an entirely different pot of *poisson*.'

'I can't tell whether you're joking or not, Chief Inspector Maigret.'

'You'll find out soon enough if you try to sneak a MI6 snooper into Paris on my watch, *mon ami.*'

★

Megan tried four times to contact Philippe Maigret that morning. Four times! And each time his phone either went straight to voicemail or was engaged. Eventually the three women, plus Nat, and Brodie, the Scottish terrier, had a long discussion to decide what to do next.

Rosa, as was her way, immediately came up with a number of enthusiastic but harebrained suggestions, most of which involved her wearing weird disguises while she staked-out the bread shop. Even Brodie rejected those outright!

Finally, against Megan's better judgement, they agreed that she, Rosa and Nat should walk Brodie to the park while Louise Maigret remained in the apartment and kept trying to contact Philippe or a senior member of his team.

It was further decided that Rosa would go into the *boulangerie* to buy a large baguette for lunch and while there would try, by means unclear, to discover whether Akram had by chance been at Les Invalides the previous day but without any mention of photography. And if he had – why?

They spent half an hour in the park, then left to undertake the mission. *Why are we even doing this,* Megan asked herself. *What do we hope to achieve?* It was a question she had asked the others in the apartment but she had been overruled. *Never undertake any significant course of action without knowing what you hope the outcome will be,* her subconscious reminded her. This was one of Philippe Maigret's favourite mantras. 'We'll know more than we know now,' Rosa had said by way of rebuttal and there was no arguing with that, so here they all were – *clueless in Paris*, Megan thought.

Nat and Megan remained on the corner of the park with Brodie which was far enough away from the *boulangerie* to avoid being seen, while Rosa went inside full of nervous excitement.

No Akram. Not so much as a glimpse of him. *What can that mean,* Rosa thought. *He's always here. He never seems to have much time off. Although I didn't see him yesterday, now that I think about it. Was he here the day before? I can't remember. Should I ask for him? Or will that make the others suspicious. What shall I do? Should I say something about Scarborough Fair – or will that give too much of the game away?* But it wasn't a game: it was deadly serious. And this was something that Rosa had only realised at the moment she crossed the threshold of the *boulangerie*.

The man behind the counter had now asked her three times if he could help without receiving an answer. He knew Rosa, he'd seen her many times before, and she had always been vivacious and talkative. But he'd never known her to be as subdued and tongue-tied as she was that day.

Finally she managed to compose herself enough to

stammer out a question as to Akram's whereabouts. She was given short shrift – 'Not here today,' was the reply. As Rosa, knees now trembling, turned away from the counter to make a hurried escape from the shop without remembering to ask for the baguette, a voice behind the screen at the rear of the counter whispered, 'What was wrong with her today?'

His colleague shook his head, 'No idea,' he said, 'and the dog wasn't with her either, nor the old lady Maigret. Why didn't you come out when she asked about you?'

'I don't know,' replied Akram. 'Something didn't *feel* right, she's never asked for me personally before.'

'You think she knows anything?'

'How could she? She's only a girl, and from Colombia! How could she know anything? Anything at all?'

But Rosa knew *plenty!*

On the walk back to the Maigret apartment Rosa refused to say a single word. This was partly because she was mulling everything over in her mind, and partly because she was embarrassed that she had so miserably failed her mission. And not only *that* but now there would be no fresh bread for their lunch, so she had failed Madame Maigret as well.

'He was there,' she said finally, after Louise Maigret had twice assured her that the absence of fresh bread was of no importance. 'I *know* he was. I could smell his aftershave.'

'That horribly strong musky cologne?'

'Yes, Madame.'

'Maybe someone else there uses it too.'

Rosa shook her head. 'No, Akram is the only one I've ever smelt it on before.'

'Hmm – *curiouser and curioser, said Alice,*' Megan commented.

'Alice?'

'I was just thinking out loud, Louise,' Megan replied. 'Did you manage to get in touch with Philippe while we were gone?'

'I'm afraid not. And I don't like it. I never do when I can't reach him or his team. It always suggests that there's something big going on and that means he's in danger.'

This was something Louise Maigret always said. At first it had worried the new Madame Maigret, but now she tended to dismiss it as something an elderly mother *would say*. However, this time she couldn't seem to dismiss it. Quite suddenly she felt uneasy. And afraid. *I'll send him a text,* she thought. *Even if he can't phone he'll usually reply to a text.*

He did, an hour later -

No time to speak, madness here. Home late don't wait up. Will try not to wake you when I come to bed. Love you.

'He's okay,' she said as she read the text. 'Thank God, Philippe's okay.'

'Amen,' replied his mother. 'But what about giving him the news about Akram, and what we've discovered?'

'I'll tell him in the morning, Louise,' Megan replied. 'I'm sure it is something that can wait until tomorrow.'

She was wrong.

SIX

Philippe Maigret spent two hours at the Pitié-Salpêtrière that afternoon. He reviewed all the security arrangements; he visited Henri Masson and checked his progress with the medical staff. Then he moved on to talk with the team of doctors and consultants who were taking care of David Quinn.

Sergeant Masson was well enough to be discharged from the hospital that very afternoon, the chief inspector was told. *Not so fast,* he thought. *Let the poor man stay in here for another night or two. In here, where he's safe. I know what it's like to feel Death's hand on my shoulder and see his face. I could tell you, if you were inclined to listen, that it is one thing to be patched up in a hospital then sent off into the world again but an entirely different question as to how one finds the means to deal with what remains. The unseen damage, the scars: the loss of confidence and the walk across the tightrope of fear. Not to mention the bouts of paranoia and the nightmares. That kind of trauma can't be shrugged off in a day or two as the unfortunate Masson will discover soon enough, if he hasn't already, God help him.*

But what of David Quinn? He had made good progress; much better than had been predicted by his medical team but then he was young, healthy and athletic, all of which had worked in his favour. The most recent tests indicated that the swelling in his brain had subsided at a dramatic rate: consequently an attempt would be made the next day to bring him out of the coma and into full consciousness again.

'When precisely?' Philippe Maigret had asked.

'Not sure yet,' was the reply. 'Depends on the results of the monitoring overnight.'

'Let me be quite clear,' the chief inspector had said in his best expert witness, courtroom voice, 'this is a matter of national security and I insist on being present when you bring him round again. I can, if necessary, get a court order for this within the next thirty minutes.'

'Relax, Chief Inspector,' the senior consultant had said. 'No probs – you'll be there; we'll give you plenty of notice before we start the procedure.'

'I'll be in the actual room, watching everything?'

'No, this is a hospital! We do procedures like this under *sterile* conditions. You will not be sterile, therefore you will not be in the room but you can be on the other side of the glass. And that's not more than a few metres away. Okay? Understood?'

Chief Inspector Maigret nodded. 'Understood,' he said, signalling to Sergeant Jacques Laurent that he was ready to be driven back to HQ. And there he had stayed for the remainder of the day, and a good part of the night, as he had told Megan he would.

Long after he had sent the rest of the squad home he worked on in his office, one of the few remaining sources of light left in the snake pit, with tie off, shirt open-necked, shoes off, head throbbing, sinews screaming, bones aching with exhaustion.

Over and over the question insinuated itself into his brain like a determined worm attacking a fertile garden patch.

Should David Quinn's reference to the Ides of March – at a time when he was semi-conscious and in considerable pain – be taken literally, or symbolically? In other words, was an actual political assassination planned for the 15th March in the Reichstag in Berlin, or something else? Something with the potential to be as politically *significant* as the assassination of Caesar in the Senate had been in 44 BC?

If it was the former, who was the potential target – the German Chancellor, currently the most powerful woman in Europe, or someone else? And if the latter, who, or what? And how could the words of a 400 year old English folk song, given a new lease of life in 1968 by a couple of American singers, possibly have anything to do with either of these options?

Then there was David Quinn himself. *A riddle wrapped in a mystery, inside an enigma,* as Churchill had said of Russia. *To which we might as well add, in the case of David Quinn, and packaged in a paradox,* thought Maigret. Thirty-three years old, born and raised in Leeds, West Yorkshire, in the valley of the River Aire, with history that can be traced back to the 5th century when the Kingdom of Elmet was covered by the forest of Loidis, the origin of the name Leeds. Present population around 758,000 souls; third-largest city in the United Kingdom;

fourth largest urban economy; largest legal centre after London; three universities. *And a mere 58.12 miles, or 93.54 kilometres from Scarborough.* Coincidence? *Not likely.* Chief Inspector Maigret did not believe in coincidences!

So: David Quinn, only son of an Israeli mother, and an English Christian father. First class PPE degree – Philosophy, Politics and Economics – from Oxford University, recruited straight from university by GCHQ Cheltenham, the British Government's listening-post in Wiltshire. Hebrew speaker, French speaker: a first-class, top-notch MI6 operator in the making if that was what someone in authority should eventually desire.

And then, somewhere along his career track, a spectacular derailment. He had left his job and disappeared from sight for almost a year. Why?

The only clue of any note was that not long before he left GCHQ, without offering a formal resignation, he had joined *Peace Now,* an organisation founded in 1978 during the Israeli-Egyptian peace talks. At a moment when these talks appeared to be on the brink of collapse a group of 348 reserve officers and soldiers from Israeli army combat units wrote an open letter to the Prime Minister of Israel calling upon the government to make sure this opportunity for peace was not lost.

Tens of thousands of Israelis sent in support for the letter and the movement was born. When Egypt and Israel signed their historic peace treaty in 1979 members of *Peace Now* and the wider Israeli public realised that public pressure and action in support of the peace process could dictate the course of history. In 1994 *Peace Now*, and its supporters, celebrated another breakthrough when Israel and Jordan signed a peace treaty normalising relations between the two countries.

Over many years *Peace Now* supported any steps promising to promote a resolution to the conflict in the Middle East, while lobbying Israeli parties to take all means to bring an end to the occupation of the Palestinian territories on the West Bank and Gaza Strip. This land which Israel has occupied, in contravention of numerous United Nations resolutions, since the Six-Day War of 1967.

A majority of Israelis and Palestinians continue to support a two-State solution to the long-running conflict between their countries, as do people of all faiths around the world. They remain convinced that it is the only way there will ever be lasting peace in this volatile region.

So – *Peace Now*, a worthy and influential organisation. *Where's the harm if a man like David Quinn should decide to join it? No harm, no harm at all,* Philippe Maigret thought. *But the real question is what had brought him to this decision? And why did he feel the need to leave GCHQ after making it? Was he a genuine innocent supporter, or had someone ordered him to join so he could spy on the group? Had he joined – or infiltrated? And if so, whose orders had he followed? That's the question. Many questions and no answers,* Maigret thought wearily.

He had shared nothing of David Quinn's history or his possible *dark history*, with Chief Inspector Scott of the Met Police in London. All he had been sent was a brief résumé with Quinn's photograph attached, which, in the

American gangster films watched by Inspector Georges Martin, is called a rap sheet. But the main file that the French State had on Quinn had been kept from Clive Scott. No need for him to know that the reason Quinn had come to their attention was firstly, the places he had been during the past year – here, there and everywhere in the Middle East – and the *company* he had kept.

Some of those people were, not to mince words, *undesirables* in the eyes of the French authorities. Terrorists, even – maybe. *But then one man's terrorist is another person's freedom fighter and history shows that yesterday's terrorist can sometimes be tomorrow's head of state: best to avoid bandying words around like terrorist too widely. And, for all I know, Clive Scott is already in possession of far more information about David Quinn and his recent activities than the French State is ever likely to discover,* Maigret thought ruefully, sighing again. *Wheels within wheels: and secrets kept from our friends and allies that our enemies almost certainly knew long ago!*

He eventually dragged his body home just before 11pm; too tired to eat the food Megan had left for him, too exhausted to think any more about the enigmatic David Quinn. *Peace activist or cunning infiltrator? Poacher turned game-keeper or game-keeper turned poacher? Which one was he?* He poured himself a glass of Cabernet Sauvignon from a bottle he found open in the kitchen, ate three Jacob's cream crackers (a staple in the Maigret apartment since Megan's arrival) without butter or cheese and crept quietly into the marital bed.

Megan stirred briefly, 'You're so cold,' she murmured, 'and I have something important to tell you.'

'Tell me in the morning, darling,' he whispered, snuggling closer to her warmth.

'Okay.'

*

Thursday 10th March.

The next morning it was Megan who carefully removed herself from the bed, determined not to disturb the sleeping Philippe. She gently lifted his mobile from his bedside table, taking it with her as she tip-toed down the hall to the kitchen. Nat was already sitting at the table, engrossed in a game he was devising on his tablet, a glass of orange juice in front of him. He looked up as she joined him, but she put her finger to her lips before he could speak and whispered something in his ear. He nodded. *Okay,* he mouthed back to her, and speedily sent the three photographs they had identified the previous day to Philippe's phone.

Some twenty minutes later, as Megan was cooking their bacon and eggs, there came a roar – Philippe's version of a long, luxurious yawn – from the direction of their bedroom. As Nat looked up in surprise, the follow-up came – the anguished cry of, 'Where's my phone, Megan?'

Looks like my Lord and Master is finally awake, she thought, calmly continuing with her cooking.

Philippe Maigret padded down to the kitchen in his bare feet, boxer shorts and t-shirt, a few moments later.

'Good morning, my loves. Where's my mobile, Megan?' he repeated.

'Eat first, talk second,' she said, placing his plate on the table. He looked down at the bacon, eggs, tomato and toast and realised that he was famished. 'And eat *slowly* – otherwise you'll get heartburn.'

Philippe ate his breakfast slowly and with relish, feeling the strength coming back into his body as he did.

'Thank you, darling,' he said when he'd eaten every last morsel and was enjoying a steaming cup of coffee, 'please may I have my phone now?'

Megan retrieved his mobile from the odds and sods drawer and handed it to him. 'Take a look at the three photographs that Nat sent you a while ago.'

'What am I looking at?' he asked as his brain attempted to reach top gear. 'Two photographs obviously taken at Les Invalides and one that looks like somewhere near the Eiffel Tower. But why?'

'The man talking to me is the one who said *Are you going to Scarborough Fair?*'

He did a double-take and looked more closely. *There's no doubt about it,* he thought. *Even with the facial injuries he has now I can tell that this man is David Quinn. And it's also him at the Eiffel Tower.*

'So,' he said carefully, not wanting to give anything away, 'that's our mystery man, is it?'

'Yes. But there's actually another mystery man in the photos and I'm surprised you haven't noticed him yet.'

'The man in the background who seems to be taking photographs of the three of you? I noticed him.'

'Yes. And lucky for you, Chief Inspector, Nat and I know who he is!'

'Who, Miss Marple?'

'Akram, who works at the *boulangerie* near the little park where your mother and Rosa walk Brodie.'

'Who? What? It can't be!'

'And yet it seems that it is. Both your mother and Rosa are quite sure about that.'

'What have you and *maman* been up to, Megan?' he asked, frowning.

So then, of course, she had to tell him everything. He was not amused. But he was grateful. Very grateful.

And also very worried.

SEVEN

Thursday 10th March

As Philippe pondered this information his phone rang. The caller ID indicated that it was Georges Martin.

'Excuse me my loves, I need to take this in the study,' he said, leaving the room.

'Good morning, sir. I've read the notes you left on my desk last night and I'm now looking at the photographs you've sent to me. I was just…'

'*Bon, bon,* and good morning to you, Georges. And yes, you need some explanation regarding the photos. Obviously you can see my wife at Les Invalides and again near the Eiffel Tower?'

'Yes, Chief.'

'The man she's talking with is…'

'David Quinn.'

'Exactly – so now we have confirmation of the Scarborough Fair connection. But have you also noticed the man in the background of all the three photos that Nat took?'

'Yes. Do we know him?'

'We don't, but apparently my mother and her housekeeper *do*. His name is Akram and he works in the *boulangerie* where they buy their bread. Where are you now?'

'Still at HQ, Chief.'

'Then who's keeping security under control at the hospital?'

'Lapotaire, boss. Is that okay with you?'

'Yes, yes. Robert Lapotaire's a good man. Careful too – sometimes I think he has eyes in the back of his head the way very little escapes his attention.'

'My thoughts exactly.'

'I want a watch put on the *boulangerie* in question, Georges. And as soon as possible. You know where it is – near the park, ten minutes or so from my mother's apartment.'

'I know it, sir; best bread in Paris.'

'Get the tech guys to enlarge the photo of Akram I sent you and make it as clear as possible. Put two men on the surveillance; one to take photographs of everyone in and out of the bakery that doesn't look like they're one of their regulars. The other one is to follow Akram when he leaves. And make sure you send a good team; if Akram makes a move we don't want to risk losing him. For all we know he could hold the key to this puzzle although I can't see what possible connection there could be between Quinn and him.'

'Apart from the politics of the Middle East perhaps, sir.'

'Yes, God help us, apart from the unholy mess that

is the politics of the Middle East and the Palestinian question.'

'Chief, I forgot why I actually phoned you this morning! It was to ask you what time you want me to drive you to Gare du Nord.'

'Damn and double damn, Georges! I'd forgotten about Clive Scott's arrival! Thanks for reminding me. But I won't go to Gare du Nord now. I need to stay in the apartment this morning: I'm expecting some important news from the hospital.'

'So no Gare du Nord at all today, sir?'

'Not for me but you should still go. Take Michel Evreux with you for back-up and Luc Nicolas too. I want all of you to carry clear plastic files with very visible photographs inside – but make sure you don't let Clive Scott or his buddies get close enough to identify them otherwise the game will be up. I want you to put on a show for the chief inspector and whoever else he might have brought with him from London.'

'Photographs? Do you mean mug shots, Chief?'

'No, no, no! *Decent-looking men*: or, at least, *half-decent looking men* who, at a distance, might possibly pass for MI6 officers.'

'You've lost me, sir.'

'I've led Clive Scott to believe that we know their MI6 agents by sight...'

'And do we?'

'Of course we don't! How could we possibly know something like that? We're good, Georges, but not *that* good!'

'So we're *scamming* Scotland Yard?'

'I prefer to think that we're keeping them *honest*, just in case anyone should be tempted to sneak one or two agents in with Clive, and the photographs are part of the illusion. Smoke and mirrors stuff.'

You wily old operator, Georges thought admiringly. *You never cease to amaze me, Philippe Maigret!*

'Did you hear what I just said, Inspector Martin?' his boss said loudly.

'Er, yes, sir – smoke and mirrors.'

'No, what I said *after that.*' Georges Martin squirmed in his seat at HQ. His boss could almost *hear* him squirming right down at the other end of the line.

'I said, that because I want you to put on a good show for Scotland Yard – a very, very good show – there's to be no creeping around in the shadows as if you are doing surveillance. Everything out in the open and as obvious to the Brits as is the difference between night and day. That's what we need! Got it? Think you can pull it off?'

'Got it, sir. And we'll certainly give it our best shot. Then we drive him to the embassy, do we?'

'No need, I'm sure the embassy will send a car and probably a couple of minders too. A few photographs of the car would be useful – no need to be shy about anyone seeing you taking photographs of the numberplate, either.'

'We're really just going to Gare du Nord as *window-dressing* are we, Chief?'

'*Exactement.* But you could also pass on a message to Chief Inspector Scott from me, if you would. Tell him that sometime this morning the medical team at Pitié-Salpêtrière Hospital will attempt to bring David Quinn out of his coma. The consultant will give me as much notice as he can before they start the procedure. Tell Clive I'll text him as soon as I've heard from the hospital. And ask Jacques to be on standby because I'll need him to drive.'

However, Clive Scott brought no one with him from London. At least not as far as Georges and his colleagues could tell. But then the Eurostar is a long train and many passengers alighted from it that morning, so Georges could not be completely sure that someone hadn't escaped their notice. Or arrived on an earlier train. Or on an earlier day. *Maybe the chief is not the only wily old fox in this policing game,* Georges thought. *But in that case, who is actually the fox, and who the rabbit?*

While he was enjoying his third cup of coffee that morning Philippe Maigret received the all-important news from Pitié-Salpêtrière Hospital.

'We will start the procedure in one hour, Chief Inspector,' the chief consultant said. 'With or without you – one hour.'

'I'll be there. Does this mean that the brain monitoring overnight was good, Doctor?'

'Not good – *excellent!* I've never seen anyone make the rapid progress that David Quinn has especially considering the condition he was in when he arrived. Frankly I expected him to die the first night.'

Philippe Maigret immediately sent a text to Clive Scott. *The balloon goes up at Pitié-Salpêtrière in 60 mins. Want us to pick you up – we'll have an outrider or two. P*

An immediate response from Chief Inspector Scott.

Not on your life! I've seen the way your lot drive! Maniacs! More like low-blasted-flying – will meet you there. C

The process of restoring David Quinn to full consciousness worked in text book fashion.

'You've got to hand it to these guys,' Clive Scott said admiringly, 'they certainly know their stuff! I don't know about you but I thought it would take a lot longer than it did.'

'Indeed, *mon ami.*'

But what took longer was the head consultant's insistence on Quinn being given at least an hour's respite before he was questioned. Both chief inspectors protested but with no success.

'On the street you're the law – in here it's me,' the consultant said. 'And what I say goes. Understood?'

When they were eventually allowed into Quinn's room there was another surprise. Chief Inspector Maigret spoke to him in French, as he'd done before, and was pleased to see that the patient not only *remembered* him, but seemed friendly and amenable to questioning. However when he introduced Chief Inspector Scott of the Met Police in London it was an entirely different matter: *instant hostility*.

'I will speak with you, Chief Inspector Maigret, but not *him*,' he said with an inclination of his head towards

Clive Scott. 'Not to him under any circumstances and not to *you* while he's in the room.'

'What did he say?' Clive Scott asked. 'Can't you get him to use English?'

'I don't believe I can, Clive, but I'll try.'

'I heard what he said, Chief Inspector Maigret,' Quinn said, 'and I think you know what my answer will be.'

'Do you know him, David?' Philippe asked. 'Seen him before?'

'No and no.'

'Then why the hostility?'

'Because he's part of the problem. Or he might be.'

'I don't understand.'

'I *know* that he's not the *solution,* ergo he must be part of the *problem*. How can the... *establishment* ever have a part in the solution – *any* solution?'

'Look you – *Quinn!* I may not understand what you're saying but you can damn well understand me! So understand this and understand it *perfectly*: you are in a lot of trouble, my friend, and you need my help.'

'You are not my *friend*, Chief Inspector Scott,' Quinn said in English. 'And I am not yours. You can't help me, nor do I seek your help.'

'This is not getting us anywhere, Clive,' Philippe Maigret said. 'I'd ask you to please leave now.'

'And if I refuse?'

'Then neither of us will get *anything* this morning – isn't that right, David?'

'Yes, not another word from me until *he* leaves the room,' he said, again in English.

At that point the senior consultant, who had been standing in the doorway observing the interview, intervened.

'Look at his blood pressure,' he said also in English, pointing to the figures on the monitor behind the bed. 'It's going through the roof now! Are you trying to *kill* this man? Is that what the two of you want?'

'Alright, alright,' Clive Scott replied grudgingly. 'I'll go.'

'Thank you,' the consultant said, 'and by the look of you I should check *your* blood pressure, Chief Inspector Scott, because you're showing classic signs of hypertension. And you could certainly afford to lose a kilo – or five.'

'Take care of your *real* patient, Doctor,' Clive Scott said curtly as he left the room.

After Clive had gone, Philippe Maigret showed Quinn the photographs that Nat had forwarded to his phone earlier that morning.

'Recognise anyone, David?' he asked, deliberately keeping his tone light.

'Oh yes – yes, of course. That's the woman I saw at Les Invalides.'

'And near the Eiffel Tower too, *mon ami.*'

'Yes, and near the Eiffel Tower too.'

'Why?' Philippe Maigret asked.

'Why what?'

'Why did you… *engage* with her at both places? Was she your contact?'

'Contact?'

62

'*Oui.*'

'Do you think I'm a *spy*, Chief Inspector Maigret? I'm not a bloody spy. I hate spies – I *loathe* spies.'

'Then what are you?'

'I'm a *concerned* citizen. A peace-worker, one might say.'

Shall I tell him who Megan is, Philippe thought. *Or is it too soon? Will it spook him if I do?*

Neither of them said anything for the next five minutes. But Philippe noticed that Quinn's blood pressure was gradually returning to normal.

'Good,' he said.

'Good?'

'Yes, your blood pressure is perfect now.' Then he took a deep breath and said, 'The woman you spoke to at both the Eiffel Tower and Les Invalides is my *wife*. Her name is Megan and the lad with her is my grandson, Nathaniel.'

'What? Is that really true, Chief Inspector?'

'Yes, I promise you that it's true, David.'

'She's Jewish?'

'No.'

'Nathaniel is a name that is popular in Jewish circles,' Quinn said.

Philippe Maigret shrugged. 'Maybe so, it's certainly an Old Testament name. You say that you are not a spy. So why did you speak to her?'

'I can't remember.'

'I think you remember very well! Because if you *can't* I'm supposed to believe that out of the two million people resident in Paris – not to mention the thousands of tourists here at this time of the year – you managed, quite randomly and without any plan or instructions – to speak to the wife of one of *Police Nationale's* chief inspectors. Now what do you suppose the odds of that might be as an accidental occurrence? Tell me. What are the chances, David?'

'Have you never heard of a coincidence, Chief Inspector?'

'Oh yes – I've *heard* of them! I just don't *believe* in them, that's my problem. And certainly not a coincidence of the magnitude that this one is supposed to be. Don't insult my intelligence, David.'

Silence from David Quinn.

'And that's why you asked her the question, *Are you going to Scarborough Fair,* isn't it?'

'Did I? Maybe.'

'Which is it, David,' Philippe asked, losing patience with him. 'Why did you speak to Megan, and why did you say what you did to her? Tell me now or I swear I'll turn you over to the damn British; so help me God, I will! And they can do with you as they wish!'

'Er… I *might* have known the time and the place for Les Invalides but that's all. She was there at that time and I'd seen her before near the Eiffel Tower so I assumed she was the person I was to meet. But obviously she was not. End of story,' he said, turning his face to the wall.

'Were you expecting a woman *and* a lad too?'

'No, just a woman. A woman standing in front of the souvenir shop reading a guide book at 3.30pm.

That's what I was told. I didn't notice the boy taking the photographs until... er... afterwards.'

'After you'd asked her the code question. But she made the correct response, didn't she? So why did you walk away?'

'I don't remember – did she?'

'Tell me about Berlin and the Ides of March.'

'I don't know what you're talking about, Chief Inspector Maigret.'

'And now you're lying to me, David! You *do* know about Berlin. You even told me that's where Scarborough Fair will happen!'

'I was obviously delirious when you questioned me before, Chief Inspector. Scarborough is in North Yorkshire. It has nothing at all to do with Berlin!'

Let's try a different tack, Maigret thought.

'Do you know this man, David?' he asked, pointing to the man in the background of all three photographs.

'No, never seen him before. Who is he?'

'If you really don't know him then there's no point in me telling you.'

'Tell me – please.'

So that got his attention, Philippe thought. *Let's try a little carrot and stick.*

'Okay, David, this is how we're going to proceed from now on. I give you some information then you return the favour. Agreed?'

'Hmm. Maybe.'

'No *maybe* about it. And if I'm not happy with your replies, I *will,* no ifs or maybes about it, abandon you to the devices of Chief Inspector Scott and his British Embassy hard boys.'

At that pivotal moment, Philippe's phone rang. It was Georges Martin. 'Sir… sir…' he stammered.

'Spit it out, Inspector Martin – what are you trying to say? And why do you sound so… er, *weird*?'

'Oh sir! It's… a… blood bath,' Georges stammered. 'I've never seen anything like it before my life. It's a total, literal, blood bath!'

EIGHT

'Where?' Chief Inspector Maigret shouted as he rushed out of Quinn's room, almost colliding with Clive Scott, who was lurking in the corridor a few metres away holding a polystyrene cup.

'Steady on, mate!' Clive warned, 'You nearly had me *wearing* my blasted coffee then.'

'In the 10th,' Georges Martin said from the other end of the line, 'roughly halfway between Gare du Nord and Gare de l'Est. I'll text you the address.'

'How many, Georges?'

'Six.'

'Survivors?'

'None. It was professional – two bullets each. One in the head, one in the heart.'

'Weapon?'

''Looks like it might have been a Baikal handgun, obviously with a silencer because no one heard anything. The would-be assassin at the hospital had the same weapon.'

'Do we know this firearm?'

'Not really, sir – although I think a few of them might have turned up recently. Very popular in England I understand: originally designed to fire teargas pellets, produced in Russia, made lethal in Lithuania, smuggled into the UK by a well-run eastern-European gang. With the silencer it can be used at close quarters, which means targets rarely escape with their lives. And it's so cheap, so reliable and so accurate that it has become the favourite kill machine for British gang culture and street crime. In fact, it's so popular that on both sides of the law it's known as the hitman kit.'

While he'd been talking to Georges, Philippe Maigret had been walking at a brisk pace towards the elevator with Clive Scott tagging along behind. 'Hold on a moment, Georges,' he said as he stabbed the down button impatiently. 'Not you, Clive,' Philippe said, his outstretched arm preventing Scott from getting any closer to the elevator, 'this is as far as you go. I've got er... a *situation* to get under control. I suggest you think about returning to the embassy.'

'Can I question Quinn without you being present?'

'Well, you can certainly *try* but I don't like your chances. He'd pretty much clammed up on me at the end: denied he'd even mentioned Scarborough Fair, Berlin, or the Ides of March. Claimed he must have been confused when I questioned him before. Why don't you come to HQ around five o'clock – I should be back by then – and I'll fill you in on what he told me. But I warn you that it wasn't much to go on.'

'Okay.'

But when Clive Scott went to Quinn's room he found that the door was now closed and the head consultant was barring his entry.

'Come back in the morning, he's asleep now, and he'll stay that way for hours,' he said. 'He complained of serious pain so we've given him a strong sedative.'

Strong sedative my ass, Clive Scott thought as he followed in Maigret's footsteps towards street level and the embassy car. *The crafty sod wanted time to create a plausible yarn to spin us later. I bet he didn't even swallow the damn painkillers! He might fool the French with that trick, but he won't put one over on me!*

When Chief Inspector Maigret reached the crime scene in the 10th *arrondissement* he saw that Georges was right. A blood bath was exactly what had occurred at this address.

The bodies of the six victims – all men – lay sprawled in various locations around the shabby room in one of the few remaining old-style boarding houses in the area. The curtains were drawn against the daylight, and the windows were closed. The atmosphere in the room was heavy with the foul-sweet stench of blood. Airless, bordering on fetid, but the men were far beyond such concerns now. An old-fashioned ceiling light hung low over the table: a glimpse of mercy in an otherwise wretched scene.

A pile of photographs had been strewn around the room. The ones remaining on the table were soiled with the blood of a man of middle-eastern appearance who was slumped across it.

He had been the boss. A tough battle-wearied man of around sixty years of age. His face was heavily tanned and lined by the sun but a scar was visible on his right cheek. All the other men had respected him. In life, none would have dared to cross him, or even contradict him. But they were all *equal* now: death – the great leveller. This man's temper had been legendary; quick and sometimes ruthless. But no one, least of all his comrades, need fear him any longer.

And no need for him, Ibrahim, to worry that his people would get the blame if the atrocity planned for Berlin on 15th March should come to pass. His prayer had been answered. Allah had called him home. It was for someone else to take up the struggle now: a war-weary warrior had departed for Valhalla. They had *all* gone to Valhalla. All, except for fair-skinned Jamal; educated, precise, English faultless, the son of his younger, favourite sister. Jamal was not there. Jamal had escaped the blood bath. Or Jamal was the killer.

'What happened here, Georges? I mean what, apart from the grim *obvious*, happened here?' Chief Inspector Maigret asked as he scanned the scene.

'I followed your orders, Chief, I set up a surveillance team near the *boulangerie*...'

'When, and who?'

'About half an hour after you asked – as soon as the tech guys had isolated and enlarged the photographs of Akram. I assigned Guy Chabois and Antoine Morel.'

'*Bon, bon*. And then?'

'Well, not long after Chabois and Morel took up their position, Akram rushed out of the shop. He was on foot but clearly panicked, and going at a fair old speed: as if the hounds of hell were after him, Morel said. He managed to keep him in sight while Chabois followed discreetly in the car for as long as he could. Then Akram ducked down the first Metro he came to, with Morel behind him, and caught the next train that arrived. He changed lines twice, finaxlly ending up at Gare du Nord. Then he walked for about ten minutes, still obviously in a hurry, with Morel following until he reached this place. He went inside; Morel waited on the street. After about five minutes, or maybe a little longer, Akram came haring out of the building, face white as a sheet, and on the point of collapse. Morel couldn't get any sense of him so he called the emergency services and did what he could until they arrived. Then he, and some uniformed lads, went inside and found – well... *this!*'

'Where's Akram now?'

'Either still on his way to Pitié-Salpêtrière – or already receiving treatment at the hospital.'

'Under guard I trust, Georges?'

'Yes, sir, under guard. Morel went with him in the ambulance.'

'Where's Chabois? What's he doing? I hope he questioned the people at the *boulangerie* after Akram left. And I also hope that it wasn't the arrival of Morel and Chabois that spooked him.'

'No, the people at the bakery hadn't noticed the surveillance. Apparently Akram took a call on his mobile after which he *literally* dropped everything and rushed out the door without a word to anyone. The bakery staff didn't have a clue what was going on! And Chabois is also on his way to the hospital now to help guard Akram.'

'*Bon, bon,* well done, Georges! Has anyone touched the bodies yet?'

'No sir, nothing's been touched, or disturbed – apart from me when I checked for signs of life. There were none, but the bodies were still warm.'

'Put your gloves on again and we'll examine the bodies together. Remove whatever identification we might be lucky enough to find, and also their phones – let's see if one of them made the call to Akram. I presume you confiscated his mobile before he went to hospital?'

Inspector Martin nodded. 'Yes, Chief, we very carefully followed standard procedure.'

All of the men had phones, none of which had been removed by the killer, which Maigret found curious, although he said nothing to Georges.

'Give me Akram's mobile, Georges,' he said, when they'd finished their examination of the bodies. Georges handed over a phone in a plastic evidence bag and Chief Inspector Maigret listened to the last call received on it. It was in Arabic as he'd expected it would be. But the tone of voice used was far beyond anxious; the sense of urgency was palpable. And one word had been repeated three times. That word was Jamal.

It had been the eldest victim, Ibrahim, who had made that final call. His mobile was still clasped in his hand. He had clung to life just long enough to do it. The final message from the battle-weary soldier. The call to warn Akram.

NINE

'So, by the look of their ID two were Palestinian, one Jordanian, and three are nationality unknown. But which one was this Jamal?'

'One of the unknowns, Chief?'

'Hmm – maybe. But, more to the point, *what* were they?'

'A terrorist cell in the making?'

'It's possible. But if so who killed them? And why? Has the post-morten on the shooter at Pitié-Salpêtrière been done yet?'

'Yes, sir, not long finished. Doc Lambert says he was a well-nourished man of about forty or fifty years, he had expensive dental work in his mouth and an appendectomy scar from an operation done about five years ago. Oh, and his fingernails had been manicured. Doc Lambert says that based on his teeth, the appearance of the appendectomy scar, and the manicure he thinks he might have been American, maybe from New York. He said no other red-blooded men he'd ever known would *dream* of having a manicure!'

'He might be right. I know I wouldn't!'

'Me neither! But I know that many young guys these days – the ones the media calls *metrosexuals*, have them regularly – and lots of other stuff as well: facials, or highlights in their hair and that kind of thing!'

'A *metrosexual*, Georges?'

'Yes, sir. In other words, a heterosexual *urban* man who enjoys shopping, fashion and similar interests once thought to be the territory of women or homosexual men.'

An infinitesimal shudder from Philippe Maigret. 'Any… er… *metrosexuals* at HQ, Georges?'

'Not a one, sir,' Georges laughed. 'They're an endangered species in our neck of the woods!'

'Thank the Lord for that!'

★

At 5pm that day, Chief Inspector Scott arrived at *Police Nationale* HQ as scheduled. He and Philippe Maigret sat alone in the latter's office with the door closed. The troops knew what that meant: do not even *think* about knocking! Each chief inspector wanted the *other* one to be the first to reveal what information he had, so in the end they tossed a coin to decide. Clive Scott lost the toss.

'*Bastard EU coin*,' he muttered, 'and you probably used a double-headed one, didn't you, my *former* friend?'

Chief Inspector Maigret chuckled. 'You know you checked the bastard EU coin before we tossed, Clive,' he said. 'Here – check it again if you think I cheated.' But, of course, Scott didn't.

'Okay, this is what we know. At least *some* of what we know: my Whitehall masters won't allow me to tell you everything, and even so I'm probably risking my pension by telling you what I'm about to.'

'Get on with it, Clive!'

'Okay. How well do you remember your European history from school days, Philippe?'

'Fragments, mainly – and some of *them* better than others.'

'But you remember the division of Germany after the end of World War Two?'

'Yes – fragments.'

'Then let me refresh your memory: the Victors – the United States, the Soviet Union, Great Britain, and France – divided the spoils between them. Don't ask me *how* they did it, but they did. The Soviet Union took control of the eastern half; the western half was divided between the United States, Great Britain and France. So far, so good, Philippe?'

Philippe Maigret nodded.

'Then the capital city of Berlin, which happened to be sitting smack-dab in the middle of the Soviet controlled eastern half, was also divided into four parts, one half being Soviet controlled, and the rest divided, as before, between the other three parties.'

'The Soviets must have had a better negotiating team,' Maigret observed, 'because they certainly got the best deal.'

'Yes, but remember that they also suffered far greater casualties in the war; something like 20 million dead, which is probably how they ended up with the lion's share of the spoils.'

'Indeed. But what does any of this have to do with Berlin on the Ides of March, Clive?'

'I'm getting to that! When Berlin was divided, you French got the north-west sector, including Tegel airport. We Brits were given the central-west sector, including Gatow airport, while the Yanks ended up with the south-west, a large part which abutted the Soviet controlled area in the east, and Templehof airport.'

'I'm losing concentration here, Clive, and possibly also the will to live,' Philippe Maigret grumbled.

'Okay, pay attention now because here's the important bit. One of the prominent people negotiating on the British side was a tall, fair-haired, good-looking Lieutenant-Colonel by the name of Giles Scarborough, who was apparently much admired by the ladies despite being happily married.'

'Ah,' said Maigret, sitting upright in his chair, 'perhaps now we're finally getting to the salient part of your story.'

'He was also a scrupulously *honest* man, well, at least as far as the intrigues of post-war Berlin permitted, so he came to be known as…'

'Scarborough fair!'

'Yes, or rather Scarborough *the* fair, but in time the *'the'* was dropped, and he was just referred to as Scarborough. And from the division of Berlin in 1945 until he eventually retired in 1960 he pretty much ran the show in the British sector. And that's how the British sector became colloquially known as Scarborough Fair.'

'Hmm – so nothing to do with Scarborough, North Yorkshire.'

'Nothing at all.'

'Which means that whatever's happening in Berlin on the the Ides will happen in the old British sector of Berlin?'

'Or, rather, *might* happen there. That's about the size of it, or that's what my political masters believe, based on an increase in what the spooks call *chatter* about Scarborough Fair picked up recently by GCHQ, Cheltenham. Although you didn't get that last part from me. Understood, Philippe? In fact this entire conversation never actually happened, did it?'

'*Oui.* Understood; it never happened. But I have to tell you, *mon ami,* that this entire scenario sounds pretty far-fetched to me: the division of Berlin stuff happened eighty years ago. Who would remember these kinds of details?'

'You'd be surprised, Philippe! Second World War buffs, intelligence agencies; spooks; history aficionados; crossword puzzle creators and their addicts; other assorted geeks and weirdos – they have this kind of information at their fingertips.'

'Hmm. I take it that you've checked for any significant events that are planned in the area for the Ides. So what are they?'

'We don't know, Philippe.'

'You must!'

'We have identified some er… possibilities, but that's the part I really *can't* tell you. Official secrets and all that kind of malarkey. And none of it makes much sense to me anyway; all the important landmarks are in other parts of Berlin, especially the old eastern sector.'

'Might be a flesh and blood target, not a monument,' Maigret said, looking grim.

'The spooks seem to have eliminated that possibility, Philippe. I can tell you that much at least.'

'Tegel airport then?'

'The Germans have that kind of target well-covered – extremely well-covered,' Clive Scott said. 'Just out of curiosity, where does your missus stay when she's in Berlin?'

'These days she prefers to stay at Myers, a small hotel in the Prenzlauer Berg district of the former East Berlin. It's an old Jewish area with great restaurants, and it's very trendy now. It's also convenient for the main tourist sites.'

'Oh.'

'Oh what, Clive.'

'I think it might be best for her to avoid the main tourist attractions on the Ides, just in case.'

'I knew it! Not all of the *possibilities* MI6 has identified are in the old British sector, are they? When are your spooks going to let the Germans in on what they know?'

'The German Government has been fully briefed; they know what we know. Or, more accurately, what we *suspect.*'

'And your other allies – like the French? When can they expect to be fully briefed?'

'Not my call, Philippe. That's a decision for someone far higher up the food chain than I'll ever be. For all I know they've been told already. Now it's your turn to tell me what you got out of Quinn.'

So he did. But he didn't mention Akram. Nor the massacre in the 10th *arrondissement*.

'And what about the shooter at the hospital? Any clues on his identity? Tattoos or other distinguishing marks?' Scott asked as Maigret finished speaking.

'No. All we've got to go on is that he'd had his appendix removed within the last five years, and that he had expensive dental work in his mouth. No trace on his fingerprints. Ever had a manicure, Clive?'

'What?'

'A manicure – surely you've heard of them.'

'Yes, I know about them, my missus has them regularly. I see the charge on our credit card statements. I *pay* for them but that's as far as I go!'

'Well, our shooter had his nails manicured, so we think there's a chance he was American.'

'And the weapon?'

'A Baikal handgun. Georges Martin tells me you know all about them in England.'

'Yes unfortunately we do. They've spread like wildfire. The Russian–Lithuanian killing machine: unfortunately we know them all too well on our patch!'

'There's just one more piece of information I can give you, Clive,' Maigret said, turning over the three photographs that had been laying face-down on his desk throughout their conversation. 'Take a look at these photos of my wife and grandson, and tell me if you recognise anyone else.'

Clive Scott studied the photos. 'Well, obviously Quinn's in every one, interacting with your wife.'

'Yes. And the man in the background? Do you know him?'

'Got a magnifying glass handy, Philippe?'

Maigret opened the top drawer of his desk, retrieved the object in question, and handed it to Clive Scott. He studied each photograph carefully for a few minutes, and then nodded, looking pleased with himself.

'Yep – I thought I knew that guy,' he said with a grin. 'He's been off our radar for a long time but I'd know that face anywhere.'

'Who is he?'

'The former third in command of the security service of the Hashemite Kingdom of Jordan, Akram Momani.'

'What! He can't be! My mother buys her bread from him.'

'Well, old Akram always was a *talented* man,' Clive Scott chuckled. 'Didn't know he'd turned his hand to baking though; that's certainly a turn up for the books!'

'How do you know him?'

'Well some time back – like ten years or so – we er... Akram and I, er... *liaised* on a... er... *delicate* matter connected with middle-eastern politics. And that's all I'm prepared to say on the subject.'

'You must be mistaken, Clive. A man with his background wouldn't be working in a Parisian *boulangerie*.'

'I don't see why not. How long has he been there?'

'Don't know. I could ask my mother, but better still, let's ask Akram. Fancy a car ride?'

'Yes. But are you sure the *boulangerie* will still be open?'

'Not there, Clive; the Pitié-Salpêtrière Hospital.'

'Akram's working there, too?'

'No, he's a patient. He was admitted this afternoon.'

'I don't understand.'

'You will, after I've told you about the murders in the 10th *arrondissement* this afternoon.'

'Good God. Was there an attempt on Akram Momani's life?'

'No, he wasn't there when the murders happened, but he obviously knew the victims: he's being treated for severe shock. Let's see if he's well enough to be interviewed.'

'You'll let me sit in while you question him?'

'No, I want *you* to do the questioning on my behalf. I won't even be in the room. If the two of you know each other, he's much more likely to open up to you than me. Find out why he was following David Quinn; it was obvious to me that Quinn recognised him but he denied that he did.'

'Well, well, well, perhaps this day is not going to be a complete waste of time after all,' Clive Scott said approvingly.

Nor would it.

TEN

As Akram *was* well enough to be interviewed Clive Scott went straight to see him. He was propped up in bed, still pale but otherwise unscathed. When Clive entered the room he blinked a few times as though he couldn't believe what his eyes were telling him then held out his hand. 'Clive, my friend,' he said, 'is that really you?'

'Yes, it's me, Akram old lad – pleased to see you after all this time, but sorry that it has to be in a hospital,' Clive boomed, giving him a quick hug. Then, following Jordanian custom, Akram kissed him on each cheek.

'That's enough of that, matey, don't want people to think we're a couple of...'

Akram laughed. 'You haven't changed a bit, Clive,' he said. 'You've put on a few pounds, but otherwise you're exactly as I remember you: never in much danger of being politically correct, were you?'

'And too old to change now!'

'Yes, me too. But what are you doing in Paris of all places?'

'Er... just a bit of police business, Akram – liaison work mostly, and that's why I've come to see you. I heard you found yourself in a spot of bother this afternoon. Nasty business from what I've been told, which isn't much. I'd like to help if I can. Feel like filling in some of the blanks for me?'

'You want to interview me, Clive?' Akram asked, suddenly wary.

'No, no – not at all. We're just two old mates having a conversation, aren't we? Nothing heavy, nothing like that.'

'Are you sure, Clive?'

'I'm sure. And remember, this is France, and I have no authority here.'

Akram hesitated while Clive bided his time, saying nothing but remaining relaxed. After five minutes Akram took several deep breaths and said, 'Late this morning I received a call on my mobile. It was from a friend. He seemed...' Akram's voice broke and he was unable to continue. Clive Scott poured him a glass of water, and he drank it slowly, trying to regain his composure. Eventually he took up his story again. 'He... he... *Ibrahim* said that he was... near... that his time had come. His voice was faint and difficult to hear. He said they had been attacked... a man... Ibrahim warned me to be careful; my life was in danger. He was worried for his nephew. He said I should watch out for him.'

At that point Akram slumped back on his pillows and began to weep.

'There, there, old man. You're safe now. I won't let anyone hurt you.'

'My life is of no concern to me,' Akram said quietly. 'My wife and son are both dead, and my daughters are in hiding in Canada. It's the young man who I'm…'

'I didn't know about your wife and son, Akram – and I'm so sorry to hear about it now. What happened?'

A long sigh from Akram. *A story told too many times already,* Clive thought. *Was I wrong to ask for the details? Does the pain dig deeper into his heart every time he has to tell it? Or does it help in some way? Poor man. Merciful God help him.*

'Wrong place, wrong time.'

'Where?'

'A suicide bomber in a crowded bazaar in Lebanon. Seems that they were looking for a birthday present for me. Twenty other people died too.'

'Oh dear God, Akram. What can I say – it's too terrible –a senseless *outrage!* I can't find the words to…' Clive cleared his throat, dabbed quickly at his eyes with his handkerchief then blew his nose loudly, looking embarrassed.

'The tears of a friend are as water from Heaven to a soul in torment,' Akram said, squeezing his hand. 'But now we need to talk about the living – the young man that…'

'Jamal,' Clive Scott said.

Akram started in surprise. 'You know him, Clive?'

'I've heard mention of his name.'

'Where – how?'

'Afraid I can't tell you, mate. Not yet, anyway. I don't suppose you have a photograph of Jamal in your wallet do you?'

'No. But I'm sure Ibrahim did. Jamal was his favourite sister's son – he thought the world of him. Did you...? Or did the French...?'

'No, the police found no photographs on any of the people in the 10th.'

'Then the killer...'

'Yes. The killer probably has them now.'

While this conversation was taking place, Philippe Maigret took the opportunity to interview David Quinn. Or, more accurately, he went to his room to *attempt* to ask him some further questions. There was no sign of him, but the bed was neatly made and a full carafe of water was on the side table. When he finally tracked down the head consultant to ask him Quinn's whereabouts he looked both agitated and uncomfortable.

'Gone, I'm afraid, Chief Inspector,' he said.

'He's dead! But he was almost fully recovered – you said so yourself, Doctor!'

'Not dead – gone.'

'Gone?'

'Disappeared, escaped, and totally vanished! We can't find him. We're searching everywhere.'

'Where are my men – the officers who were guarding him?'

'They're leading the search team.'

'Why wasn't I informed immediately?'

'You were *about* to be informed, Chief Inspector, but we thought he might just have wandered off... he had been sedated, he couldn't have gone far in that condition! It's just not possible.'

Heavily sedated my Aunt Fanny's fan, Maigret thought. *He planned this from the beginning. He's made fools of us.*

'Sound the security alarm, Doctor! Sound it immediately.'

'Look, we can't…'

'Now, Doctor, right now, or I'll be forced to arrest you for obstruction.'

As he spoke, Philippe Maigret bent down and unstrapped the revolver he sometimes wore on his right leg, a few centimetres above his ankle, and held it firmly in his hand, pointing it downwards. It was a deliberate action meant to intimidate the doctor and while it made him uncomfortable he knew it had to be done. *It feels heavier than usual,* he thought. *Oh yes, Jacques loaded it a few days ago – must remember that!*

'Now, I said. Right now!' he repeated. 'And I mean the police emergency alarm not the fire alarm. This hospital is going into full lockdown mode now. No one in or out until David Quinn is found, and that's an order.'

Without a further word the consultant went over to a keypad on the wall a few metres down the corridor and keyed in a four digit number. The alarm began immediately. After that came pandemonium. People running, loud shouting, and more than a whiff of panic.

First on the scene was Chief Inspector Scott who emerged from Akram's room as soon as the alarm started.

'What's with the blasted siren and all the damn noise

and shouting?' he called, noticing Maigret halfway down the corridor.

'Quinn's gone, Clive!'

'What?'

'He's disappeared – vanished. Gone!'

For the next three hours the hospital was searched from top to bottom. Every nook and cranny, every storage cupboard and equipment room; every last conceivable hidey-hole. Robert Lapotaire was found after the first hour: naked, bound and gagged with surgical tape and bandages, fast asleep in the cleaning team's auxiliary storeroom. The sedative that had been meant for Quinn had been forced down his throat: it would be mid-morning the next day before he was in any state to answer questions about how it had all happened.

Meanwhile, detectives Guy Chabois and Antoine Morel were going through the CCTV footage for the main entrance of the Pitié-Salpêtrière Hospital. *And, eventually, there he was.* Large as life, and twice as handsome, as Clive Scott commented when he and Philippe Maigret watched the footage, calmly leaving by the front door wearing Lapotaire's clothes.

'He looks a bit shaky on his pins,' Clive said. 'But apart from that he's not doing too badly for a man who was on the brink of death a couple of days ago. But he must be in a lot of pain if he hasn't been taking his meds.'

Or he's gone through the full counter-interrogation program and has learnt how to over-ride pain. Brutal, but effective. I wonder if the Brits use the same techniques as the Israelis and Russians, Maigret thought.

'And he also looks like he knows where he's going,' Maigret said. 'But where? A safe house? A friend?'

'He won't get far without money.'

'He's got money, Clive. He lifted Lapotaire's wallet, his police ID and his loaded weapon, as well as all his clothes – he even took his underpants!'

'*Blimey,* you wouldn't catch me wearing someone else's *used* underdaks, I'd rather go commando than do that! But heads might roll over this blasted fiasco, mate: they certainly will if MI6 chooses to turn *really* nasty. I hope those heads are not yours and mine!'

'Calm yourself, *mon ami*. If you blame *me,* and I blame *you,* we might just survive with our heads intact,' Maigret said. 'I suppose I could always apply for early retirement although I doubt my wife would approve!'

'Let's not make any rash moves; time to think rationally now! The thing that's been puzzling me is this: if kick-off's supposed to be happening in Berlin on the Ides, why has Quinn even been in Paris in the first place? What's he been doing here?'

'*Précisément.* My best guess is that he's either waiting for someone else to join him or he's expecting further orders. Or, and this is a frightening prospect; he's a red herring designed to keep us busy while someone else is really doing the heavy-lifting stuff.'

'Do you want me to go back upstairs and continue to… er talk with Akram?'

'Yes – good idea. Right now he seems our best chance of getting any useful information.'

'Okay.'

'What was all the fuss about, Clive?' Akram asked as he re-entered his room.

'I'll tell you all about it in a minute, old boy,' he said, 'but first I'd like you to take a look at some photographs I have here.'

As he spoke he fished the three photos Philippe had given him out of the inside pocket of his suit coat, and passed them, without further comment, to Akram.

He studied the photographs, one by one, but his hands were trembling as he did. For a time he tried to control the shaking, then gave up the fight and sank back on his pillows.

'He's a bad man, Clive; a very, very bad man,' he said, his voice scarcely above a whisper.

'Who – the man talking to the woman?'

Akram nodded, but said nothing.

'Were you following him, Akram? It *is* you, isn't it – in all three photos? You are watching the man talking with the woman at the Eiffel Tower, and again at Les Invalides.'

'Yes.'

'Why? Do you know him?'

'I was shown a photograph of him – many photographs of him – that's how I know him. And that's all I can tell you, except that it was *he* who killed my friends.'

Chief Inspector Scott ignored that comment, knowing that it was impossible for Quinn to have been the murderer, and determined to press ahead on what was proving to be a fruitful line of enquiry.

'Who showed you the photographs?' he asked.

'Ibrahim. He showed them to all of us.'

'And where did he get them?'

'I don't know. Ibrahim was a good man. A very good man, but he didn't... *encourage* us to ask too many questions!'

'Let me tell you what I and the French police know. This man's name is David Quinn. He's an Oxford graduate and a British civil servant. He is not, as far as we know, a killer.'

Before he had finished speaking Akram had started shaking his head again. 'No, you are wrong, Clive. This man works for Israeli Intelligence. And he's planning something very big – and very bad – which will happen next week in...'

'Berlin.'

Akram started again in surprise. 'You *know* about that, Clive?'

'Yes, we know. But we don't know *everything,* not by a long way – so how about an exchange of information, Akram? I swear, by everything I hold dear, that I will tell you *everything* I know about this matter. And I will tell you the *truth* – *if,* and only if, you will do the same. Do we have a deal?'

Akram nodded. 'Yes.'

'Wait one moment,' Chief Inspector Maigret said, standing in the doorway. 'I want in on this deal too, Clive.'

'This is Chief Inspector Philippe Maigret of the *Police Nationale,*' Scott said.

Akram looked astonished. 'Maigret?' he queried. 'But... I know someone...'

'My mother,' Philippe interrupted. 'She buys her bread from your *boulangerie*.'

'And the pretty Columbian girl?'

Maigret nodded. 'Yes, Rosa's my mother's housekeeper.'

Akram stared at Philippe Maigret in amazement. And then he began to laugh. He laughed and laughed until Clive Scott and Maigret joined in with him although they didn't know why.

'What idiots we are,' he said, wiping his eyes. 'What a bunch of fools to imagine we can pit our feeble wits against such a nest of *vipers!*' Then he began to recite

'Rub-a-dub-dub! Three men in a tub,
And who do you think were there?
The butcher, the baker, the candlestick maker,
And all of them gone to the fair!'

'Is he delirious?' Philippe Maigret whispered to Clive Scott.

'No, he's quoting the words of an English nursery rhyme. I'm guessing you had an English nanny for your children when they were young, Akram – am I right?'

'Yes,' he said. 'And still I can't get that damn rhyme out of my head even after all this time.'

'So if you're the baker,' Maigret said thoughtfully, 'who is Clive, and who am I?'

'You two must be the candlestick makers.'

'And the butcher?'

'The butcher is the man in the photographs you

have. No matter what you say I *know* that it is him. I saw his… *handiwork* today and so did you, Chief Inspector Maigret.'

'And the fair?'

'Berlin, of course. You told me that yourself, Clive – didn't you?'

ELEVEN

It took the best part of an hour to prove to Akram that David Quinn could not have murdered his friends. Firstly, he was shown the police report of the deliberate run-down of Quinn near Les Invalides and the numerous photographs of his injuries. *He was not convinced.* Then he was shown the *medical* reports with the doctors' assessments of his injuries, his blood-soaked clothing, and the details of the treatment he had received. *Still not convinced.* Finally he was invited to look at the copy of Quinn's brain scan, the senior consultants' evaluation of this, and the list of the drugs used to induce his coma. *The doubts remained.* Even the date and time-stamped CCTV footage of Quinn leaving the hospital wearing another man's clothes failed to convince him.

Finally, Philippe Maigret had a timely dose of lateral thinking. He excused himself from Akram's room, went out into the corridor, and phoned Dr Lambert, the *Police Nationale's* senior pathologist.

'Will do, Chief,' Doc Lambert said cheerfully after Maigret had outlined what he needed. 'You'll have them in five minutes give or take.'

Philippe Maigret waited in the corridor until the data alert on his phone signalled the arrival of the post-mortem photographs of the dead would-be assassin of David Quinn.

He walked briskly back into Akram's room and held his phone in front of Clive Scott. 'Are these okay, Clive – or too er... *unsanitised?*' he asked quietly.

Clive took a quick look and nodded. 'They're okay.'

'Thanks. Now, Akram, I'd like you to look at the three photographs I have on my phone. I warn you that these show a man we have in our morgue. However, and I emphasise this, he is *not* one of your friends from the atrocity at the 10th. But even so, be prepared.'

Akram was surprised, but said nothing.

'Okay?' Maigret asked.

'Yes – show me.' He viewed the photographs quickly, and then glanced from Maigret to Scott with a surprised look on his face.

'But how did you...?'

'Do you know this man, Akram?' Clive Scott asked.

'Wait!' Philippe Maigret said quickly before Akram could answer. 'That's not the *right* question. The question *should* be: is this the man who showed you the photographs of David Quinn? And was it also he who told you that Quinn worked for Israeli Intelligence?'

After a brief hesitation, Akram nodded. 'Yes, and yes,' he said.

'Crikey Akram! Who was this character? How would he even know those things?'

'Well er...'

'Because he said he worked for the American CIA?' Maigret interjected, taking another lateral stab in the dark. 'Is that what he told you?'

Another start of surprise from Akram. Then he nodded, 'Yes.'

'And showed you some ID to back up his story?'

'Yes, Clive. I may be a baker now but I'm not likely to take someone's *word* for something like that, now am I?'

'No, you're not, sorry mate.'

'You're sure that the ID was *authentic?*' A sceptical Maigret asked, determined not to overlook any possibility.

'Well, Chief Inspector, it has been many a long day since I was last shown a Central Intelligence Agency ID but it certainly looked authentic to me!'

'What the hell's going on here, Philippe?' Clive Scott said, completely exasperated.

'We're being played, Clive, that's what is happening.'

'By whom?'

'By the forces of evil,' Maigret said, looking from one man to the other.

'What? For Pete's sake don't talk in riddles, man! I warn you that my short fuse has been cut in half by all this... this mess, so it is very, very short now!'

'Fine, straight-talking, Clive. I'm willing to bet my pension against yours that this *supposed* CIA operative showed David Quinn some photographs of Akram, or Ibrahim, or even Jamal and told *him* that one or other of *them* was a very, very bad man. Or that they were *all* bad men. It's the old playing both sides against each other con trick and the aim is to make as much mischief, and create as much chaos as possible to further whatever cause you're supporting. Akram, the man in the photographs I've just shown you is no more a CIA agent than I am. In fact, my money's on him being a professional assassin!'

'But… but that's not possible, Chief Inspector! He had an American accent…'

'So?' Clive Scott interrupted. 'Philippe's not saying he wasn't American. He's just saying that he doesn't believe he worked for the CIA. And neither do I!'

'Why not?'

'Because two days ago he came to this hospital with the sole intention of killing Quinn,' Maigret said. 'And if it hadn't been for the quick thinking of one of my officers he would have succeeded!'

Then, finally, Akram was convinced!

'But if this Quinn fellow didn't kill my friends who did?' Akram asked.

'If we knew that we'd know a hell of a lot more than we know right now, Akram,' Clive Scott said ruefully. 'But we've put our cards on the table, so now it's your turn to tell us what *you* know. And you could start by telling me why a man with your background is working in a *boulangerie* in Paris.'

'Very well. After my wife and son… died, I was in a very deep, dark place for a long time. Then Ibrahim, a friend from my childhood days, found me. Found me, and *rescued* me. He had contacts in a great many places:

you would say he had fingers in numerous pies, and one of those pies was a small organisation committed to working for a *peaceful* solution to the problems, the many problems, in our region.'

'Before we go any further answer me this,' Philippe Maigret said. 'Do you support a two-State resolution to those problems?'

'Of course, it's the only reasonable position to take!'

'*Bon, bon.*' Maigret settled himself more comfortably in his seat, satisfied.

'*Peace Now?*' Chief Inspector Scott volunteered.

'No – but an organisation similar to *Peace Now* – the name is not important.'

'It's important to me, Akram!'

Akram sighed. 'Very well, the name is *Hailemariam.*'

'The power of Mary,' Philippe Maigret said.

Akram was astonished.

'Not *all* my friends are Christian, Akram.'

'I'm lost,' grumbled Clive Scott.

'The blessed Virgin, Clive – Mary, Mariam, or Maryam – they all mean the same person. Islam venerates Mary in much the same way that Christianity does. Hailemariam, sometimes written as Haile Mariam in the West, means the power of Mary.'

'You never cease to surprise me, Philippe Maigret,' Scott said, 'but we seem to be getting off the track – get on with it, Akram!'

'Wait, Clive. I'd say that the name Maryam, or Mariam, held special significance for someone within this budding organisation. Am I right, Akram?'

'Yes, Chief Inspector – right, and perceptive. Maryam was the name of Ibrahim's wife... and my beloved wife too.'

'Crumbs.' For once in his life Clive Scott was almost lost for words. 'How did you know that?' he whispered to Maigret.

'A lucky guess.'

'I doubt that,' Akram said. 'I doubt that very much! However, to continue, Ibrahim realised that he had to get me, and my daughters, away from the world we used to know: that once perfect world that no longer held two cherished members of our family. And it suited him to leave Jordan too. I don't know why; as I said, Ibrahim did not like to be asked too many questions. It was he who brought me to Paris, and he who persuaded me to revert to my father's trade, that of master baker. And that's how I came to be working in the *boulangerie* in which the police found me, and my daughters went to live with my cousin in Canada. But, when the time is right, they will join me here. Paris is to be our family home now.'

'And the Berlin affair – how did you come to hear about that?' Clive Scott asked.

'Through *sources*... in my former way of life with whom I am sometimes in contact.'

'Jordanian Intelligence?'

'I can't believe you expect me to answer that question, Clive. We are now in danger of swimming out beyond our depth into very murky waters, and if we do it might happen that none of us survive,' Akram said. 'And that's all I'm prepared to tell you.'

★

For the next few days the *Police Nationale* almost literally turned Paris upside-down and inside-out. Every *arrondissement* was searched thoroughly, not once, but twice – and then searched again. Every known criminal haunt, every likely place where a man on the run from the police might disappear into the local scene without attracting attention. Montmartre; La Defense; Montparnasse; the Marais – every area searched again, and again. Airports, bus and train stations – every way known that someone could escape undetected from the French capital.

Patrick Evremond arrived during those frenetic days, and was quickly put to work looking for Quinn too, armed with nothing more than a couple of photographs and a brief download to his mobile of what was known about him, followed by a conversation over a cup of coffee with Philippe Maigret. And still the search went on. The *fruitless*, frustrating search.

The chief inspector wanted photographs of Quinn to be splashed across the media, and wherever else it might, just might, prove useful. He wanted to advertise a reward for information leading to the whereabouts of the wanted man, but the British Embassy intervened to prevent every one of those options. Quinn was, the embassy said firmly, a British citizen who had not been charged with any offence in France, or anywhere else, no matter what might be *suspected.* Therefore the Mission could not, *would not,* sanction any course of action that might lead to him being hunted down like a common criminal by a posse of vigilantes hell-bent on making a fast buck. *And especially not on French soil!*

★

And so the days passed without Quinn even being sighted, much less apprehended. Then suddenly, it was the morning of Monday 13th March, and Megan was packing for the trip to Berlin with Nat.

How much should I tell her? Philippe thought, as he watched her. *Or should the question be how much can I tell her? And does it really matter whatever I tell her? She'll still go no matter what I say. I know she will.*

Finally he decided to show her a photograph of Quinn in the hospital recovering from his injuries, and to say as little as possible.

'Oh – but that's the man from the Eiffel Tower and Les Invalides, isn't it? But why's he in a hospital? I hope he's alright? Is he?'

He's alright – so damned alright that we can't find any trace of him, her husband thought.

'He's fine, Megan,' he said. 'He's er… out of the hospital now.'

'Good, I'm pleased to hear that, he seemed like a pleasant man.'

'Hmm. Will you promise me something, my love?'

'If I can – why so mysterious?'

'Sorry, can't say – ongoing investigation.'

'As per usual,' she said, patting his face affectionately to show that she didn't mind.

'Yes.'

'So?'

'Will you promise me that if by chance, while you are in Berlin, you see this man, you'll move away from him as quickly as you possibly can?'

'Why?'

'Let's just say that he might have some very dangerous friends and associates.'

'That can't be true, darling! He was perfectly charming when we spoke. Why would a man like that have dangerous friends? It doesn't make sense.'

'Tell me Megan, who is the patient police officer in this marriage and who is the… *pesky* civilian?'

His use of the word *pesky* made her laugh, as it always did. And he knew that very well. Since their marriage it had become his weapon of choice to win some, but by no means *all,* disputes between them. It was a word he had never even *heard* until she introduced him to it. Now he used it whenever he could, sometimes merely to tease her, but with his accent he still couldn't pronounce it correctly. To his ears yes, he could; to hers, no, he most definitely could not!

'Okay, you win,' she said, still laughing. 'I promise. But at least you should tell me the man's name if I'm supposed to run for cover if I ever see him again!'

'His name is David Quinn.'

However, Megan would not cross paths with David Quinn in Berlin. She would meet him again long before the Night train had even left French soil that night.

TWELVE

Philippe Maigret and Patrick Evremond met again that afternoon over a late lunch. The chief inspector, the perfectionist, wanted to make certain that his young protégé *fully, completely, and totally*, understood his task. He did. His mission was to follow Megan Maigret to Berlin and keep her out of trouble, while at the same time being on the alert for David Quinn.

'Perhaps I should give you my revolver,' Philippe pondered, 'in case of any trouble.'

'No, sir, I mean, Philippe – no revolver.'

'Do you know how to shoot?'

'Yes, I've been clay pigeon shooting since I was eleven.'

'Well, then...' Maigret bent down, removed the revolver from his leg, and slid it across the table to Patrick. 'Careful,' he warned, 'it's loaded.'

'Sir! Philippe – we're in a restaurant!' Patrick quickly covered the revolver with his napkin. 'You can't go waving weapons around in places like this!'

'I did not... *wave*, young man, I pushed!'

'Even so. Why do it at all? I told you I don't want to

take a revolver with me; that is not the *English* way,' he said. 'And I'd never get it through the train's security checks anyway. I have my Swiss Army knife and that's the only protection I need. That was fine on Eurostar because it has a folding blade not more than three inches in length.'

'There will be no security checks on the train, Patrick you won't even have to show your passport or ticket. You could take a surface to air missile on that damn train if you wanted to and no one would be any wiser!'

'What?'

'It's the Schengen Agreement which guarantees the free movement of people between all the EU States that signed up to the Agreement in 1985, or those who have subsequently signed.'

'But the UK didn't sign up to Schengen.'

'Yes, I'm aware of that fact. However, in 1999 the UK asked permission to cooperate in *some* aspects of Schengen, mainly with the police and judiciary in criminal matters, and the fight against drugs and terrorism. Ireland made almost the same request in 2000 and both were agreed to by the EU.'

'You seem remarkably well-informed on the Schengen Agreement, Philippe.'

'Have to be, *mon ami*. It became a big part of my job once France and Germany signed-up and all *internal* borders were abolished. We just have one single *external* border now. There's full co-operation and co-ordination between police services and judicial authorities too. We can even, in cases of hot pursuit, chase criminals across the borders of other countries.'

'Hmm, useful,' Patrick said thoughtfully. 'But aren't you worried about security?'

'Do you think I'd tell you if I were?' Maigret replied. 'But shall we just say that some passengers are more er... *acceptable* than others and so undergo only minimal scrutiny. Not that we do the checking, the train company has that responsibility.'

'I get the picture: the security is negligible and any safety concerns are dealt with at the time the ticket is booked online,' Patrick said.

'I'm afraid I couldn't possibly comment on that statement except to say that I've always felt that you were a very *astute* young man,' Philippe said, winking as he spoke. 'But now we need to get down to business again. I'd like you to board as soon as the boarding message appears on the monitors at Gare de l'Est which will probably be shortly before 8pm. I'll delay my wife in some way so that she doesn't see you. Okay?'

Patrick nodded.

'*Bon*. Now when you go to board you'll find that it is a very long train. That's because it goes to three different parts of Germany, despite the company's advertisements which state that it is non-stop from Paris to Berlin in a mere twelve hours.'

'Three places?'

'Yes; Berlin, Munich and Hamburg.'

'But how?'

'German efficiency, or not, as the case might be. Passengers for Berlin board the front part of the train which goes to Berlin. Then, at some time after midnight

– zero dark thirty to use American-speak, the middle part, which goes to Munich, will be divided from the rest of the train – *uncoupled* is the correct term – to go in a different direction. The same thing will happen about forty-five minutes later for the end part which will go off to Hamburg.'

'And does it all go like clockwork?' Patrick asked.

'That's what you're about to find out! But you must promise me that you'll go beyond... *vigilance* on the train. It will be carrying a very precious... *cargo* tonight. Cargo that for me is irreplaceable. Understood?'

'Yes. I'll keep them safe for you, Philippe. I give you my solemn word that I will. And don't forget that you saw me take down the Purple Vegetable at Montmartre when I worked with you in Paris last time.'

'Purple Vegetable? I don't...'

'Yes, the Purple Vegetable – Rene Aubergine – that's how I always think of him. Haven't landed a monster punch in anyone's solar plexus since him, but then no one's had the nerve to proposition me since him either!'

'Oh yes, the Purple Vegetable indeed. You were impressive the way you felled him, no doubt about that!'

I see that you are also adroit at diffusing tension within the space of a heartbeat, Philippe Maigret thought. *You saw the emotional track I was headed down and you threw in the mention of purple vegetables to change my direction. Clever, and subtle. You'll go far my young friend, and you deserve to because you are an unusual combination of brilliance and humanity.*

'Here, take this, Patrick,' he said, placing an envelope on the table. 'And use it as you please. I won't need to see any receipts or invoices. It's for your use, no questions asked, and for any emergencies.'

'There won't be any emergencies, Philippe,' Patrick said, opening the envelope. 'What the…?'

'There are a thousand euros in various denominations – mostly fifties, in that envelope – and the account for your hotel in Berlin has been paid in advance as has your air fare to London.'

'I don't understand… sir…'

'Philippe – remember?' the chief inspector said. 'Right now I'm just another anxious husband, not a police officer – no sirs or chief inspectors necessary.'

And you're only just managing to keep your anxiety under control aren't you, Patrick Evremond thought as he looked across the table at Philippe Maigret. *You think that, whatever he says, David Quinn has deliberately approached your wife twice, and now he's disappeared and you can't find him. And you can't stop thinking, and worrying, about whether he'll try to contact her again. But why should he? What's his agenda, and how does Megan fit into it?*

'I said,' Philippe repeated for the third time, 'that if you've quite finished with your wool-gathering it's time to go. I'll drop you at your hotel on my way back to HQ. And remember this: my mobile will always be switched on, never off or on silent, until…'

'Until *after* 15th March,' Patrick said, helping him out.

'*Oui.* Until after *Wednesday – long after* Wednesday has come and gone. So contact me and only me, if anything er… unusual should happen. Day or night – yes?'

'Yes. Now stop worrying, Philippe. Madame Maigret is a sensible woman and she…'

'She's a heat-seeking missile!' Philippe Maigret snorted. 'But she's *everything* to me.'

'I know that, Philippe. Still there's just one thing that's been bothering me…'

'What? Tell me,' Maigret said, as they left the restaurant.

'The Scarborough Fair folk song…'

'What of it?'

'I can't seem to get the third line out of my head,' Patrick said.'

'They, Quinn and Megan, didn't get to the third line. He said *are you going to Scarborough Fair,* and she replied…'

'*Parsley, sage, rosemary and thyme.*'

'Yes, so what's your point?'

'My point is this: what if the third line was the important one?' He could see Philippe Maigret running the folk song through his memory.

'*Remember me to one who lives there…*'

'Exactly. So who does your wife know in Berlin?'

That question, left suspended in the air between then, would haunt Philippe Maigret for the rest of that afternoon, and most of the night to come.

Four hours later he had asked Megan the same question as they drove to Gare de l'Est. She had looked at him as though he'd gone mad.

'Well, Julie and Nick are there,' she had said. 'But

they don't *live* in Berlin, they just visit three or four times a year.'

Was there no one else, he'd persisted. No distant relatives, long-lost pals, old lovers, *former husbands* – or other assorted miscreants that she had forgotten to mention? He had actually used the word *miscreants* – he couldn't fathom why – and that had made her angry. Very angry.

'Some people told me that it would be a mistake to marry a police officer,' she had said coldly. '*And especially a foreign one.* And now I think they were probably right.'

'What's going on with you two?' Nat had asked from the back seat. 'Why are you fighting?'

Then Megan had apologised, and told Philippe that she knew no one in Berlin, as far as she could tell, apart from her daughter and her husband, and that she loved him and couldn't imagine herself being married to anyone else – *in this or any other Universe.* Then they'd both laughed and kissed and made up.

But even so…

Patrick Evremond boarded the train as soon as the announcement appeared on the monitor at Gare de l'Est. He took his bearings as he did and noticed that a young woman, of about his own age, was busily directing passengers to their compartments or seats. He deliberately engaged her in light-hearted conversation. He knew a little German, but his French was considerably better, so he started with that language. Hildy answered him in French, but immediately suggested they speak in English because she would welcome the practice. By then he felt they were on their way to becoming friends; Hildy hoped that they were actively flirting!

He spun a credible story to her about the possibility of his aunt and cousin being on the same train; she checked her passenger log, confirmed that they were, and gave him their compartment number but added that they hadn't boarded yet. Philippe had already given him those details, but he thanked the young *fräulein*, and said he hoped to see her again later. She smiled sweetly and said she hoped for that too. Oh, but one more thing, Patrick added, would she please not mention their conversation to his aunt as she had no idea that he would be on the train, and he wanted to surprise her. Hildy nodded, smiled again, and said she would be *diskret*.

While this was happening on the train, two young men were standing back in the shadows observing the people boarding the Berlin section of the train. But they were not together, nor even very close. Nor was either of them aware of the presence of the other.

One of them was David Quinn. And the other one was Jamal Ahmadi. Jamal had a ticket for the train – a reclining seat, like Patrick's, but he was not ready to board yet. For his own reasons he wanted to board at the very last minute.

David Quinn had no ticket, but he had a big advantage over Jamal; he had seen a photograph of him, so would recognise him if they should ever meet, whereas Jamal had not been present when Ibrahim had shown Quinn's photograph to his comrades. But Quinn also delayed his embarkation. He would not board until he saw Megan Maigret get on the train. How could he? She was vital to his plans. She was his *insurance.*

Philippe escorted Megan and Nat on to the train, found their compartment, and made sure they were comfortable. Then they heard the guard's whistle; the first of three, five minutes apart, which advised passengers that departure was imminent.

'Don't wait, darling,' Megan said, kissing him again, 'we won't be able to see you, and you look tired. Besides, you need to walk Kitty, and she'll be hungry now. You will remember to walk her – won't you? You *did* promise.'

'Yes, my love. I've already informed the Minister of Police and the Judiciary that all crime investigation in Paris will be suspended for the next few days while I assume my official role of Chief Inspector cat carer!'

When the second whistle sounded he left the train. As he did he collided with a young man who was hastily boarding.

'So sorry, sir,' the young man said politely in English, 'my fault entirely.'

Philippe Maigret smiled, 'You are too kind, *monsieur.* I do believe the fault was mine.'

While this conversation was taking place, David Quinn was anxiously waiting for a chance to break cover and board. He could see Philippe Maigret talking to another man, but that man's back was turned towards him.

If Maigret sees me, I've had it, Quinn thought, *but when the guard blows his whistle a third time the train will leave immediately. What to do?* He saw the guard raise his whistle towards his lips, and now Maigret was walking in his direction.

At that moment there was a loud scream from a woman at the other end, the Hamburg end, of the train. A commotion followed with more loud screams and shouts. The guard hesitated, not sure whether he should blow his whistle or not. Maigret, seeing the guard's indecision, yelled, 'Don't start the train yet,' flashing his police ID as he did. 'I'll find out what's happening at the other end, and signal you when the train can start. Tell the driver he's not to proceed yet. Understood?'

The guard nodded. 'Yes, sir.'

Chief Inspector Maigret walked quickly down the platform, and as he did, David Quinn left the shadows behind him and walked confidently towards the train, entering by a door immediately to the rear of the one by which Maigret had left. Meanwhile the guard, whistle still in hand, was walking towards the front of the train to speak to the driver.

Quinn found a great deal of confusion inside the carriage as people, of all different ages and nationalities, tried to discover the reason for the delay.

He had intended to walk from that section towards where Megan Maigret had boarded. No one took any notice of him, but the door between these sections was locked. He went back to where he'd boarded and looked carefully in both directions, then, in a smooth movement, left and re-boarded through the forward door.

There was confusion in that section too: some people were getting off the train in search of more information, while others were already standing around on the platform discussing theories and possibilities. The distracted Hildy was desperately trying to round up her troublesome flock to get them back on the train again. She didn't notice him, nor it seemed did anyone else.

He made his way against the tide of excited passengers, and saw Megan and Nat standing at the open door of their compartment halfway along the corridor, speaking with another passenger. They didn't see him.

When they went back into their compartment he walked quickly past the door, continuing towards the front of the train where he knew the reclining sleeper-seats were located. Just before that area he saw what he'd been looking for – a door marked 'toilet'. He went inside, locked the door, and waited for the train to start. Ten minutes later, drama or false alarm over, Philippe Maigret signalled the "all clear" to the guard who blew the third whistle and the train slowly pulled away from Gare de l'Est.

I'll stay in here for as long as I can, Quinn thought, *then, when we're well on our way, but before the start of the dinner service, I'll find out if Madame Maigret is prepared to give me sanctuary. Sanctuary – and support.*

THIRTEEN

Tuesday 14th March. Paris

'Come on you *cat*,' Chief Inspector Maigret said, dangling the leather harness in front of her nose, 'it's time for your walk. And trust me I'm not looking forward to it either but if Madame says it must be done, then it must be done.'

The cat sat quite still and looked at him as though he had lost his senses. *But you don't walk me,* was clearly written on the little tabby's face. *You don't even like me – and I know that. I'm not going anywhere with you!* Then she yawned, lifted her leg in the air and began to wash her intimate parts: Philippe recognised that this was the ultimate feline insult.

'How about a little treat?' he said, walking towards the kitchen. He opened the cupboard where the moggy indulgences were kept and suddenly Kitty appeared at his feet. 'Hah – fell for the old treats trick again – didn't you, Missy?'

'Meow,' Kitty said.

'If that means "yes my lord, you win", you may have one.'

'Meow,' the cat repeated.

'That's good enough for me,' he said, bending down to offer her three of the treats from the palm of his hand. 'And I hope that there will be no further... *unpleasantness* between us.'

She ate the treats delicately, one by one, and then licked his palm with her rough little tongue.

'Oh, I see – it's rude to speak while you have food in your mouth, is it? We humans, superior beings as you should always consider us, have the same etiquette.'

'Meow,' she said walking out of the room with her tail held high. *You're the one talking to a cat so how superior is that,* was quite obviously the sub-text.

Some days ago Megan had pointed out that he was *not the triple pillar of the world,* and he had reluctantly agreed. However, now that the reputation of *Police Nationale* was under threat he was determined *not* to walk through the entrance lobby with the cat on a lead. *No sniggering behind their hands from the concierge and doormen,* he thought, *and no denigration of the police on my account. I'll have to carry her.* She scratched him twice as he tried to fit her harness but immediately looked apologetic. He lifted her into his arms, stroked the soft fur under her chin and she began to purr. *Not a bad start,* he thought, *Megan will be impressed.*

As soon as they were in the street he put her down and let her walk. *She really did have an air about her. Or were all cats like that?*

They walked for twenty minutes in the neighbourhood park, and to his surprise he enjoyed it.

He found himself feeling strangely protective towards this contrary feline scrap that walked so gracefully across the grass, sniffing the air and kowtowing to no one. Two dogs presumed to menace her with loud barks and bristling hackles, and she hissed; he quickly scooped her up, resisting the urge to lash out at the brutes with his shoe. Her little heart was beating furiously against his shirt; he soothed her with gentle reassurances until she began to purr again.

When they turned the last corner on their way home he was surprised to see Inspector Georges Martin standing next to an unmarked police car outside of their building. He was trying desperately to suppress a grin, but without success.

'*Bonjour*, sir,' he said before he completely lost his composure and began to laugh. 'The sights one sees on a fine morning in Paris – quite amazing!'

'I take it, Inspector Martin,' Philippe Maigret said sternly, 'that you are looking for a spell of policing in the open-air again, perhaps in the Place de la Concorde at peak hour while wearing a nice new shiny uniform. Are you?'

'Not really, sir…' Then he dissolved into laughter again.

'Hmm. Well, *mon ami,* that's where you'll be, and that's what you'll be doing if one word – *one single, solitary word* – of what you've just seen finds its way back to HQ. *Comprendre?*'

Georges Martin made a Herculean effort to pull himself together. 'Yes, sir,' he said.

'*Bon.* The things we do for love, eh Georges!'

'Yes, sir,' he managed to say before he started to laugh again, 'only I've never been so enamoured that I would walk a cat on a lead in a public street! And I'm sure I never will be.'

'Yes, and that's exactly what I would have said not so long ago. Yet here I am, complete with cat. And what's more, it wasn't such a bad experience for either of us, was it Miss Moggs? But what are you doing here, Georges? I didn't ask you to drive me this morning.'

'I thought that with Madame away you might need a coffee and a croissant, Chief. And there's been a development.'

'What?'

'David Quinn was seen near Gare de l'Est last night.'

'We have a witness?'

'Yes, of sorts; he was picked up on a CCTV camera.'

'How far from the station?'

'Very close to one of the entrances.'

'Well, well, well,' Maigret said pensively. 'I wonder where he was going. What time was he filmed?'

'7.45pm.'

'And it's definitely Quinn?'

'Oh yes, Chief; it's a clear image.'

'So – where do you think he was going – Berlin?'

'That would be my bet.'

'Hmm. As soon as we're at HQ I want you to get on to the train company in Luxembourg. Tell them we want a copy of the passenger Log from last night's train. And make sure they send it pronto! And while you're doing that Jacques can issue a European arrest warrant for Quinn.'

'The Brits won't like that, sir!'

'To hell with the Brits, and what they like or don't like! It's a different story now: he's assaulted and drugged a police officer, bound and gagged him, and robbed him of his clothes, ID and weapon. Not even the Brits will be able to spin that little lot into simple misdemeanour no matter how hard they try. Okay, coffee and croissant now, then fast as you can to HQ, Georges.'

'Wait, sir – the cat!' Georges said, looking down at the moggie who was now engaged in full-scale washing on the pavement.

'Oh, hell! Yes, the blessed cat, and my coat and tie! Give me five minutes to settle her down then we can be on our way.'

'I can probably get the Log from the train company *and* ask Jacques to prepare the warrant in that time, Chief.'

'How?'

'From my new phone. It's an absolute little marvel. You must let me demonstrate what it can do some time, Chief.'

'Hmm. Yes, *sometime* – just not in this *present* lifetime!'

At 10am that morning, fed and watered, Chief Inspector Maigret received an incoherent phone call from Berlin. It was Julie, Nat's mother, and Megan's daughter.

'Please, Julie, slow down,' Philippe Maigret said, 'I can't understand what you're saying.'

'They're not on the train,' she said. And then she began to cry.

'*Comment?*'

'*Bonjour,* Philippe, Nick speaking now. We seem to have a *situation* here, and Julie's too upset to speak.'

'A situation? What's happening, Nick?' Philippe Maigret asked, holding his breath.

'They're not on the train and neither's answering their mobile. We couldn't reach them last night either.'

'I haven't been able to reach them since they left Paris, it seems the wi-fi on the train was pretty hit and miss. But this morning – do you mean the train's been delayed?'

'No, Philippe,' Nick said, speaking slowly and deliberately, 'the train arrived right on time but Nat and Megan were not on it.'

'But that's impossible! I put them on the train myself last night! Tell the transport police to search the train. They must be there.'

'The train's already been searched but they've agreed to search it again. I'll go with them this time. I think they're about to start so I'd better…'

'Wait! Who's coordinating the search? Transport police, or regular…?'

'The transport police seem to be in charge right now, but I've made a fuss and apparently there are a couple of cars from the *Berliner Polizei* on the way. The main problem is that they don't believe that Megan and Nat were ever on the train. They're saying they must have missed it!'

'Listen to me, Nick – that's rubbish! I boarded the train with them and there was a young woman from *Deutsche Bahn* checking people off her Log as they boarded. I saw her do that for Megan and Nat. Don't let them get away with this nonsense about them never being on it – understood? Better still, put someone from the transport police on and let me speak to him!'

'Do you speak German, Philippe?'

'No, not really. But don't they all speak English?'

'Not the guys I've dealt with so far – better to let me handle it…'

'I can't just sit here and do nothing!'

'I'm sure there's a simple explanation. Maybe they got off at the wrong station – *Spandau*, for instance. I think that's the last stop before Berlin. Or is it Zoo? I can't remember.'

With every one of the thirty-seven trillion cells in his long lithe body, Philippe Maigret wanted to believe that comforting explanation but the police officer in him would not let him. Not when David Quinn had been sighted near Gare de l'Est, and not when there was a simple way to find out.

'Their luggage, Nick; was it still on train?'

A small pause on the other end of the line: a moment of hesitation before delivering uncomfortable news.

'Yes, it was.'

'And did everything look er… completely *normal* inside their compartment?'

'There was no blood, or any sign of *trouble*, if that's what you're asking. It looked like the bunks might have been slept in, but otherwise everything was neat and tidy. That's why the police are convinced that they were never on the train.'

'Despite their luggage being there?'

'Yes, despite that, Philippe.'

Then a moment of total mental clarity as the police officer exerted full control over the anxious husband.

'Were any other passengers missing?' Maigret asked.

'I don't think so. All present and accounted for as far as I'm aware. Why?'

'Because I know another passenger was on that train too. His name is Patrick Evremond and he's English. Find him for me, Nick. See if he's waiting around anywhere.'

'Okay. What does he look like?'

'He's about twenty-three, 183 cm, or six feet tall, longer than average fair hair, and at the moment he's quite tanned. Oh, and he speaks excellent French.'

'Well, I haven't seen anyone that matches *that* description, Philippe. Just about all of the other passengers have left the platform. The only people still here seem to be Julie and me and the police and station officials.'

'So Patrick's also missing,' Philippe said thoughtfully. 'See if the train people think he missed it too! And see if his overnight bag was still on the train like Megan's and Nat's. He had a reclining sleeper-seat near the front of the train. I booked it for him, myself.'

'What's going on, Philippe? What's this all about?'

'Patrick Evremond was on the train at my request.

He was there to make sure Megan and Nat were kept safe.'

'Why wouldn't they be safe?'

'Long story, Nick,' Philippe said wearily. 'And for another time, not now. Suffice to say that Patrick would not have left them... *unguarded*. He just wouldn't. He's a most responsible young man, and he took his assignment very seriously. I'll bet you anything you like that if they're not on the train then neither is he.'

Nor was he. Nor his backpack. But his overnight bag was still there.

FOURTEEN

There were actually *four* passengers missing from the previous night's train although the train company was only aware of three – the ones that were on the passenger Log. The one they didn't know about was the stowaway, David Quinn.

By 11am Chief Inspector Maigret and his friend Christophe Saint-Valéry, the Minister of Police, had pulled about the same number of official strings as the racquet mishaps at the French Open that year, and the Luxembourg train company had accepted reality: three passengers were definitely missing. Consequently a full-scale police search was underway on both sides of the Franco-German border.

But there was another name on the passenger list that, after he'd finished his string-pulling and given it the attention it deserved, leapt off the page at Philippe Maigret. That name was Jamal Ahmadi. *A coincidence,* he wondered? Maybe. *But how could it be? You don't believe in coincidences – do you?* This Jamal was listed as a British citizen. *Oh hell,* the chief inspector thought, *Clive Scott doesn't know anything about this and Patrick Evremond's British too. Serious oversight, Maigret,* his subconscious rebuked, *and it's because your heart is currently running the show. That's not the way to find them! Think man; use your intellect. But I don't want to be here, sitting behind a desk in Paris! I want to be out in the field leading the search for them. Yes, but you can't. Christophe is right: you can do more good by using your brains in Paris than you can on the ground searching. Leave that to the uniformed officers, that's what Christophe said. Yes, but it's not his wife who's missing – it's mine! God help them. And me.*

He picked up his phone, called Clive Scott, and, as succinctly as he could, told him everything. There was shocked silence from the other end of the line for a few moments.

'Hells-bells!' Scott exclaimed, whistling through his teeth. 'What can I do to help, Philippe? Anything. I don't care what it is – tell me, and I'll do it. How are you coping?'

'*Merci, mon ami.* I'm not really... most of me feels... I feel numb.'

'Stay strong, my friend – you're not alone. Want me to get in touch with Akram again? He'll tell us if this Jamal Ahmadi is the Jamal he knows. If he is, I could run some checks on him – see where he's been lately, that kind of thing, and if he's had any brushes with the law.'

'Yes please, Clive, do that. And what about Quinn?'

'Quinn? I've told you everything that my political masters would allow, and then some, actually. What more is there for me to tell?'

'Berlin, Clive. Isn't there something more you could tell me about Berlin, and the Ides?'

'Not now. But I'll let my embassy people here know about these developments and maybe they'll allow me more *latitude*. One thing I *know* they'll say for sure is this: *don't assume that Quinn was on the train.* Yes, he was captured on CCTV near Gare de l'Est, but that doesn't mean he went *into* the station or that he actually *caught* the train. And he wasn't on the passenger list. He might just have been in the neighbourhood for some reason.'

'That's not what my entrails are telling me, Clive.'

'Nor mine, mate – nor mine. Leave this side of things to me. I'll get back to you pronto.'

As soon as his conversation with Chief Inspector Scott had finished Maigret knocked on the glass of his office to summon Inspector Georges Martin and Sergeant Jacques Laurent.

'Close the door behind you,' he said as they entered the room, 'and listen carefully to what I'm about to tell you. You know, of course, that my wife and grandson *disappeared* from the night train between Paris and Berlin last night. What you don't know is that there was another person missing from the train, too.'

'We know that, boss – the Luxembourg people have admitted that three passengers are missing now,' Georges Martin said.

'Yes, but now I need both of you to give me your assurance,' he said, glancing from one to the other, 'that what I'm about to tell you will not be discussed with anyone at HQ or anywhere else, with the exception of Chief Inspector Scott who I have just informed because the third missing person is a British citizen. *Comprendre?*'

Georges and Jacques nodded.

'Good men, I knew I could count on you. The third person missing from the train is young Patrick Evremond who, as you will remember, worked at HQ some months ago.'

'But how, sir?' Jacques asked.

'And why?' Georges added.

'This is the strictly confidential part now, *mes amis*. Patrick was on the train because I'd asked him to follow my wife and grandson to make sure they arrived safely in Berlin, and that they were kept safe during their time there. It was a *private* arrangement between Patrick and me, although Chief Inspector Scott had given his er... *tacit* approval.'

'You didn't believe David Quinn's meeting with your wife at the Eiffel Tower and Les Invalides was accidental.' Georges Martin said.

'A small correction, Georges. I wasn't *convinced* that he mistook her for someone else. Once I might have believed, but twice? No. Not from someone with a First from Oxford who worked for GCHQ Cheltenham. That would be stretching things too far. Nor was I satisfied with either his answers or attitude when I questioned him the second time in hospital.'

'Did Madame Maigret *know* that Patrick would be tailing them?'

'Look at me, Jacques – am I in hospital? Do you see any injuries?' Maigret said. 'Do you think I'd be sitting here in one piece if she had known?'

At that moment Maigret's phone rang; it was Clive

Scott. 'The answer's yes, Philippe,' he said. 'I've spoken to Akram and the Jamal on the train's passenger list is the one he knows. Jamal Ahmadi is the nephew of Ibrahim from the massacre in the *10*th. It came as news to Akram that Jamal's in Berlin, although I don't think he was particularly surprised: "where else would he be the day before the Ides?" he said. He doesn't have Jamal's mobile number but he's promised to let me know if he hears from him. And I've done a quick check: Jamal Ahmadi is a British citizen born in Birmingham and has no criminal record. At least not under that name, nor has he been anywhere recently that should give you cause for *concern.*'

'I don't believe that Jamal, or any of those who were murdered in that room in the 10th were criminals, Clive.'

'Then who were they? And who killed them?'

'It's think it's possible they were working in the same way as Quinn; trying to stop something horrific happening in Berlin tomorrow. They might have been two strands of the same story: Quinn, a member of *Peace Now*, and Jamal and his friends with the fledgling Hailemariam organisation, always running *parallel* – so never aware of what the other side was doing. Or *trying* to do. If only they *had known*, and shared their resources, what a difference that could have made. As for who killed them; I think that was probably an associate of the man who tried to kill Quinn in the Pitié-Salpêtrière Hospital a few days ago.'

'You know what, Philippe, as far-fetched as all that sounds, it does have certain er... whatever it is that you

French always say when you're stuck for the right word?'

'*Je ne sais quoi?*' Maigret said, helping him out.

'Yes – that. And a kind of weird logic, too. You might just be on the right track, my friend.'

'*Merci* for the reassurance, Clive. And what about the other er *stuff?* Have your compatriots at the embassy agreed that you can tell me more?'

'Not yet. But they've gone into a huddle behind closed doors and I take that as a good sign. Well maybe not *entirely* good but at least they're still discussing it. Leave it with me. I'll work on them as much as I can and maybe that will help. Any news from the search?'

'No. Nothing at all. And that's the frustrating part. There were only two opportunities for anyone to leave the train; firstly when the Munich section was uncoupled at about thirty minutes after midnight, and secondly when the Hamburg section repeated the same process forty-five minutes later.'

'The Munich section would then have headed in a south-easterly direction, while later the Hamburg section would have gone north-west,' Clive Scott said thoughtfully.

'And your point is…'

'Do you know what speed the train was doing between the Munich uncoupling and the Hamburg?'

'Somewhere between 125 and 150 kilometres per hour we think.'

'Think?'

'Yes, Clive – the train company's not very precise on that point.'

'No black box technology?'

'Afraid not. Old train due to be taken out of service at the end of the year. Probably wouldn't do us much good anyway. Anyone leaving the train at either the Munich or the Hamburg uncoupling could have gone in any direction they liked.'

'So you're dealing with a large search area, Philippe.'

'Very large – annoyingly so.'

'Any contact from their mobiles?'

'None. Patrick's phone wasn't on the train, but it's currently out of range or out of service. Megan's and Nat's mobiles were left in their compartment.'

'What I don't understand, Philippe is this: why would anyone want to get off that damn train in the first place when the final destination was Berlin and that's where the action's supposed to be happening tomorrow?'

'Precisely. I'm certain that Megan and Nat would not have left the train unless they were *forced* to go. But by whom? Person or persons unknown or David Quinn if he was actually on the train at all? And, either way, for reasons unknown! But Patrick must have realised what was happening and he *chose* to go with them. Or *after* them. At least that's the hope I'm clinging to! If Patrick's with them I feel slightly better about everything. But if he's not, well then...'

'There's a lot of ifs and buts and *suppositions* in what you've just said, my friend.'

'And don't I know it! But it's all I've got to go on. And it's the only thing that's keeping me relatively *sane*, too.'

'Any time you fancy a fast trip over the German border, Philippe, just let me know,' Scott said. 'And the same goes for a good, fast, *German-speaking* driver. I happen to know where the keys to a late model XJ Jaguar are kept; and it's gassed up and ready to go. Could be very *unofficial* and *entre nous*. And it is a very fast beast, very fast indeed – far better than any of your clapped out Citroens or Peugeots.'

'Is that offer for real, Clive?' Maigret asked, ignoring Clive's gratuitous slur on the French car industry as well as the *Police Nationale's* transport budget.

'Very much so, my friend.'

'And legal?'

'As me no questions and I'll tell you no lies,' Clive chuckled.

'For the love of all things holy Clive tell me that it's not the Ambassador's car!'

'Of course it's not – the Ambassador's always using his car! But it does have *diplomatic* plates which I consider an advantage.'

Chief Inspector Maigret sighed and looked at his watch. *Noon,* he thought, *and it won't get dark until seven – or later. But what would this move of Clive's accomplish? Anything? Nothing? Do you really care? At least it would be better than sitting behind a desk going crazy!*

'How does thirty minutes sound to you, Clive?'

'Your place or mine?'

'Better be ours. I may be *persona non grata* as far as your place is concerned.'

'Deal! See you soon.'

Immediately after his conversation with Chief Inspector Scott had ended, Philippe Maigret started gathering items from his desk.

'Going somewhere, boss?' Georges Martin asked. It was a rhetorical question: he already knew the answer.

'Yes, and so are you, Georges. Grab your overnight bag from your locker but say nothing to anyone. You can probably guess where we're headed.'

'And the cat, sir? The feisty little furry one – is she going too?

'Oh, hell no – Jacques, here please. These are the keys to my apartment. Take the car, collect one cat. There's a travel basket in the laundry, and the harness for her twice-daily walking is hanging on the back of the door. There are cat treats in a cupboard in the kitchen. Take them; you might need them for bribes. Then drive her over to my mother's. But be careful, she scratches and she might bite too – the *cat,* I mean, not *maman!* Ask *maman* to look after her for a few days but don't tell her where I've gone: use your imagination, make up a plausible story, and don't breathe a word about the disappearance of Madame and Nat. Understood? And after all that, get back here as quick as you can and keep your phone turned on 24/7, we'll need you to be our liaison while we're away. If anyone else asks where we are, tell them we're in Luxembourg for meetings with the train's security people and their insurers. I'm sorry to load this on you, Jacques, but I can't think of anything else to do.'

'There's no problem, Chief. All the lads in the squad

know the score, and they will rally around to help. And none of them would ever say a word to the media. You can count on that, whatever happens.'

'*Merci,* Jacques. Please tell them I'd be lost without them: they're a remarkable team as they've proved many times before.'

'But the media, and the train company, boss – they might…'

'They'll keep quiet for the next thirty-six hours! Christophe Saint-Valéry has taken out an injunction on behalf of the Republic to prevent any reference to me or mine. He's also threatened them with the wrath of God if they drop even a *hint* that I may be personally involved.'

'I shouldn't think that the train company would want it known that they *misplace* passengers – not good for business,' Inspector Martin said.

'*Exactement.*'

What none of them mentioned *was the elephant in the room.* The obvious *truth* that they all chose to leave unaddressed. The obvious *risk* that no one wanted to discuss. The possibility that Megan Maigret might have been deliberately targeted by Patrick Quinn himself, or persons unknown, *precisely* because she was Chief Inspector Maigret's wife.

And there was a second elephant in that room: if the answer was that she *had* been chosen that way was it for blackmail, ransom or worse still, *revenge?*

FIFTEEN

The little tabby might have stayed in Paris but those two elephants most definitely went with them: they were determined to haunt Philippe Maigret no matter where he went. And they were making their presence felt by everyone.

Chief Inspector Scott was well aware of their presence – these two elephants were the questions that any half-competent detective would have asked at the outset of any missing persons enquiry. However he had not yet found a way – a *considerate humane* way – to broach the subject with his French counterpart. And to do so, without using the right form of words, would have turned the screws even tighter on a man who was already stretched on an emotional rack. *But what, exactly, would be the right words,* Scott asked himself. *There were none. At least none that he had been able to think of yet.*

If Megan had been deliberately targeted because she was Philippe Maigret's wife then was David Quinn the most likely suspect? Philippe thinks the answer's yes, but I'm not so sure, Clive Scott thought. *I didn't like the smart-mouthed prat; far too clever for his own good in my book, but I can't believe that he'd stoop this low. Don't want to think more likely,* his subconscious corrected; *you just don't want to believe that a fellow Brit could do such a thing. And yet you know that these things happen all the time.*

But if not Quinn, then who? An opportunist? Someone who didn't have any idea who Megan and Nat were? Is that why no ransom demand has been received so far? Or has Megan Maigret gone off on another one of her adventures? Not without letting Philippe know that they're okay. She may be a force of nature but she's not an irresponsible idiot. And she loves him.

'Why are we on the Strasbourg auto-route, Clive?' Philippe Maigret demanded, interrupting Scott's train of thought. 'We're going too far east – the train went almost due north after it left Gare de l'Est.'

'Keep your hair on, Philippe; we're not going as far as Strasbourg: we'll turn westwards long before we get anywhere near there. Trust me, this is the fastest route into Germany and where we want to end up. We'll be there in less than three hours.'

'We're running out of time; tomorrow's the Ides.'

'Yes.'

'Is that all you've got to say?'

'Yes – now please shut up and let me drive!'

'I can't, you know I can't. Why don't you let me drive for a while? I know these roads very well.'

'Let me tell you a little story, Philippe. A posh black tie affair was being held in London – Mansion House, I believe.'

'*Comment?*'

'Sorry. For the benefit of our *foreign* passengers I should explain that Mansion House is located opposite the Bank of England in the City of London – at the business end, one might say. It's the home and office of the Lord Mayor of the City of London and a magnificent venue for business functions, fundraising events, receptions and dinners. Cabinet ministers, visiting heads of government and other prominent public figures often attend high profile events there.'

'Get on with it, Clive,' Maigret growled. 'And spare us the PR spiel.'

'As I said, a posh dinner was taking place in Mansion House. As the guests took their seats, but before Grace was said, a young Aussie waiter made his way down the table, allocating one bread roll to each side plate as instructed. One of the guests, a man very er... *conscious* of his own importance, said "Waiter, I'd like *two* bread rolls." The waiter looked at him and replied, "I'm sorry sir, but it's only one roll per person." "Don't you know who I am," the man said haughtily. "No sir, I'm afraid I don't. But do you know who I am?" This reply surprised the man who said, "No, who are you?" The waiter paused for a few seconds, then, with a satisfied smile replied, "I'm the guy with the bread rolls!" And with that he continued on down the table doling out *one* bread roll per person as before!'

'So?'

'So in this operation I'm the guy with the bread rolls. Okay?'

'*Touché,*' Philippe said, 'I take your point, Clive. But I know what you're thinking. And you too, Georges!'

'I'm... I'm not *thinking* anything, Chief – I'm just er *admiring* the scenery.'

This was such a fatuous remark that they all laughed.

'Admiring the sodding scenery are you, Georges? All I've seen so far has been blasted trees, concrete, more trees, and cars. I suppose we should look forward to the pretty little toll booths and charming motorway services before too long.' Clive Scott chortled. 'I've never heard such a load of old toilet contents in all my born days!' And they all laughed again.

Then suddenly Philippe Maigret was serious. 'Let me ask the question that is on both your minds. If Megan was chosen because she's my wife then *why* was it done? Was it for money, or to blackmail me in some way? Or was it...'

The question went unanswered.

'If it is for money, I can handle that; it's common knowledge that I'm not without financial resources. I could even find a way around blackmail: the early release of a criminal perhaps, or maybe vital evidence that might be... *mislaid,* or some other way I could be forced to break the law. And then, of course, I would immediately resign. But if it's...'

'Let's not go there, Philippe,' Chief Inspector Scott said quickly, glancing over his shoulder, 'and Georges, I hope that you will forget what you just heard.'

'Did someone say something, sir? I'm afraid I was too busy map-reading to hear if anyone did.' Georges Martin replied.

'Good man. And as for you, Philippe; there's never any point in crossing bridges before we come to them – understood? So no more alarmist talk or I'll be tempted to thump you!'

They drove on in silence for the next forty kilometres, then turned westwards as Clive had said they would and headed towards Neuwied, a town lying on the right bank of the Rhine, twelve kilometres northwest of Koblenz, on the railway from Frankfurt am Main to Cologne.

Neuwied was founded by Count Frederick of Wied in 1653 as residence of the Lower County of Wied. It grew rapidly due to its religious tolerance. Among those who sought refuge there was a colony of Moravian Brethren who were Protestants escaping persecution in their own country.

Besides being known for its tolerance, Neuwied was something of a German railway hub having two railway stations, Neuwied and Engers, on the Right Rhine line, while a third station was under consideration by the state agency for northern commuter services connecting to Koblenz Hauptbahnhof in the south and Koln Hauptbahnhof in the north. Via either of those stations, the German high-speed rail network and the interCity network were accessible.

And, as far as the detectives had been able to ascertain, Neuwied was very close to where the first uncoupling of the train, for those passengers wanting to travel to Munich, had taken place.

When they eventually reached the outskirts of Neuwied they could see something in the distance that looked suspiciously like a roadblock. As they drew nearer it was obvious that a roadblock was exactly what it was. Every car was being stopped for questions to be asked, IDs examined and car boots searched. When the officer in charge noticed the diplomatic plate on the Jaguar he indicated that he would wave it through the roadblock.

'Let's find out what's going on, Clive,' Maigret said.

'Okay.'

'No need to stop sir, please proceed,' the police officer said to Clive. Clive produced his Scotland Yard ID and asked 'What's going on here, officer?' in German.

'Nasty business, Chief Inspector,' said the officer. 'Crime scene in a cottage on the other side of town.'

'Fatalities?'

'Yes, sir – three.'

With those words Philippe Maigret was out of the car, flashing his *Police Nationale* ID and holding his breath. Georges Martin followed suit.

'Ask him if he speaks French,' Philippe said to Clive.

'No, sir, I don't. But I do speak some English,' the officer replied before Clive could speak.

'Who were they?' Philippe asked.

'We don't know their identities yet, sir.'

'No. I mean were they men or women?'

'All men, sir. They were all quite young men.'

'Thank God,' Philippe said without thinking.

'Sir?'

'No, no – I mean, it's a tragedy of course. But I thought… we thought that…'

'We thought the victims might have been the three missing passengers from the train from Paris to Berlin last night,' Clive Scott said by way of explanation.

'Oh. I understand.'

'May we visit the crime scene, officer?' Philippe asked. 'It's very important to us and especially to me.'

'His wife and grandson were two of the missing from the train,' Clive Scott said in German, 'that's why he's so worried.'

'This is very unusual, Chief Inspector. I'd like to help but I'm not sure I can. I'm not really involved in the murder investigation; all I know is what I've heard on the grapevine. I'm just in charge of the roadblock.'

'Then tell me this officer, how were the victims killed? Was it, perhaps, by two shots each – one to the head, one to the heart – using a Baikal handgun?'

'How did you…? Yes,' the officer replied.

'Over to you, Chief Inspector Maigret,' Clive Scott said.

'Merci. Officer, these murders could be – most probably are – connected to the very recent murder of six men in the *10th arrondissement* of Paris. If you don't have the authority to allow us to visit the crime scene then please, I beg you; contact your superior officers for their permission.'

'And…?' Clive Scott prompted.

'And tell them that the murders are very likely linked to an *atrocity* which is scheduled to take place in Berlin tomorrow!'

'Atrocity?' the officer repeated.

'Yes – I used that word advisedly – but other than that I have no real information. If I did I would tell you!'

'And so would I,' Clive Scott added.

The German officer signalled to a motorcycle cop who was standing on the side of the road taking note of everything, including their intense conversation and their anxious appearance.

'Officer, escort Chief Inspector Scott of Scotland Yard, and Chief Inspector Maigret of *Police Nationale de Paris*... and er...' he said, looking enquiringly at Georges Martin who hadn't said anything yet.

'Inspector Martin, also from *Police Nationale de Paris*,' Georges said, producing his ID.

'Escort our *colleagues* to the crime scene as quickly as you can and ask the officer in charge to give them his full co-operation! Lead the way and use your siren. I'll clear it with our superiors.'

The motorcycle outrider jumped on his bike and set off at high speed with loud siren, while Clive Scott kept pace.

'I told you a diplomatic car would come in handy – especially a hot little number like this one!' he said, clearly enjoying himself.

'Yes – but I'd be a lot more relaxed if I was convinced that the car was being used *legitimately!*'

'Of course it's being used legitimately, Philippe. What do you take me for – a common car thief? Do you really think I'd risk my pension if the car wasn't completely kosher?'

'Then tell me how.'

'Well, the way I pitched it to my superiors at the embassy was that David Quinn, being ex-GCHQ and therefore most likely the keeper of a great many official secrets, is someone that the British Government should probably be keen – nay *desperate* – to get back to our green and pleasant land er *intact,* and well before he is tempted to divulge any state er *clangers* or, as you would say, *faux pas*. And without any international incident having been triggered in the process. However, I *may* have forgotten to mention that you and Georges would be coming with me into Germany. But surely I can't be expected to remember every little detail at my age – can I?'

Philippe Maigret chuckled. 'Listen and learn, Georges, because a master has just spoken! That's a perfect example of how to bend the rules without the risk of penalty or fall-out afterwards. You should have been a con man, Clive, you have all the natural attributes,' Philippe Maigret said admiringly.

'Or a diplomat,' Clive countered. 'And, talking of penalties, I also happen to watch a lot of football. I've noticed that a good many of the top players have perfected the art of taking a dive without the referee noticing, and they always end up with a penalty for their rule-breaking. Your lot seem particularly good at it!'

Before either Philippe or Georges could defend their country's sporting honour Philippe's mobile rang.

'Oh, sweet Lord,' he whispered as the person on the other end spoke. 'Is that really you my love?'

'Yes it's me,' Megan replied, 'And I'm fine, and so is Nat.'

'But how?' he asked, quickly checking his phone: *ID withheld.*

'Where are you?'

'I'm not permitted to say.' She paused then said 'Cambridge' – and the call was immediately terminated.

SIXTEEN

For the next few minutes Philippe Maigret said nothing at all: at least nothing to either Clive or Georges. He just rocked gently in his seat murmuring words of thanks to the Lord God Almighty, the saints, and any other luminaries of the Holy Mother Church that he could call to mind, with a few *Hail Marys* thrown in for good measure.

Clive Scott, with his Presbyterian background, albeit somewhat lapsed, found this behaviour strange, but apart from a few glances in Philippe's direction wondering when his ecclesiastical phase would end, said nothing. And neither did Georges Martin.

Then, as suddenly as it had begun, Philippe snapped back into the venal world. '*Cambridge,*' he said. 'Megan said Cambridge. Was that to tell me Patrick was with them?'

'That's my bet,' Clive Scott said. 'Must be, in fact. Patrick doesn't come from Cambridge, but he's in his final year there. And that was the best your missus could do under the circumstances.'

'Yes and grateful thanks for that small mercy.' He tapped a number on his speed dial. 'Jacques, is that you? *Bon.* I've just received a call to my phone. Ask the tech lads to trace where it came from – and as fast as they can, please. And from now on, make sure someone monitors my phone 24/7. *Comprendre?*'

'Yes, Chief, will do,' Jacques replied.

They reached the crime scene just as the pathologist – a grumpy older man lacking any of the warmth and *bonhomie* that HQ's Dr Lambert always displayed – was about to give consent for the bodies to be removed. He was not pleased to have his plans interrupted by the arrival of the three foreign detectives, nor the instructions received from higher up that he should extend all possible assistance to them.

'No,' he said taciturnly, there was no ID on any of the bodies. 'Yes,' he said, in the same tone of voice, the murders had taken place sometime before. How did he know? Because rigour had come and gone: the bodies were no longer stiff, they had begun to return to a more normal pre-death state.

'How long for rigour to come and go, Doctor?' Clive Scott asked.

'Depends on age of the victim and ambient temperature,' the pathologist replied. 'At this time of the year the nights are cold and there's not much heating in the cottage.'

'Make an educated guess, Doctor,' Clive urged in German.

'Anywhere between forty-eight and seventy-two hours. I'll know more when I get them back to the Lab.'

'So definitely not less than twenty-four hours?' Maigret asked.

'No, completely out of the question. More likely to be forty-eight to sixty hours – something like that.'

'Personal effects, Doctor; may we see them?' Georges Martin asked, attempting some schoolboy German.

'Watches yes, those we have, but there wasn't much else.'

'No passports?'

'*Nein. Nein Päss.*'

Looks like we're getting nowhere fast, Clive thought. *This bloke has somewhere else he'd rather be and I'm not convinced that it's back in his Lab!*

'Anyone got any spare gloves to hand?' he asked, pun intended. Only Georges Martin seemed to appreciate his attempt at humour.

'Here, Chief Inspector,' he said, fishing a pair of forensic gloves out of his trouser pocket.

'Ta,' Clive said. He put on the gloves and turned to the pathologist who was shifting impatiently from foot to foot, obviously desperate to make his escape. 'Do you mind if I take a quick look at the bodies,' he asked in German.

'*Nein, aber machen es schnell, bitte.*'

Clive Scott examined the bodies quickly, silently, and efficiently, while Maigret and Georges stood back observing. 'Hello,' he said after a few minutes, 'and what do we have here?'

'What?'

'These two are probably British,' Clive said, indicating the bodies of two of the victims.

'How so?' Philippe Maigret asked.

'Because the shirts they are wearing have M & S labels in them – Marks & Spencer's, I mean.'

'So? They might have been tourists who bought them while on holiday,' Georges Martin said. 'They could be from anywhere.'

'Well, yes, but this one's definitely from Israel. Or, at least he's a Jew.'

'And how do you arrive at that conclusion, Clive?' Philippe asked.

'See for yourself,' he said, opening the top two buttons of the victim's shirt, 'he's still wearing the Star of David around his neck.' The pathologist looked embarrassed; this was a serious oversight on his part and he knew it. 'Do you want me to remove it now, Doctor?' Clive asked in German.

The pathologist nodded, *'Bitte.'*

'Another tourist,' Georges said dismissively as he watched Clive Scott pass the religious symbol to the pathologist. 'These three could be from anywhere. Anywhere at all.'

'Have any of the others er…had the snip too, Doctor?' Clive Scott asked.

'The snip? What is that, *bitte*?'

'Have they been circumcised?'

'No, just the one wearing the star.' The pathologist looked pointedly at his watch. 'Do I have your permission to remove the bodies now?' he said.

'Okay with you if he does, Philippe?' Scott asked.

'No, not yet. Why don't you take a break for fifteen minutes, Doctor?' Chief Inspector Maigret said.

'There's something here that I'm not quite satisfied with at present.'

'What, sir?'

'That's it, Georges – I just don't know,' Maigret said, with a subtle nod in the direction of the irritated pathologist.

The pathologist hesitated for a moment then, huffing and puffing petulantly went outside. Maigret glanced at the two young police officers standing off to one side; saying nothing, missing nothing.

'Find out if they speak English or French, Clive,' he said.

'Righty-O,' Clive said obligingly. He walked over to the two officers and engaged them in friendly conversation. After a minute he looked back at Philippe and shook his head.

'In that case, ask them who moved the bodies,' Maigret said.

'What?'

'You heard me! Ask them, because I'm sure someone did: this crime scene looks *artificial* to me. It's too er neat and clean, and I wonder why the pathologist didn't comment on that fact.'

Philippe Maigret watched as Clive asked the question. He couldn't understand their language but it was perfectly obvious that they were annoyed by the suggestion. No one had *touched* the bodies or anything else; at least not after they'd arrived they were declaring with all the vehemence of the German language. And what's more they resented the suggestion and the slur on their professionalism.

'Did you get all that, Philippe?' Clive asked from the other side of the room.

'Yes, I believe I did.'

'And so did I,' Georges Martin said, 'including the unflattering words they used to describe you, Chief, and the doubts that were cast on your parentage!'

Chief Inspector Maigret grinned. 'Never hurts to push a button or two. And now we know the bodies were moved *before* the local constabulary arrived.'

'Do we?' Clive said, strolling over to them. 'This scene looks okay to me; certainly it doesn't set any bells ringing.'

'No, I'll give you that, Clive. Whoever moved the bodies was a professional; he, or *they*, knew exactly what they were doing.'

As Chief Inspector Maigret spoke his mobile rang.

'Sir, the tech boys have the answer to your question,' Jacques Laurent said, 'but I don't think you're going to like the answer.'

'Tell me anyway, Jacques.'

'The last call received on your mobile came from outside of Hanover on the autobahn to Berlin.'

'*Merde!* And where is the caller now?'

'The techs can't tell, sir – phone's switched off.'

'How long ago did the phone go silent?'

'They don't know; still working on that.'

'Keep me updated. They do realise this is urgent, *very* urgent, don't they?'

'Yes, Chief, they know. As soon as the phone's turned on again they'll find out more, and I'll be in touch the minute I know anything.'

'*Bon.* Good man.'

'Oh, and one more thing, sir. The British Embassy's been on the phone: the First Secretary I think he said he was, wanted to speak to you.'

'About what?'

'Er *apparently* Chief Inspector Scott has er gone walkabout, or drive-about, in one of the embassy's cars, and they'd quite like to receive confirmation that both the chief inspector and the car are er currently *undamaged,* and likely to remain that way. *If it's not too much trouble.*'

'Extraordinary, Jacques! What did you tell them?'

'I said I'd pass their concerns on to you the next time we spoke, Chief. And now I have.'

'Yes, and now you have. Please phone the embassy on my behalf and inform them that I'm quite sure there's no cause for er… *disquiet* on either the condition of the car, or that of Chief Inspector Scott. Oh, and add that I believe there's a very good chance that both will reappear at the embassy within the next day or so.'

'Will do, Chief.'

'You *charlatan*, Clive,' he said as he ended the call. 'You led me to believe that the car was completely above board and so was your offer!'

'Well, *maybe* I felt *obliged* to tell you what you obviously wanted to hear at the time, my friend, especially when you were so worried about the disappearance of your missus and grandson.'

'You're not in the slightest bit embarrassed by the deception either, are you? And I think that's the most annoying part of all!'

'Needs must, sometimes. And rules were made to be broken. I have a great many similar clichés that I'd be happy to spout if it would make you feel better.'

'I should wring your damn neck,' Philippe said, but he was smiling.

'Ready to go now, sir?' Georges asked.

'Almost. Clive, will you sooth the officers' ruffled feathers for me? Tell them I've been under a lot of pressure and didn't mean to cause any offence, and ask them two questions. Firstly, how long were the scene of crime people here, and secondly, what did they take away with them?'

'Okay.' Clive Scott went over to the policemen, and said something to them that immediately caused uproarious laughter. Georges Martin caught some of the words: idiot, eccentric, demented – and *wirkt wie eine alte frau* – which Georges judged to be highly derogatory to both his boss and old women! Clive and the officers engaged in friendly conversation, with many a side-ways glance and snigger at Chief Inspector Maigret, then Clive walked over to the pedal bin in the corner of the room, opened it noisily with his foot and peered inside. Maigret had no doubt that this had been done for his benefit.

'Walk with me, Georges,' Philippe said, 'while we take another look around the cottage.

It didn't take them long. There were only five small rooms: two bedrooms, each with two single beds; a tiny sitting room with four chairs that was almost overwhelmed by the large television standing against one wall; a bathroom; and the kitchen – the largest room in the bungalow – in which all the bodies had been found.

'Satisfied now, Chief?' Georges asked as they returned to the kitchen.

'No, not yet.'

As that point Clive Scott rejoined them. 'I told you that a German-speaker would prove useful, Philippe, and I was right.'

'I'm very grateful, Clive. So what *had* been in the pedal bin?'

'Drug paraphernalia.'

'Aha, so that was it,' Philippe Maigret said, finally satisfied. 'Let's take a closer look at the bodies now.'

So they did. They inspected the bodies in minute detail: on the victims' arms, in their hair and behind their ears, between their fingers and toes, and under the soles of their feet, but no needle marks were found.

'These men were not part of any drug cartel, nor were they users,' Clive Scott said. 'But the trappings were left behind to make it seem that they were, and that their deaths were drug-related.'

'Precisely. And how long did the scene of crime officers stay here, Clive?'

'Just over an hour.'

'We need their fingerprints, Georges; anything we could use to take them?'

'I could always follow your lead and nick a glass, sir – but perhaps not while the Germans are watching us like hawks.'

'Yes, I take your point. Oh, and some photographs

would be useful too. You take them, Georges, you're a better photographer than me, then send them to Jacques and ask him to run both prints and photos through the system at HQ.'

'Leave it me guys, but be quick,' Clive said. 'I'll take the German lads walkies in the front garden for five minutes or so. I'll say I'm looking for clues.'

'They'll have searched the garden, Chief Inspector,' Georges Martin said. 'Any clues that might have been there will have been found by now.'

'I didn't say I'd *find* any clues, laddie – just that I'd look for them.'

'Okay, Clive, off you go.'

However, much to everyone's surprise, not least of all his own, Clive Scott did find a clue. And a significant clue at that: a Eurostar boarding pass from London to Paris in the name of Patrick Evremond.

SEVENTEEN

Tuesday 14th March.
Neuwied, Germany. 2.30pm

'So much for the Aryan master race,' Clive Scott said as he returned to the cottage with his trophy tucked in his pocket. 'By the looks of things these guys couldn't organise a you know what in a you know where! But to be fair to them, although I don't know why I should be since they keep beating us at football, it was very well concealed; tucked right in the middle of an overgrown shrub planted well back from the path. I might have missed it myself if I hadn't bent down to tie my shoelace. And that's probably how it was hidden there in the first place.'

'Did the German lads object to you taking it away?'

'No because they didn't see me do it! As soon as I spotted it I asked them if they'd mind checking on the car for me and they were happy to oblige. After they'd gone I retrieved and pocketed it. Simple!'

'Perhaps we shouldn't judge them too harshly, sir. By the look of things Neuwied's a small place, it's not exactly Paris or Berlin.'

'Granted, Georges, but I wouldn't tolerate the oversight of a piece of evidence like this. And I doubt Chief Inspector Scott would in London, either.'

'You're right, Philippe. But the German police don't know about Patrick Evremond, do they? Nor how important finding his boarding pass is for us.'

'That's true,' Philippe Maigret conceded. 'But even so…'

'Yes, even so it was sloppy policing to miss anything that *might* possibly have been useful to a murder investigation,' Clive agreed.

They took their leave of the German policemen then walked back towards the British Embassy's newest addition to the diplomatic fleet. A small crowd of locals had assembled to admire the car but their motorcycle escort was making sure none of them came too close.

'How about I ask this officer if there's somewhere good in the area where we could have a late lunch?' Clive said. 'I don't know about either of you but I'm starving.'

'No time to eat, Clive and no guesses as to where we're going next,' Philippe said firmly. 'We can pick up a baguette somewhere on the way.'

'Over my dead body! I'm the one with the bread rolls, remember? Or, in this instance the car keys and I'm not going anywhere until I've had something *decent* to eat!'

'And I'm with Chief Inspector Scott, Chief,' Georges said. 'We'll be no help to anyone if we don't look after ourselves.'

'Okay,' Philippe said, 'but let's make it snappy.'

At that point the motorcycle cop intervened. 'Follow me, sirs, and I'll take you to the best brasserie in Neuwied,' he said in English. And they did.

As they finished eating and their coffee arrived, Philippe Maigret said quietly, 'How much do you think they saw, Clive? I mean Megan and Nat? Why were they even at the cottage?'

'Don't go down that road, my friend. Not when we can't be sure whether they actually *were* there. Yes, it seems very likely that Patrick was present, but that doesn't necessarily mean that your missus and Nat were too.'

'No, Patrick would not have left them on their own. If he was there, they were; I'm sure of that.'

'Chief, what if David Quinn *did* actually board the train, and what if these three men were his contacts?' Georges Martin asked while his boss was staring silently into space.

'And Quinn murdered them?'

'No, Chief Inspector Scott. What if someone else got to them before he could meet with them?'

The two chief inspectors mulled over Georges' words for a few minutes without saying anything, and then Clive Scott spoke again.

'You know, Philippe that idea's not as farfetched as it might seem. Georges could have a point.'

'Hmm, maybe.' As Philippe Maigret contemplated Georges' theory his phone rang. It was Jacques Laurent with an update.

'Sir, we have a trace of two of the victims.'
'Which ones?'
'The two who were not er… Jewish.'
'And who are they?'
'Well, as far as we can tell both of them are… er *were* active MI6 field officers.'

★

Monday 13th March (8.30pm)

Twenty minutes after the train pulled out of Gare de l'Est in Paris there came a gentle knocking at their compartment's door. Megan assumed that it was the German concierge to tell them that dinner was about to be served. She opened the door and David Quinn pushed his way inside: with one look she realised that he was on the verge of collapse. *I know Philippe said I shouldn't have anything to do with this man,* she thought, *but I wouldn't turn a stray animal away in the state he's in! Why was he discharged from hospital? By the look of him he should still be there.*

Nat glanced up from his tablet as Quinn entered. He recognised Quinn and was about to speak but Megan shook her head so he said nothing. She sat Quinn down on the lower bunk, brought a glass from the bathroom, opened one of the small bottles of Italian red wine that had been left for them – along with two bottles of still water – and poured him a glass. He gulped it down quickly and immediately proffered the glass for a refill.

None of them said anything but gradually the colour started seeping back into Quinn's face.

He needs something to eat, Megan thought, *but I've nothing to give him.* Then she remembered the chocolate bar in her handbag. She gave it to him and he ate it greedily.

'Rest now,' she said, when he had finished both the wine and the chocolate.

'No time,' he muttered.

'We'll make time,' she said, gently lowering him back on the pillow. He offered no resistance, closed his eyes and within a minute was asleep.

'What's he doing here, Megs?' Nat whispered.

'I don't know. But it seems he needs our help.'

'He can't sleep here – there are only two bunks.'

'Yes, I know. Maybe he has his own compartment or a seat somewhere.'

'If he *does* what's he doing asleep in ours?'

'Good question, Nat. And I don't know that answer either but I'm sure he'll tell us after he's had a rest.'

'What if he wants to sleep here for the *whole n*ight? Where will you sleep?'

'In the bath,' she joked.

'We don't have a bath, just a miniscule shower.'

'Hmm, I thought there might be a flaw in my plan,' she said, smiling at him. 'Don't worry; we'll sort something out after we've had our supper.'

'He can't stay here; Philippe wouldn't like it!'

'I'm sure he wouldn't. But remember the story of the Good Samaritan, Nat?'

'Yes, of course!'

'We have to be good Samaritans now. What else can we do?' As Megan spoke there was another knock on their door. She opened it gingerly and this time it actually was the train concierge.

'Dinner is ready to be served, Madame,' she said.

'Thank you, miss, we'll be along in a couple of minutes.'

'Are we just going to leave him here while we have our dinner?' Nat said, looking incredulous.

'Yes. Why not?'

'What if he does something weird?'

'Like what?'

'I don't know,' Nat said, losing patience. 'Something; anything!'

'He won't.'

'He might.'

'No. I *know* he won't, Nat. He doesn't look like that kind of man. Now let's go.'

They walked down the long corridor unsteadily: the train was lurching from side-to-side although it didn't seem to be travelling at top speed. But they managed to keep their balance and eventually arrived in the restaurant car. They appeared to be the last to arrive.

'Can you get a signal on your mobile, Nat? I can't.'

'No. Maybe the train doesn't have wi-fi.'

'But you'd think it would; I'll try later, Philippe will want to know how we're doing.'

'Will you tell him about David Quinn?'

'Hmm, I'm not sure. How many people do you think are in the restaurant car?' she asked, changing the subject.

'About thirty, maybe – not as many as I thought there would be.'

'Nor me,' she said, studying the menu. Two choices of soup to begin with, followed by a main course of fish, fowl, or vegetarian, and dessert. Or cheese and biscuits, or both, apparently. *Obviously the soup's out as far as snaffling something in my serviette to take back for Mr Quinn,* she thought, *although the cheese and crackers will be useful. But maybe that's not enough; the poor man looked very hungry.*

'Why are you frowning?' Nat asked.

'I'm wondering what food we can take with us to feed our needy guest.'

'Obviously not the soup!'

'No, I'd worked that out for myself. When the waiter comes with the bread basket take as many of the rolls as you can and I'll do the same.'

'He'll need more than just bread!'

'Yes, well we can also take lots of cheese and maybe some fruit. And perhaps more wine to help him sleep.'

'He's not sleeping with us!'

'No, of course he's not. Did you hear me say that he was?'

They finished their dinner, taking pleasure in filching as much extra food as they could. *If only my husband the chief inspector, the upholder of the law, could see me now,* Megan thought, smiling to herself as she wrapped a large piece of roast chicken in her napkin and stuffed it into her handbag. *Here I am, stealing food for a stranger who's hiding in our compartment! Why is he hiding? Does he even have a ticket,* her conscience pressed. *I don't know, and what's more I don't care right now!*

The waiter, watching their pilfering, was both amazed and amused. *They're welcome to have as much food as they wish,* he thought, *so why do they steal instead? English,* he decided, answering his own question, *all as mad as the March hare, isn't that what everyone says?*

But he was more than happy with the large tip Megan left for him. So much for German rectitude!

When they arrived back at their compartment they were surprised to see that Quinn, having had a solid hour's sleep during their absence, was awake and looking considerably more alert than he had been on arrival.

'We brought some more food for you,' Megan said as they entered the room. 'I'm afraid it's only a piece of chicken, some bread, cheese, a pear and a banana. Oh, and another small bottle of wine.'

'Thank you, Madame Maigret,' he said, taking the food-filled serviettes from both of them and depositing them next to him on the bunk. 'And you too, young man. I'm grateful for the help you've given me.'

'That's okay,' Nat said before Megan could speak. 'Megs says you're our Samaritan project.'

'What?'

'You know my name?' Megan asked. She watched as he tore a roll in half, buttered it with the knife she'd misappropriated from their table, inserted a large chunk of cheese between the two pieces and wolfed most of it down in a couple of mouthfuls. *Looks like there's not much wrong with his appetite,* she thought, *and that must be a good sign.*

He nodded, mouth still otherwise engaged.

'Yes, and I know your grandson's name is Nathaniel, but everyone calls him Nat,' he said as he finished chewing and looked eagerly at the chicken piece.

'How so, Mr Quinn?'

'Your husband told me when he interviewed me in hospital, Madame. But please, my name is David. If you keep calling me Mr Quinn I'll start looking over my shoulder expecting to see my father standing behind me.'

'And my name's Megan, David. Now what's all this about?'

He didn't answer immediately, but rummaged through his pockets looking for something. Eventually he found it; a somewhat crumpled photograph.

'This is what it is about,' he said, 'or rather *who* it's about. Take a look for yourself, Megan – I'm sure you'll recognise this man.'

She said she didn't.

'Think back thirty years or so. A time when you did work experience in New York. Isn't this a man you knew then?'

She looked at the photograph again. 'No. I've never seen this man before.'

'Oh, but I think you have. And you knew him. In fact you knew him very well! Surely he hasn't changed so very much over the years. He's still an attractive man, isn't he?'

This time she took a longer, *closer* look at the photograph. 'Is it, perhaps? I wonder? Could it really be?' she said, as though talking to herself. 'Is this a man who used to be an art critic in New York? I don't remember his name but perhaps it is. It might be.'

David Quinn looked amused. '*An art critic,*' he repeated. 'Is that what he told you?'

'Yes, and that's what he *was*,' she said. 'I read every one of his reviews while I was in New York. He was a fine writer and very knowledgeable about all kinds of art.'

'Good. So now, can you remember his name, I wonder?'

'Give me a few minutes,' she said. 'Nat, why don't you get ready for bed? You could change in the bathroom.'

'Okay.' David and Nat said simultaneously.

When Nat had gone, closing the door behind him, Megan said firmly, 'No more questions about New York, David: and never in front of Nat.'

'You've remembered. In fact I believe you recognised him the first moment you looked at the photo. Just tell me his name and that will be enough for now.'

'His name was Tom,' she said reluctantly.

'And?'

'Aitkens. His name was Tom Aitkens.'

'Very good. Now let me tell you something. Mr Thomas Jefferson Aitkens is the reason I'm on this train. He's also the reason that you, and I – and Nat – will leave this train at around half-past midnight when the Munich section is uncoupled.'

'You can do whatever you want,' she replied, 'but there's no way that Nat and I are leaving this train before Berlin!'

'You will, Megan, when I tell you more. The Tom Aitkens with whom you had a passionate love affair during your three months in New York arrived in Berlin this very morning. And your Mr Aitkens is involved in something very nasty that will happen in Berlin tomorrow unless you help me stop him.'

'No,' she said defiantly. 'You've got the wrong man! Tom Aitkens was a respectable art critic and a good, decent man. He wouldn't get involved in something like that. He just wouldn't!'

The door to the bathroom opened a couple of centimetres and Nat peered through. 'Is it safe for me to come out now – or is one of you about to clobber the other one?'

'Not yet,' Megan said. 'Wait until I call you, Nat.'

'Okay,' he said, closing the door again.

'Thirty years ago, Tom Aitkens might have been a good decent man, probably was, in fact,' Quinn said. 'But don't you think the world has a way of corrupting even the best of men, Megan?'

'No, I don't. I'm not that cynical.'

'Then you're incredibly naïve.'

'So those are the alternatives are they, Mr Quinn? Either I'm as *warped* as you are or I'm as thick as a brick?'

'Warped? Well, maybe I am. But three days ago I considered myself to be a good man and I think you might have thought me that too. Then I was deliberately run down by a car outside of Les Invalides not long after speaking to you, and left for dead. I was taken to the Pitié-Salpêtrière Hospital where I was placed in an induced coma. But before that was done, and while I was in a very poor physical state, your husband ruthlessly attempted to interrogate me.'

'No, Philippe wouldn't behave like that.'

'Yet he did. He even brought in a Scotland Yard officer to question me too: a great brute of a man but he didn't speak French and I decided that he was not to be trusted.'

'If you're referring to Clive Scott he's a friend of ours. A very *good* friend.'

'You have my sympathy, Madame!'

'And my French is fairly basic so perhaps you shouldn't trust me either!'

'Then while I was still in the coma,' he continued, ignoring her disingenuous interruption, 'an armed man came to the hospital to kill me. To cut a long story short I figured that it was time for me to get out of that hospital before someone actually succeeded. But to do this I first had to overpower one of your husband's officers, force drugs down his throat and then bind and gag him and steal his clothes, wallet, police ID – and revolver. And that's exactly what I did. Now tell me, Madame, am I still a *good* man, or not?'

EIGHTEEN

'How should I know? I only have your word for it that you were *ever* a good man,' Megan said.

'Fair enough. How could I convince you?'

'Tell me about yourself; where do you live, where are you from? How do you earn a living?'

'At present, to use police-speak, *I have no fixed abode, nor do I have a job. I was born and raised in Leeds.*'

'And that's not far from Scarborough, is it? Is that why you asked me if I was going to Scarborough Fair?'

'Yes, Leeds is not far from Scarborough,' he sighed, 'but no, that's not why I quoted the first line of *Scarborough Fair* to you. Why don't you ask me…?'

'Then why did you?' Megan interrupted.

'To awaken the memory of your time in New York all those years ago. Why don't you ask me how I come to be so well-informed about your old lover, Tom Aitkens?'

'Because I might not like the answer.'

'Ask anyway. You've really nothing to lose, have you?'

'I think you could be some kind of spy. Are you?'

'No, but some of my friends *might* be.'

'You work for the security service then?'

'Hmm. I think I'll pass on that one.'

At that moment Nat began knocking loudly on the bathroom door.

'Can I come out, please? I'm cold and it's boring in here.'

'Two minutes, Nat, then I'll call you.'

I can hear everything you're saying anyway!

'Then you'd better come out now,' David Quinn said, and Nat did.

'If the bad thing you're talking about is happening in Berlin on Wednesday why don't you just stay on the train until we get there in the morning? Why do you want to get off now? It doesn't make sense,' he asked.

'You're a pretty sharp cookie, aren't you, Nat?' Quinn said. 'And you really did hear everything, didn't you?'

'Yes and yes.'

'Where to begin?' Quinn said, talking to himself.

'At the beginning.'

'Can't do that, Nat. Not yet. There are two reasons for leaving the train when the Munich section is uncoupled. Firstly, I have some friends who are er… *should be…* staying in that area. And if they are they'll get us to Berlin *safely*.' He paused giving himself time to do some mental redacting before he continued.

'And?' Megan prompted.

'And secondly I'm worried that some very unpleasant people might be waiting for me when the train arrives at Berlin Hauptbahnhof. And if they are, they'll get rid of me and anyone with me. I'm not ready to die yet – are you?'

Nat and Megan looked at each other but said nothing. *Whoa!* Nat thought, *this all getting too serious for me. Why didn't Philippe come with us? Oh yes, he would have, but Megs wouldn't let him!*

No one said anything for a few minutes then Megan asked, 'Why?'

'Because they think I know too much, which is ironic because I know very little!'

'But you know about Tom Aitkens and New York, so obviously more than you're telling us, yet you expect us to leave the train with you. That's not reasonable. We're going nowhere with you until you give us something more. Something *concrete*. And even then, we may not go!'

'Okay. Let me ask you a question; why do you think there are so many shocking events happening these days? Planes being blown up in flight, or shot out of the sky; innocent civilians being massacred while going about their legitimate activities; unexpected conflicts, insurgencies, rebellions; militancy and civil wars? And that's without even mentioning the Middle East migration question. Why?'

'It has to be human nature, doesn't it? People, countries – everyone wants more money, territory – everything – than they have. It's a combination of greed and envy,' Megan said.

'Partly correct, but not the whole story.' He rummaged through his pockets again and produced another photograph. It was of a smiling man in uniform seated with a woman and three young children. 'Take a look at this.' They did.

'Some friends of yours, David?' Nat asked.

'Yes, Simon was a very good friend of mine. My best friend in fact. We grew up together in Leeds. When I went off to university he went into the army. That's him with his wife Lyn, and his children. He worked his way through the ranks and became a major.'

'Was?'

Quinn nodded. 'Yes, sadly past tense. Major Simon Pascoe was posted to Afghanistan supposedly on peace keeping operations. He was killed by a Taliban sniper. The bullet was later removed from his body and guess where it came from? Made in the UK – that's where the bullet that killed my best friend was made. And that's probably where the sniper's rifle came from too. The country that sent Simon to Afghanistan – his *own country* which he loved and served – *made* the bloody weapons that killed him! And how do I know that? Because until recently I worked at GCHQ, the British Government's listening station in Cheltenham. And now, thanks to you, I've violated the Official Secrets Act! I monitored the reporting of that incident and many more like it. I knew that kind of thing happened but when Simon was killed it was the last sodding straw for me.'

'How *could* things like that happen?'

'Because Saudi Arabia is the largest importer of British made weaponry. And many Western Governments believe they're also the main supporters, financial and otherwise, of *Daesh*!'

'What?'

'Daesh. That's what we should be calling the poisonous barbarians who claim they've founded an

Islamic State in Northern Syria. That's what the French Foreign Ministry decided to do in September 2014. And their Foreign Minister asked journalists and media organisations to do the same. He said "this is a terrorist group and not a State. I do not recommend using the term Islamic State because it blurs the lines between Islam, Muslims and Islamists. The Arabs call it Daesh and I will be calling them the Daesh cutthroats".'

'Oh.'

'Of course you won't hear the British Government use that name very often — nor the bloody apologists on the BBC! Daesh doesn't like being called that, so we mustn't upset the naughty boys by using it, must we? Don't want them to get *cross* with us! If they do they might *hurt* us: as if they're not already torturing and beheading people and blowing people up all over the bloody place! *Dratsabs!*'

'What's a drat... er... whatever you said, David?' Nat asked.

'Sorry, Nat, I was literally *butchering* the language,' David said, calming down a little. 'I used back slang.'

'What?'

'*Back slang*, is a kind of slang which evolved in Victorian England. It was popular in butcher shops because it allowed the shopkeeper to tell his assistant to bring out the old piece of meat for a particular customer without the customer knowing it. Greengrocers used it too.'

'How'd it work?' Nat asked, greatly intrigued.

'Well, a word was turned into code by writing it backwards while trying to make a sensible pronunciation, although certain sounds like "th" didn't actually get reversed, and extra vowels were inserted as necessary. In some cases, syllables were added or dropped, vowel sounds were changed, or a single letter – such as "h" – became pronounced. Apparently back slang is popular in prisons, and some of our young tennis players use it too. The French do a similar thing, and so do other countries. So boy becomes *yob* and *dratsabs* was used instead of… well I guess can work that one out for yourself.'

'Yes, thank you very much Mr Quinn,' Megan said quickly, 'but fascinating though the etymology lesson was, haven't you rather strayed from the point, which I seem to remember happened when you mentioned Saudi Arabia?'

'Yes, you're right, Madame. So – Saudi Arabia, a repressive oil-rich regime where Christians and other religions are not permitted to practise their faith in public and their own women are not allowed to drive a car or leave the house unless covered from head to foot, and even then must have a male escort. A country that ruthlessly puts down any hint of rebellion by its own citizens, and where people are regularly executed – some by the barbarity of a crucifixion. *A feudal medieval monarchy!* And followers of the same harsh ultra-conservative strain of Islam, *Wahhabism,* which Daesh follows. Yet we consider Saudi Arabia as our friends – "a stable influence in a troubled region" – is the way the Foreign Office describes this brutal country, while Daesh is denounced. So we train Saudi officers alongside ours at Sandhurst, and their bloody princes hobnob with royalty at Buckingham Palace and Royal Ascot, while we bomb Daesh in Syria and Iraq. Where's the logic in that? There's none – just the worst kind of hypocrisy! If the Saudis are our *friends* then God Almighty help us *because what must our enemies be like?'*

'But we were talking about Afghanistan, David, and the death of your friend there.'

'Yes. So this is how it works: we sell the weapons to our *friends* with no questions asked then they sell them on to God-knows-who! Or they're captured in Iraq or Syria and passed from terrorist group to insurgency to bloody *Daesh* – may the whole murderous lot of them rot in the hottest part of hell for all eternity,' he said, spitting the words out with great venom.

'Is that true?' Nat asked.

'Yes, I'm afraid it is, young man. Do you know which countries are the largest exporters of major weaponry?'

'No.'

'And I don't either,' Megan said.

'Then let me enlighten both of you. The USA is number one – no surprises there – with 31% of global exports during the period 2010 to 2014. Number two is Russia with 27%, and no surprises there either, followed by China, Germany and France, each with 5% and the UK exports 4%.'

'How do you know that?'

'Those figures are from the Stockholm International Peace Research Institute, or SIPRI as it is known,' Quinn said. 'But more importantly, who do you think *buys* most of them?'

'I don't know.'

'Three Asian countries: Pakistan, Bangladesh and Myanmar, formerly known as Burma – that's who. And if that doesn't give you the heebie-jeebies I don't know what would, because you can be sure they're not too worried about where they end up! The entire planet is awash with weapons right now, yet politicians and other politically correct idiots are fixated on gay marriage, transgender issues, and bloody climate change while more weapons are produced every day! Madness! Climate change, the biggest con trick of all, is being used as camouflage for what's really killing us!'

'And Tom Aitkens is somehow part of all this madness?'

'Yes, but I need to tell you how this whole arms trade works. Firstly, *peace* is bad for business! If everyone's playing happily in the global sandpit the weapons industry slows down, their order books look forlorn, and their shareholders get grumpy. So, what to do to fix that situation?

They call in someone to throw a spoke in the wheel, to create dissent, uproar, *mayhem* which leads to havoc! These particular people flit from group to group, drumming up business for the arms trade by whispering in the right ears – or to be more accurate, the *wrong* ears.'

'What? No – there can't be people that… wicked!'

'I'm afraid there are. Haven't you wondered how Daesh or Isil suddenly appeared on the scene? All some of these *facilitators* had to do was spread stories about how decadent and immoral the West had become. And then go on to suggest that maybe it would be a wonderful idea for the faithful – the *truly faithful* – to establish a pure Islamic antidote for all this idolatry and evil and – voila! A caliphate emerges out of the slime of northern Syria. And now the good times are rolling again for the arms trade! Or someone whispers to Putin that Ukraine rightfully belongs to Russia and the next thing there's a major conflict going on and a passenger aircraft is shot out of the sky. Russian arms sales go up and the West supplies Ukraine and everyone's happy because they're all making shed-loads of money again.'

'Who are these people? Where do they come from?'

'Everywhere. Greed knows no boundaries, nor does it recognise any borders.'

'And you think that Tom Aitkens – *my Tom Aitkens* – has become one of these... *dratsabs?*'

'Yes and maybe he always was.'

'You're mad. Deranged! I'll never believe that.'

'Just out of curiosity, why did you end your relationship with him?'

'I had my reasons,' Megan said, shooting a quick look at Nat, 'but I don't intend to go into them now.'

'Then you calmly returned to England and subsequently married the man to whom you were already engaged.'

'Yes, but the engagement was *unofficial* when I went to New York.'

'So that's alright then!'

'I don't need any lessons in morality from you, Mr

Quinn. Michael Lisle knew everything about New York before we were married.'

'Hmm. And I wonder how much Chief Inspector Maigret knows about your past?' Quinn mused. 'But now it's time to get a couple of hours sleep: we have a long day ahead of us tomorrow and the Munich uncoupling will happen soon enough.'

'How can three people sleep in a compartment with two bunks?' Nat said, returning to his earlier theme.

'Simple. You'll sleep down one end of the top bunk and I'll sleep down the other,' Quinn said.

'No – you'll kick me!'

'I promise I won't, Nat, and I don't want to be kicked either. Now can one of you set an alarm for two and a half hours from now, so we'll be sure to wake in time?'

'Are we really going with him, Megs?' Nat asked.

'I'm not sure. Mr Quinn – David – the people waiting for you in Berlin don't know Nat and me. Why can't we continue on to Berlin? Why do we have to go with you?'

Quinn smiled before he spoke. 'Haven't you worked that out yet, Megan? You and Nat are my *insurance*. When Chief Inspector Maigret discovers that you are missing he'll do whatever it takes to find you. I'll have him eating out of my hand! You two are my trump cards.'

'And what if we *won't* go? What then?'

'Then I'll have to resort to force, which I really don't want to do. I told you that I took the police officer's revolver at the hospital. It's loaded and I know how to use it.'

'So you'd threaten a woman and a lad, would you, Mr Quinn? I don't believe you were ever a good man! Not now – not after you've shown your true colours at last.'

'Megan, Megan, Megan,' he sighed. 'If even a miniscule part of what I suspect might happen should actually take place in Berlin on Wednesday, many people will die. What is your life, or mine against that nightmare?'

'It's my life too,' Nat said quickly. 'And I'll go with you David, even if Megs doesn't.'

'How old are you Nat?'

'Thirteen.'

'You're a very brave and intelligent young man.'

'And so will I,' Megan said, with a lump in her throat. 'And so will I, David.'

'God bless you,' Quinn said, preparing to climb up into the top bunk. 'Now give me your phones then try to get some sleep. We have a long day ahead of us tomorrow.'

Megan and Nat handed over their mobiles without protest or further words.

But David Quinn was the only one who got any sleep that night.

★

David Quinn's facts were not entirely correct: Tom Aikens had arrived in Berlin that afternoon, not the morning. He'd left his home, which some might have described as a mansion, in Connecticut at 7am and was chauffeur driven to JFK to fly from New York to Berlin in eight hours.

There was no one to farewell him: his two children were living away from home, one at university in Boston, and the older one already working in New York. There was no *current* Mrs Tom Aitkens, the previous one – his second wife – had divorced him two years earlier. However, he was never short of female companionship: his wealth was as honey to the predatory bees, mostly half his age, who ruthlessly seek out men like him. Successful men, wealthy men and, in his case, men not far from their prime with the looks to prove it. Six foot two inches tall, permanent tan – real from his regular Caribbean holidays – fair hair with a sprinkling of grey that fell foppishly over his forehead in the style of an Elizabethan dandy. Tom Aitkens was at the top of his game in more ways than one!

And with a residential address to match. Connecticut, the southernmost state in New England. Bordered to the east by Rhode Island, Massachusetts to the north, New York to the west, and Long Island Sound to the south; the third smallest state in the Union.

Connecticut's first European settlers were Dutch, who established a small, short-lived settlement in present day Hartford, the State's capital. Half of Connecticut was a part of the Dutch colony of New Netherland, which included most of the land between the Connecticut and Delaware rivers. But the first major settlements were founded in the 1630s by England and with the Connecticut and New Haven Colonies instituted documents of Fundamental Orders, which are considered the first constitutions in

North America. In 1662 the three colonies were merged under a royal charter, making Connecticut a crown colony. This colony was one of the Thirteen Colonies that revolted against British rule in the American Revolution. Now it is one of the wealthiest states in the US by most economic measures, although the income gap between its urban and suburban areas is unusually wide.

Tom Aitkens was every inch a son of this historic State, descended from the early Dutch pioneers and already upwardly mobile when, aged twenty-seven, his path crossed that of a young unsophisticated English girl, newly-graduated from a minor university by way of an insignificant public school. Her father, a well-educated man but a rather erratic provider for his family, had a friend in New York who owed him a favour: that was how the young Megan Ross came to New York for her three months' work experience.

And it was that gauche girl, with her sweet-smelling hair swishing from side to side as she walked – that innocent girl with her brown eyes that seemed to know the innermost yearnings of his soul. It was that girl, that *all-unknowing* girl with the gentle air and the sweet temperament; that girl, the one whose laugh that he still imagined he heard sometimes as he drifted off to sleep; that was the girl, the one with the smooth skin and the tender touch, that had first stolen, and then broken, Tom Aitkens' heart during that heady Simon and Garfunkel New York summer of 1985.

And his was the heart that had not yet completely healed.

NINETEEN

Tuesday 14th March. 12.45am

Patrick Evremond, watching from towards the front of the train, saw them leave. He had been thoroughly rehearsed by Philippe Maigret and his catechism had gone thus: no sleep, stay awake and alert until both the Munich and Hamburg uncouplings have been executed. Then sleep, provided all is well. If it is not, phone me no matter what time it is. Stay in touch; stay on guard.

But how could he, when he couldn't get a signal? *Old train, soon to be de-commissioned,* he remembered. *Therefore, no signal. Why hadn't Chief Inspector Maigret foreseen that possibility?*

It was a perfect *bomber's moon* night: the moon lit the earth to near-daylight. There were, however, a few skittish clouds dancing across the sky at the whim of the gentle winds. Sometimes they skipped in front of the moon and they chose to do that at exactly the time that the three passengers climbed down from the train.

The man went first. Patrick saw the shape of his head, as the first cloud moved. *It could be Quinn,* he thought trying to visualise the details in the photographs Maigret had shown him. *Certainly the man's build is right – if only he would turn so I could see his face!*

The climb down from the train was long; 12 steps at least. Losing patience the man jumped the last metre, landing smoothly on his feet like a natural athlete. The slighter, shorter figure replicated the man's movements, stumbling as he hit the ground but managing to stay upright.

Then they helped the woman down and it was then, as the clouds moved again across the sky, that Patrick saw their faces clearly. It was David Quinn, and it was also Nat. And although he didn't see her face he knew that the woman was Megan Maigret.

He waited until they scrambled across the stony open ground towards the cover of the bushes and undergrowth on the other side, then he and his backpack followed. No one challenged him, or the three who had left first; all the action – the noisy uncoupling of the train's mechanism, the good-natured bantering between the railway workers – was happening on the other side of the train. Nor was anyone watching from the train's compartments: the other passengers were either reading in their bunks or already fast asleep.

'David wait!' Megan whispered. 'I did something to my ankle when I landed. You've got to slow down, there's no way I can keep up with you at the speed you're going.'

'Did you twist it?'

'I don't know. I hope I just pulled a muscle.'

'Then we'll keep going. We have to get clear of the train before it moves off. But we can slow down a little but that's all.'

'How far do we have to go?' Nat asked.

'About a quarter of a kilometre, maybe further. Not too far. It won't take long, if I don't get lost!'

'Haven't you been here before?' Megan and Nat asked at the same time.

'Yes, but I didn't start from where we did now so I'm still trying to get my bearings.'

They trudged on with Patrick following them, as quietly as he could, from a distance of about fifteen metres.

Suddenly Quinn stopped. 'There it is again,' he muttered. 'I think we're being followed.'

'Who would even know we were here?' Megan said.

'No one, but I know what I heard. You two keep walking, as slowly as you like, while I double back to take a look.'

'Okay,' Megan and Nat said together again.

Quinn peeled off to the right of the narrow track on which they were walking, and, dodging between trees for cover, made a wide detour back towards the train. And that's when he saw Patrick. Saw him, but didn't recognise him. How could he, when he'd never seen him before? He stayed in his hiding place until Patrick had moved a few steps past him and then he struck. He was heavier built than Patrick, and he also had the element of surprise which meant he easily over-powered him, knocking him to the ground then falling on top of him.

'What the bloody hell…' Patrick groaned.

'English?'

'Yes, of course I am! What the hell are you playing at, man?' Patrick said, breath recovering, dander fully up.

'Why are you following us?'

'Why did you take Madame Maigret and Nat off the train?'

'You know them? You a cop?'

The noise of the scuffle alerted Megan and Nat who, against Quinn's orders, had retraced their steps to see what was happening.

'Patrick! Is that you?' Megan called.

'Yes.'

'You know this man, Megan?'

'Of course I do! He stayed with Philippe and me for a couple of weeks not long ago. And if you've hurt him you'll have me to deal with! And Philippe too, when he finds out.'

'Only my pride's been hurt, Madame Maigret,' Patrick said, brushing himself off. 'Otherwise I'm fine.'

'What are you doing here?' Quinn asked.

'Let's start with who you are and why you've kidnapped Madame Maigret and Nat from the train.'

'Had to; necessity,' Quinn replied enigmatically. 'My name's David Quinn.'

'Yes, I know.'

'Then why ask?'

'To see if you'd tell me the truth.'

As Patrick spoke they heard the sound of the train starting its slow shunt out of the Neuwied siding.

'Time to get a move on,' Quinn said gruffly. 'And you'd better come with us; explanations can wait until we get to the cottage.'

'Cottage?'

Quinn nodded. 'Yes, the cottage where my friends will be waiting. I hope they'll have information and a fast car for Berlin.'

'Do you know what's going on?' Patrick whispered to Megan as they continued on their way.

'Yes, and also no.'

'And yet you and Nat left the train with him?'

'It's a long story, Patrick, and my ankle's hurting me. Let's wait until we get to where we're going, then I'll tell you everything. But why were you on the train, and why did you get off when we did?'

'Er... that's another long story,' Patrick said, desperately trying to concoct a story that would not land Philippe Maigret in the marital soup. 'And for later, too.'

They trudged on for another fifteen minutes, then Quinn gave a shout of satisfaction. 'We're almost there,' he said, 'I can see the lights up ahead.'

'Not a moment too soon,' Megan said, rubbing her ankle, which had started to throb.

'Wait here – all of you,' Quinn directed when they arrived at the cottage. 'I need to let my friends know that I have company with me. Find somewhere to sit; I might be ten minutes or so.'

'It's very quiet,' Patrick said, 'they must have heard us arrive. Maybe they're out.'

'They won't be out, they're expecting me.' He opened the door and went inside.

They found an ancient garden seat just off the path and sat down gratefully.

'We could make a run for it now,' Patrick whispered, 'while he's inside.'

'But where would we go?' Nat said. 'We don't even know where we are.'

'And I don't think my ankle would let me run anywhere right now,' Megan said. 'Do you have any painkillers in your backpack, Patrick?'

'Afraid not. But perhaps Quinn's friends have some.'

Megan shivered. 'I don't like it here, and I'm starting to feel cold. Are you okay, Nat?'

'Yes, but I'm a bit cold too.'

'What's keeping him?' Patrick said.

As he spoke, the door of the cottage opened and Quinn appeared in the doorway. 'Patrick,' he said, 'I think you should join me now.'

'What about us?' Megan asked. 'We're getting cold out here.'

'Not yet. You should stay where you are for now,' Quinn replied. 'Come on Evremond – get a move on!'

Patrick did as instructed and disappeared into the cottage. The door was closed firmly behind him.

'And then there were two,' Megan said.

'Yes. Why don't we have a look around?' Nat said. 'It would be better than just sitting here waiting. And anyway – where's their car – I can't see one. Can you?'

'No, I can't. Let's see if we can find it. The rest has

done my ankle some good; I'm sure I could manage a walk around the garden.'

They walked right around the property, but found no car.

'What about out on the street?' Nat suggested.

'Is there a street?'

'There must be, otherwise how could they get a car in here?'

'If they actually had a car,' Megan replied. 'Maybe David Quinn was mistaken.'

'I think it could be that way,' Nat said, 'at the end of the front garden. That's the most likely place for a street, isn't it?'

Nat was right, although one would hardly have considered it a street: it was more like a country track than a paved street, but there was no car to be seen. Nor were there any houses to be seen. *This place is beginning to give me the creeps* Megan thought. *It's too quiet.*

'Let's go back to the garden seat,' she said, 'it doesn't look like there's anything much to be seen out here.'

'Okay.'

They retraced their steps and sat down on the rickety garden seat again, huddling together for warmth while they waited.

As the minutes passed without either Quinn or Patrick reappearing, Megan decided to take direct action. 'Stay here for a minute, Nat,' she said. 'I think it's time I found out exactly what's going on.'

'I'm coming, too!'

'No, wait a while. Count to two hundred. Slowly,

not by tens then if I haven't returned, come inside. But knock twice on the door before you do.'

'I think I should come now, Megs.'

'Please, Nat, just do as I've asked,' she said, giving him a hug.

'Okay,' he said reluctantly. 'I will, but I don't like it.'

'Neither do I, but I won't be long.

She walked to the door, opened it quietly and went inside.

★

Tuesday 14th March (afternoon)

'Say that again, Jacques,' Philippe Maigret said, glancing quickly in Clive Scott's direction.

'Okay, sir. We know who the two non-Jewish victims in the cottage were. They were both active MI6 officers.'

'That's what I thought you said. Names?'

'Er… a Richard Ennis, and a James Stanley, sir.'

'And the other one?'

'No trace of him, Chief.'

'Have you checked with Israeli Intelligence?'

'Not yet. I'll advise you when I have. But what about the British, Chief – they'll have to be informed.'

'Agreed, but not by us, Jacques. That's a job for Chief Inspector Scott.'

'Okay, sir.'

Clive Scott pulled into the first layby he came to, stopped the car and turned off the ignition.

'What the hell was that conversation about, Philippe?' he demanded.

'Do the names Richard Ennis and James Stanley mean anything to you, Clive?' Philippe replied.

'Should they?'

'You tell me: they're the names of two of the men who we found in the cottage.'

'And?'

'And apparently they were both MI6 field operatives.'

'What!'

'You heard me. They were two of your MI6 lads on active service.'

'You're sure about this, my friend? I mean, is Jacques sure this information is kosher?'

'Yes.'

Clive Scott shook his head slowly. 'And to think that I was convinced you were bluffing when you said you knew what our MI6 agents looked like!'

'I was!'

'And yet Jacques has been able to identify them. And the worst part is that I'm not even going to ask you the hows or whys of how the *Police Nationale* came by this information because I know you wouldn't tell me.'

'Got it in one, my friend.'

'But you don't know the third man?'

'No, not yet.'

'My money's on Mossad.'

'Maybe, or some other branch of Israeli intelligence.' Maigret turned to Georges Martin who was sitting quietly in the back of the car. 'Come on Georges,' he said, 'let's stretch our legs while Chief Inspector Scott makes his phone call to the British Embassy in Paris.'

'You know what this development means, Philippe,' Clive Scott said, as they were leaving the car.

'What?'

'It means that our trip to Berlin is about to become fully sanctioned and completely legit: both the Paris and the Berlin embassies will be falling over themselves to offer us whatever assistance we need.'

'Maybe. Or alternatively they'll recall you to Paris immediately for debriefing.'

'Nah, trust me: I've got this one covered, mate – no worries!'

And, as it transpired, he did.

TWENTY

Ten minutes later Clive Scott gave a toot of the horn and Philippe Maigret and Georges Martin walked back to the car and climbed in again.

'Mission accomplished, Clive?' Maigret asked.

Clive beamed. 'Yep, job done and even better than I'd hoped. We've been guaranteed all assistance from the Berlin embassy and accommodation there as well.'

'Georges and me too?'

'Yes, you're both included.'

'Er... that's very kind, but I think we should stay at our own embassy. We don't want to tread on anyone's... er... *protocols.*'

'Fairenoughski. But the offer's there nevertheless.'

'Thanks, *mon ami.*'

They drove on in silence for twenty kilometres then Georges Martin asked, 'How far are we from Berlin?'

'You're the one with the map, mate,' Clive Scott said, 'if you don't know we're in big trouble!'

'Sorry, sir, I must have nodded off.'

'Just as well we old boys have our wits about us, isn't it, Philippe?' Clive said, nudging Maigret with his elbow.

'Watch it!' Maigret exclaimed, as the car swerved.

'Just giving Georges another wake-up call,' Scott chuckled. 'However, to answer your question Georges, we're about thirty-five kilometres from Hanover. Then it's another 350 kilometres to Berlin, but it's a straight run on a very good autobahn so it won't take long.'

As Chief Inspector Scott spoke his mobile rang. 'Damn,' he said, 'answer it for me will you, Philippe.'

'Okay… er… hello?'

'I need to speak with Clive Scott,' the voice on the other end said.

'Is that you, Akram? It's Philippe Maigret. Clive's driving.'

'Oh, I see. Good afternoon, Chief Inspector. I wanted Clive to know that Jamal has just phoned me from Berlin. I promised I'd do that if I heard from him.'

'Do you have Jamal's number?'

'Yes, I'll give it to you now.'

'Better still text it to Clive's phone please,' Maigret said quickly.

'Will do,' Akram replied, preparing to end the call.

'Wait! How was Jamal? Everything alright with him? Or did he seem worried? Has he any information about what's happening in Berlin tomorrow?'

'Er – let me see. He seemed fine. Relaxed. But he had no new information, nor did any of his Hailemariam contacts there. He asked when the bodies of our friends will be released for burial.'

'As soon as possible, we know how important your religious observances are at these times. I promise I'll let you know as soon as I'm told.'

'Thanks – I'll pass that on to Jamal.'

Philippe Maigret turned to Clive Scott. 'Did you get all of that, Clive? Any further questions for Akram?'

'Ask him when Jamal will be back in Paris.'

'I heard what Clive said,' Akram said before Philippe could relay the message. 'I forgot that I asked Jamal that myself. He said he planned to stay with his friends in Berlin until… until we can take the bodies of his uncle Ibrahim and the others back to Jordan for their funerals. It is important that they don't make that journey on their own.'

'I understand, Akram. Tell Jamal he should start making preliminary arrangements: you should er… *all* be able to leave within a few days.'

'Thanks again, Chief Inspector. I'm sure Jamal will appreciate your help as I do.'

'So nothing unusual was happening in Berlin either today, or tomorrow? Nothing that could possibly be of interest to us, I mean.'

'No, nothing er except that… but it's hardly worth mentioning. It couldn't have anything to do with… or be…'

'Tell me anyway, Akram.'

'Jamal mentioned a… er pop concert in Berlin tomorrow night. Some of his friends had tickets for it. But, as I said, nothing of any real…'

'Interested, Clive?' Maigret asked aware that he could hear their conversation.

Clive nodded. 'Might as well be; no stone unturned and all that cliché guff.'

'The concert, Akram – any details?'

'No, but I could ask Jamal.'

Clive shook his head. 'Tell him we'll contact Jamal directly,' he said.

'Thanks for the offer, Akram but Clive needs to speak to Jamal himself.'

'Okay. *Au revoir,* Chief Inspectors,' he said ending the call.

'A pop concert – come on!' Georges groaned from the back seat. 'I don't think so.'

'Wait and see, Sonny-Jim,' Clive Scott said briskly, 'sometimes the flimsiest info turns out to be the most important.'

And so it transpired. When they reached Hanover, Clive's birthplace, they stopped for coffee and it was then that he contacted Jamal, the only survivor of the massacre in the 10th *arrondissement* for which no one had yet even been questioned, much less arrested.

The concert was actually a Simon and Garfunkel one performance only tribute event. There were billboards all over Berlin advertising it, one of which Jamal had noticed as he left Berlin Hauptbahnhof. And these posters read:

Scarborough Fair – are you going? Be there!

Jamal said his friends had been lucky to get seats.

And it seemed that the sponsor of that event was an American company, *Scarborough Fair Inc.*, whose headquarters were in Connecticut.

★

'It must be a coincidence,' Georges Martin said. 'There are still many Simon and Garfunkel fans around the world – someone's just trying to make some fast money.'

'You know I don't believe in coincidences, Georges,' his chief said.

'And neither do I, Clive added. 'We must be overlooking something. Either of you fancy driving for a while?'

'Either of us insured to drive a British Embassy car?' Philippe asked.

'Probably not and I'm not sure I am either! But what can they do to us; we've just found two of their missing MI6 agents for them.'

'Yes, but both were dead.'

'And that was unfortunate but at least they know where they are now!'

'Hmm. Not sure they'd be impressed by that argument Clive.'

'Look – one of you *has* to drive because I need to make some phone calls.'

'I'll do it, boss,' Georges volunteered. 'I've always fancied driving a Jag. And if anyone asks I can say I was just following orders.'

Georges took the wheel after another brief pitstop, while Philippe chose to sit in the back. 'I have some thinking to do,' he said by way of explanation. However, before he could begin, his phone rang. It was Jacques informing him that the phone from which Megan's call had been made was in use again, and that whoever had it was not far from Berlin.

'Connect me as soon as you can, and do it quickly before the phone is turned off again. You can bet it won't be left open long.'

'Okay, Chief.'

'It's going to be a very small window.'

'Yes I know, Clive.'

'And? What will you say?'

'I don't know. It depends who answers. There's something you could do in the meantime.'

'What?'

'Get your embassy in Berlin to find out everything they can about this concert; like how long it's been planned, and anything they can dig up about the company Scarborough Fair Inc. and its management.

'You think this is what we're looking for – a tribute concert?'

'It's all we've got to go on.'

'Okay.'

Twenty minutes later the British Embassy in Berlin had phoned with the information. And that was the first time that Philippe Maigret heard the name Thomas Jefferson Aitkens, the CEO of Scarborough Fair Inc.

But it would not by any means, be the last.

Fifteen minutes later the embassy phoned again with the information that one of their staff members, going on nothing more than a hunch, had checked the passenger lists for incoming flights from New York in recent days. And one name had stood out from all the others.

'*Zut alors!*' Clive Scott exclaimed when he heard the news. 'Thanks lads, you've earned your pay this week!'

'What now?'

'A Mr Thomas Aitkens arrived in Berlin from New York earlier this afternoon. Looks like he might be planning to go to the concert tomorrow night.'

'Hmm. Maybe. Exactly what kind of company is Scarborough Fair Inc.? Does anyone know?'

'The guys are still working on that one. They said it all seems very hush-hush and it's not easy to find out much about the company except that a great many US Government contracts seem to come their way. In fact it appears the US Government is their main client.'

While the three detectives were pondering this information, Jacques phoned his boss. 'Connecting you now, Chief,' he said, 'the phone's ringing.'

'Showtime!' Clive said, as Maigret prepared to speak.

'Hello – who's this?' the voice on the other end of the line demanded.

'Quinn! My wife and grandson; what have you done with them?'

'They're both fine, if a little tired. They'll sleep well tonight.'

'Listen to me, Quinn. You're in a lot of trouble: we've found the bodies in the cottage near Neuwied. Do yourself a favour and give yourself up. Or else leave Megan and Nat somewhere safe in Berlin – we know you're there now.'

'I had nothing to do with those murders. Two of those men were my friends.'

'The MI6 agents I assume.'

'You're remarkably well-informed, Chief Inspector Maigret; anyone would think you were a detective! But you don't know everything.'

'Is that so?' Maigret said, following his instinct. 'Well I know about Mr Aitkens from New York. And I know that he arrived in Berlin this afternoon.'

'Do you now? Interesting. But do you know what happened between him and Madame Maigret *in their… er… salad days* in New York a long time ago? How shall I describe them then? *Hot, very hot in blood, but definitely a little green in their judgement*,' Quinn said, tightening the screw. 'If you don't know about that relationship then you really don't know anything at all.' And with that taunt he switched off his phone.

★

Early hours of Tuesday 14th March.
Neuwied, Germany

It was the quiet, the *eerie* stillness that registered on her brain first, even as her eyes were still struggling to make sense of the horror that they met as she stepped inside the cottage. It was not the carefully stage-managed death scene that Philippe, Georges and Clive Scott would confront later that day. No, what Megan saw was the unsanitized version: the man slumped to his knees in front of the sink in the kitchen, and the other men – one with his revolver drawn but apparently not used, and the other one lying on his back on the floor. All of them with two bloody wounds: one to the head and one to the heart. And then there was the smell. The sickly, putrid smell of blood. Everywhere. And Patrick and Quinn standing unnaturally still in the middle of this carnage both with faces as white as the shrouds that would later cover the victims.

Afterwards, when she could bring herself to talk about what she witnessed in the early hours of that morning, she would describe her reaction as a brain-freeze. Her body protecting itself from an unexpected, unimaginable horror.

She had gasped, then fell silent herself. None of them said anything for a long time and none of them moved. What was there to say? What could be said? And why move, why do anything at all, when there was nothing that could be changed, or undone, or made better?

Then she felt Nat pushing gently at her back and that snapped her back to reality. *Still lives to protect, still lives that could be saved,* she thought.

She pushed backwards against him, forcing him out of the door, using her body as a shield to shelter him from what she had seen. And that movement proved the catalyst for Quinn and Patrick to move too.

'There's nothing we can do for them now, Patrick,' Quinn said. 'You go outside with the others while I search their pockets.'

'I could help,' Patrick said. 'Just tell me what you want me to do and I'll do it.'

Quinn sighed. 'These men – well two of them, Rick Ennis and Jim Stanley, were friends of mine. I'd like to be alone for a while to say my… farewell to them.'

'And the third man? Who's he?'

'I don't know, never seen him before. But go outside, please. I don't want Nat to see any of this and I'm afraid Megan's seen too much already.'

'Okay,' Patrick said, walking slowly towards the door.

'Hang on a minute, there is something you could do for me.'

'Anything – anything at all. What?'

'They had a car, they told me they did, but I didn't see one outside. Knowing the way those two operated it will be a late model high performance car and probably German. Have a look around the neighbourhood: they'll have hidden it in plain sight if they could.'

'And the keys?'

'If the car's unlocked they will be underneath the driver's seat. But see if there's a letter-box near the front gate; they might have left them in there. Or maybe they're taped under the box.'

And they were.

Patrick walked down the little street – hardly more than a lane really – and shivered. He looked at his watch: almost 3.30 in the morning and heavy dew had chilled the air. No lights to be seen anywhere, except for a weak street light here and there. Everything was quiet. *As quiet as the grave,* he thought, shivering again. And no car to be seen either. He kept pressing the automatic opening on the keys as he walked, and, after five minutes or so, he heard a click as the car doors were unlocked. He followed the sound and found the car half-hidden in the shadows of another small tree lined street nearby. Quinn was right: the car was a BMW with only 35,000 kilometres on the clock. *Nice,* Patrick thought, *at any other time I'd enjoy driving this trendy little baby, but not now. Not under current circumstances.*

He adjusted the driver's seat to accommodate his long legs, and did a U-turn, driving slowly back to the cottage with only the parking lights on.

He parked the car in the street, opened the dilapidated gate and walked up the path towards the garden seat on which Megan and Nat were sitting, huddled together. But not for warmth this time; shock. As he reached them the door of the cottage opened and David Quinn came out.

'Find it?' he asked.

'Yes, it's outside in the street.'

'Good man. Come on,' he said to Megan and Nat, 'it's time we were on our way again.'

'We're tired and cold,' Megan said, 'and we need a hot drink.'

'We'll stop for a snack somewhere soon, I promise,' Quinn said. 'And we'll have a few hours' sleep, too.'

'Did you find anything er... useful, after I left?' Patrick asked.

'A few things and some money. But nothing of any real importance.' There was something in the tone of his voice that made Patrick doubt whether Quinn had told him the absolute truth.

'Passports?' he asked, prompting his way to more information.

'No. They'll have left them somewhere safe in case of trouble: that's SOP for MI6 field agents.'

'SOP?'

'Standard operating procedure.'

'Oh.'

'Now in the car please and make it snappy.' Quinn ordered. 'We need to be on our way.'

★

Thursday 14th March 4.30pm: between Hanover and Berlin

For the next fifteen kilometres, Philippe Maigret said nothing. He sat motionless in the back seat with his eyes closed. Several times Clive Scott and Georges Martin exchanged glances – accompanied by raised eyebrows – but neither of them spoke. *He needs time to come to terms with what he's just been told,* they thought. *And by the look of him it has knocked him for six.*

Just when they had both assumed Maigret would stay this way until they reached Berlin, he finally spoke.

'Would it be pushing our luck to ask your friends in the embassy to do one more favour for us, Clive?'

'Not at all, my friend. Our stocks are high with them right now. I think we could pretty much get anything we want.'

'*Bon, bon.* Then please ask them if they can find out where Thomas Aitkens is staying in Berlin.'

'He'll be at the US Embassy near the Brandenburg Gate, Chief,' Georges Martin said.

'Yes, that's right. With all the Government contracts his company handles he's bound to be invited to stay,' Clive agreed.

'Hmm. Maybe. Or maybe Mr Aitkens might prefer a little more... privacy than he'd get there. Humour me, Clive, just this once.'

'Will do,' he said, reaching for his phone.

Philippe Maigret was right. Tom Aitkens was not an honoured guest at the US Embassy, although he *had* been invited. He was staying in his luxurious suite in the nearby hotel where he always stayed.

'Any more requests before I hang up?' Clive asked.

'Yes, just one more. Ask your embassy if they would invite Mr Aitkens to meet us in the bar of his hotel at... er...' He glanced at his watch. 'Eight o'clock tonight.'

'Do you think he'd come?' Clive asked. 'I don't.'

'Only one way to find out.' Maigret said. 'If he's involved with something criminal in Berlin tomorrow my guess is that he'll be intrigued by a request from three detectives – one British and two French – for a meeting. And I have no objection to the embassy giving him our names and ranks. Do either of you?'

'I don't,' Chief Inspector Scott said quickly.

'Nor me,' Inspector Martin confirmed.

As the minutes ticked by without the embassy

phoning again, Maigret began to doubt his instincts. *Looks like Clive was right,* he thought.

Just as he was on the verge of giving up hope, Clive received a text. *Mr Aitkens regrets that he has a dinner engagement at 8 o'clock this evening. However he would be pleased to meet with Chief Inspector Scott, Chief Inspector Maigret and Inspector Martin at 7pm – if that would be convenient.*

'Will we be in Berlin by 7pm?' Maigret asked when the message was relayed to him.

'Absolutely. We'll be there by 5.30 if Georges gets a move on,' he said.

And they were.

TWENTY-ONE

Tuesday 14th March (early afternoon)

'How long before we get to Berlin?' Megan asked, shifting Nat's head to another spot on her shoulder.

'We'll reach our destination soon,' Quinn said.

'And then what? We need a shower and a change of clothes, except we don't have any other clothes because you made us leave everything on the train. We don't even have toothbrushes!'

'All in good time, Megan,' Quinn said. 'We'll get you everything you need; we must have you looking your best when you meet Tom Aitkens again.'

'What? Why would I want to see Tom Aitkens again?'

'Oh, you'll see him again, Megan. And you'll do whatever it takes to find out everything he knows.'

'I won't.'

'But you will,' Quinn insisted. 'Because I have Nat and I also have a revolver. A *loaded* revolver.'

'You'd *hurt* Nat?'

'Yes, if it's necessary. But I wouldn't like doing it.'

'Oh, and I'm sure that will be a great comfort to his

family. I think you're a fraud, Mr Quinn. Or a fantasist. A Walter Mitty type: you're no more a peace activist than Hitler was!'

'Walter who?'

'Walter Mitty, the main character in Thurber's famous short story. A meek man who imagines himself as a wartime pilot, or an emergency room surgeon, or even a killer. He was an inept dreamer always seeing himself in fantastic roles and situations; the very opposite of the real life he actually led.'

'And that's what you think of me?'

'Yes.'

'So tell me; did someone twice attempt to kill this Walter Mitty? Did they run him down outside of Les Invalides? Did they come into a hospital armed and ready to kill him?'

'Well, no,' Megan conceded.

'You know that's what happened to me – so why do you doubt me now after we've come so far together?'

'Because I'm not sure I can trust you.'

'Well you can certainly trust that I have the money to buy you some new glad rags because that police officer's wallet was satisfyingly fat.'

'I have money,' Patrick Evremond said, fingering his Swiss Army knife in his trouser pocket as he always did when stressed. 'I have Phi… er I mean I have euros.'

'You were about to say that you had Philippe's money, weren't you, Patrick,' Megan said quickly. 'I *knew* there was no way you just *happened* to be on the same train as we were by accident! Philippe put you up to it, didn't he? He'll have some questions to answer the next time I see him.'

'I think you might have a few questions of your own to answer at that time too,' Quinn said before Patrick could answer. 'And I doubt that many of them will be about money.'

'No one cares what you think, Mr Quinn,' Megan snapped as Nat stirred from his brief nap.

'Are we there yet?'

'No, but soon, Nat. Very soon,' she said.

'I hope we don't find any more bodies,' he whispered.

'Oh dear God, Nat – you saw... you saw... at the cottage?'

'Yes. I saw.'

'Listen to me,' she whispered. 'At some time, and I don't *when* that will be, or *where* that will be, there might be a chance for us to escape from Quinn.'

'What!'

'Ssh. A chance for us to get away. Or maybe only you.'

'Megs!'

'Ssh. Yes, Nat. Just like Celia did at Gare du Nord when she was only ten. I told her to run and she did. And she found Philippe, and then she was safe.'

'You want me to run somewhere?'

'No. I want you to stop a taxi... or a car and ask to be taken to the French Embassy. Do you know how to say that in German?'

'Sure, that's no problem – but we're not French!'

'No, but Philippe is, and I know he'll have been in

touch with their embassy or the German police. He'll be trying to find us.'

'I thought we were supposed to be *helping* David. We have to stay with him because otherwise something terrible will happen tomorrow.'

'I think if anything terrible happens in Berlin there's a good chance he'll be the one who's responsible. And I think he probably shot those men we saw in the cottage.'

'But how could he when he was on the train with us?'

'Those men had been dead for days. Maybe even before he was run down in Paris. It could be possible.'

'He said they were his friends.'

'Yes, but how do we know that's true? How do we know that anything he's told us is actually *true?* Promise me you'll run when you get the chance. Please, Nat.'

'Okay, I will,' he said after a few moments' thought. 'But I'll go to the British Embassy – and that's final. I won't let you change my mind!'

Megan nodded. 'That's fine by me; the British Embassy it is.'

'Keep quiet – both of you,' Quinn growled from the front seat. 'And no more whispering.'

'David, Nat has just told me that he saw... he saw what we saw in the cottage.'

'Oh, God! Did you, Nat?'

'Yes. But first I could smell it. So I pushed Megs to make her move and that's when I *saw* them. They all had two bullet wounds and they were very dead and very strange looking – like wax dummies, not humans.

So did you and Patrick. I thought you were going to throw up!'

'Nat, what can I say? It would have been quick for them. Very quick. And maybe they didn't realise what was happening.'

'They're still dead though, aren't they, David?' Nat said pragmatically. 'And they shouldn't be. Just like your friend Major Pascoe in Afghanistan.

★

Half an hour later Quinn told Patrick, who was driving, to pull over at the next layby so he could take the wheel. He drove carefully, making sure he obeyed all the speed restrictions: *can't risk attracting the wrong kind of attention at this late stage,* he thought. Only Patrick noticed when he took exit 19 for Potsdam. But before he could query this change of direction, he saw a sign for Berlin-Zentrum so he assumed Quinn knew this was the fastest route into the city. They continued on the A10 until the highway junction at Nuthetal where a sign indicated the A115 leading towards the centre of Berlin. But Quinn did not deviate from the A10.

'Hey, David,' Patrick said, 'shouldn't you have taken the A115 back there at the junction?'

'Are you the damn navigator now, Wonder Boy?' Quinn said. 'I know where I'm going.'

And by the look of things it's not Berlin, Patrick thought. *Could Megan be right? I didn't hear everything she said to Nat, but I heard enough to know some of what she thinks of Quinn now, and I heard some of what she's planning. Who is he? And, more importantly, what is he? I think I could overpower him if it came to that. The element of surprise was in his favour last time but if I caught him unawares then I'd have that advantage. Yes, but he has a revolver and all you have is a Swiss Army knife that you've never used in anger. God knows what combat experience he might have had. And he's strong and fit. Yes, but I'm fit too, and I'm younger.*

'What's happened to Fat Herman,' Nat said, peering out of the window. 'I thought we'd have seen him by now.'

'Fat Herman?' Patrick asked.

'Nat means the old water tower at Kollwitzplatz, one of the first water supply facilities in Berlin. It's a famous old landmark that the locals call Dicker Herman or Fat Herman because of its round shape. The area around the tower has been a park since before the First World War; we've often eaten in the cafés and restaurants in the area. It's in the former East Berlin.'

'You make it sound charming and serene, Megan.' Quinn said, 'But surely you know that it was an improvised concentration camp under the Nazis.'

'Yes, but after the war it was converted into highly desirable apartments.'

'Yes, very highly desirable – as long as you don't mind hearing the ghostly screams from the tortured souls that disturb the peace during the night hours,' Quinn said sarcastically.

'Old wives' tales and folklore.'

'Really? *For the stone shall cry out of the wall, and the beam out of the timber shall answer it,* as one of the Old Testament prophets said. That bloody building should have been torn down, brick by brick, like the Bastille prison was.'

After that comment no one spoke for what seemed like a long time. Then the silence was broken by Nat.

'Hey! This is not Berlin – we're almost in Potsdam.'

'Yes, we are. Well spotted, Nat.' Quinn replied.

'But why are we here?' Megan probed. 'You said we were going to Berlin.'

'No, I said the appalling events would happen in Berlin. I don't believe that at any time I said *we* were actually going to Berlin,' Quinn replied calmly.

'But you must have! You were on a train going to Berlin.'

'Quickest way to get to Potsdam under the circs.'

'Megan's right,' Patrick said. 'Certainly it was *implied* that Berlin was our destination.'

'Maybe. But what's the problem? Potsdam's only a stone's throw from Berlin anyway; it's considered part of the Berlin/Brandenburg metropolitan region.'

'The problem is that it's yet another lie you've told us.'

'Shut up please, while I concentrate on finding our digs,' Quinn muttered.

What did the note hidden in the cottage say, he thought. *Didn't you memorise it? Cross the Havel River and take the road to Bornstedt. After you pass Schloss Sanssouci, the Palace of Frederick the Great, look for an old white painted house on the left. Three streets after that take the next right. Continue down that street until you see a small-ish red brick apartment building. Take the lift to the third floor and apartment 3b is on the right. The key's under the door mat. Quite safe, the Hun is a law-abiding creature! We think we're being followed. If you find this note we're dead and probably Josh Weinbrenn is too. He's a Jew but not very observant. Do us a favour though and get him buried within twenty-four hours if you can – that's important to them. And thanks for everything mate. Good luck, keep the faith. See you upstairs sometime in the great Hereafter. And say a Hail Mary for us now and then.*

Quinn found the apartment without any trouble. The key was exactly where he'd expected and the flat was well-stocked. And, to Megan's relief, there were new toothbrushes, combs and brushes in the bathroom.

'Just freshen up now,' Quinn said, 'we'll have a break for an hour or so, and a snack, then we'll head off to find the clothes for your big date tonight. You can shower when we get back.'

'I've told you that I won't go,' Megan said.

'And I said you *will*. Besides, Tom Aitkens is expecting you – you wouldn't want to disappoint him would you? Not after all this time.'

'How could he be expecting me? He doesn't even know I'm in Germany.'

'Oh, but he does. Earlier this afternoon he received a text from you at his hotel. It was a very *affectionate* text. You asked if he could meet you for dinner at one of the upmarket restaurants in Potsdam. And, surprise, surprise, or not really, he sent a text to accept. He'll meet you at the restaurant at 8pm.'

'But how?'

'Your Tom Aitkens is a creature of habit; he always stays at the same hotel near the US Embassy. And I've had his business email address for some time now, thanks to some contacts in Berlin.'

'But how could he reply?'

'He sent a text, as I'd requested, in your name of course to what he thought was your mobile. Would you like to read it? It might make you blush! Your Mr Aitkens seem to have er… *great expectations* as to how the rest of the evening might proceed after dinner. We'd better get you some fancy underwear too.'

'You… you *dratsab!* How could you compromise me like that?'

'*All's fair in love and war,* my dear Megan. And this is the latter now: I regret to tell you that your Mr Aitkens is very much the enemy as far as I'm concerned.'

TWENTY-TWO

Potsdam. Germany. Tuesday 14th March (late afternoon)

David Quinn looked at his watch. 'Okay, rest time is over and I want all of you in the bathroom now,' he said.

'No,' Megan said automatically before she noticed he was holding the French police officer's revolver in his hand.

'In the bathroom, all of you – and make it snappy! You – Patrick – put the lid down and sit on the loo, Nat you sit on the stool near the hand basin – and Megan, you stand.'

They filed silently into the bathroom without further dissent. There was something in the tone of Quinn's voice that was different now: hard, determined, and ruthless – a man not to be disobeyed unless one was willing to take the consequences. *He's still coming to terms with finding the bodies in the cottage,* Megan thought. *Have I misjudged him?*

After a short delay Quinn joined them, carrying two lengths of cord about the same width as a clothes line.

'Here, take this,' he said to Megan, 'and tie Nat's hands behind his back.'

'No.'

'Do it quickly or I'll have to do worse to him. And make sure you tie the rope *tightly* because I'll check.'

'I don't mind, honestly I don't,' Nat said quickly.

Megan walked over to Nat, kissed him and whispered that she loved him. Then she did as Quinn had ordered.

'Is this really necessary?' Patrick said, as Quinn did the same to him. 'You've trussed me up like a damn Christmas turkey.'

'It's necessary. I'm not sure I could control you if you came with us so you'll have to stay here. We won't be long, an hour tops,' he said. 'Oh, and one more thing – almost forgot.'

He fished a wide roll of adhesive tape out of his pocket, tore off a strip, and slapped it roughly over Patrick's mouth. 'Not that it would matter if you yelled because I'm sure these apartments are sound-proofed, but best to be certain. And get me a cushion from the sitting room,' he said to Megan.

'Why?'

'Just damn well do it, and get a move on!'

What's he planning to do with the cushion, Megan thought, as she walked slowly into the sitting room. *Oh dear God, I think I know what. But how can I stop him?*

'Where's the cushion?' Quinn growled as she re-entered the bathroom.

'I didn't bring it because I know what you'll do with it.'

'I'll get it myself,' he said.

'Quinn, if you intend to shoot Patrick that will be the end of all co-operation from me. You can do what you want but I won't let you wound him.'

'I'll just nick his fibula; just a little nick, and a little fracture,' Quinn wheedled. 'It won't hurt much and the bone will heal quickly because he's young.'

'No: he could bleed to death while we're away. Why do you need to do that anyway? Just tie his ankles and Nat's too if you must. They won't go anywhere.'

Quinn hesitated for a moment, looking carefully at Megan. *She means it,* he thought. *She's determined. I don't think I can push her any further.*

'Okay,' he said reluctantly. He fossicked in his pocket again and pulled out the adhesive tape.

'Take this piece and stick it around Nat's ankles,' he ordered. Then he did the same to Patrick.

Crikey, that was close, Patrick thought, *he was ready to do it – I know he was!*

'Come on,' Quinn said, giving Megan a non-too-gentle push towards the door. 'Chop, chop – get a move on.' Then he closed the bathroom door, locked it and pocketed the key.

Patrick listened carefully. As soon as he heard the front door close he began to move. He stood up and wriggled his way over to Nat, shoving his side pocket towards his face. Nat nodded and began a series of contortions in an attempt to get his fingers inside the pocket. At first it seemed hopeless; then Nat felt the rope was beginning to slacken. He concentrated on loosening it more instead of trying to get his hand in Patrick's pocket. After struggling for what seemed like a long time, but was actually no more than five minutes, his hands were free. He ripped the tape off his mouth in one movement then did the same to Patrick's.

'Bloody hell, Nat! That really hurt – don't you know you're supposed to remove adhesive tape *slowly*?'

'Best to get it over and done with quickly. Now let me get your Swiss Army knife.' Still working fast Nat half cut, half *sawed* his way through the rope on Patrick's hands.

'That feels good,' he said, rubbing his wrists and stretching his arms and shoulders.

'Don't be a wimp – you only had it on for about ten minutes! Now what do we do?' Nat said, as he attempted to get the tape off his ankles in one pull. It didn't work; that turned out to be a two-pull procedure!

Patrick walked over to the door and tried the handle.

'It's locked,' he said, looking around the room. 'Our only chance is the window but I think it's too small for me to get through. But maybe you could make it.'

'I'll give it a try.'

'Let me try first.' Patrick leant across the cistern of the toilet and opened the window. *It's too small,* he thought, *only a midget would be able to get through it and even then it wouldn't be easy.* 'I don't think it can be done, Nat,' he said.

'I might be able to – if I go through it sideways.'

'Okay – it's worth a try. I'll help you as much as I can. First let me have a good deco to see how you could get down after you've climbed through the window; we're on the third floor, remember?' Patrick stood on the loo seat and leant as far as he could through the window, but not much more than his head would fit. 'There's a ledge leading to the balcony of the next apartment,' he said, 'but it's narrow. How are you with heights?'

'I'm fine. And my shoes are rubber-soled.'

'Okay, but no heroics; slow and steady as you go.'

'Okay.'

It was a tremendous effort, but Nat eventually managed to get through the window, scraping several layers of skin off his body as he went, or so it felt to him. Not many professional contortionists could have done much better.

'Can you see anyone below?' Patrick called. 'If you can, attract their attention and tell them we're trapped. Ask them to call the fire brigade or the police.'

'I can't say all of that in German,' Nat protested, hanging on for dear life as he inched his way to the next balcony.

'Then say it in English – they'll probably understand.'

'I can't see anyone in the street anyway,' was the muffled reply. 'I'm going to try to stand up now.'

'No – crawl!'

But Patrick's warning came too late: Nat lost his footing and plummeted earthwards, clipping a small tree as he did. This impeded his fall a little but even so he landed with a sickening thud that Patrick heard with awful clarity. Yet during that time not a single sound came from Nat. Not even as he fell. And certainly not afterwards, when he lay helpless on the damp lawn towards the side of the building.

And he had been right. There was no one in the street. No one to see him fall; no one to help now while he was lying motionless on his back. Not conscious, barely breathing.

For the next few minutes Patrick was lost in a state of overwhelming panic. *It's my fault,* he told himself over and over again. *I encouraged him – and he's only a kid. How could I do that? Where's my judgement, my bloody life skills? What kind of police officer will I make if I'm so lacking in any kind of nous, or sodding cool-headed commonsense?*

Eventually he became calmer. He jumped up on the toilet seat again, leant as far as he could out of the window, and called for help. He couldn't remember the German word for help but he could remember that *bitte* was the word for please.

'*Bitte* – help!' he cried for as long as he could before his voice began to fail, while simultaneously banging on the frame of the window until his knuckles were raw and bleeding. But no one heard, so no help came.

He slumped down on the loo seat and sobbed through a mixture of guilt and frustration. The last time he'd cried like that had been when his sister Ginny died. He thought he had manned up since then but knew that day that he still had some way to go. However, the tears proved positive because they released a new burst of energy. He hopped up on the loo seat and began to shout again.

And, eventually, someone heard him. An elderly lady carrying her shopping basket, walking along on the other side of the street, looked up.

'Here – here! *Bitte* – help!' Patrick called. 'Up here – *bitte!*'

The *frau* hesitated for a moment then crossed the street. And it was then that she saw Nat's body which had been obscured by shrubbery from the other side.

'*Gott im Himmel, was ist das? Was ist das?*' Then she bent over Nat and seemed about to lift his head.

'*Nein! Nein* – don't move him!' Patrick shouted.

'*Was?*'

'*Nein* – Polizei – *get the police!*

'*Polizei?*'

'*Ya* – *Polizei* – *bitte!*'

All this shouting to and fro attracted the attention of a long-haired, lanky young man who came into view riding an ancient bicycle. He jumped off his bike, threw it casually on the ground and ran towards Nat's body and the elderly *frau*.

'*Bitte* – *sprechen sie Englisch?*' Patrick shouted from the window.

'Should do,' the young man replied, 'I'm from Manchester! What's happened here?'

'He fell from the window. His name's Nathaniel and he's from Norfolk. Do you speak German?'

'*Ja sicher!* At least enough to get by. Want me to call an ambulance?'

'Yes, for the love of God, yes! And tell them to hurry! He hasn't moved since he fell!'

'Right-O. Why don't you come down and help if you know him?'

'Can't – locked in the bathroom. My name's Patrick.'

'Why?'

'Because that's the name my parents gave me!'

'No, you idiot! Why are you locked in the bathroom?' The young man pressed the emergency number and spoke rapidly into his phone in German.

'It's a long er… complicated story. What's your name?'

'Roy.'

'Roy?'

'Yeah. No; it's actually Royston, but I prefer Roy.'

'I can understand that, Roy!'

Roy knelt down next to Nat on the damp grass, felt the pulse on the side of his neck then checked his wrist pulse for confirmation.

'He's alive, his breathing seems normal and his pulse is pretty good under the circumstances.'

'You a doctor, Roy?'

'Not yet – second year med student.'

'What are you doing in Potsdam?'

'A month's goodwill exchange funded by the EU at the university here.'

'Lucky for me you came along – and for Nat.'

'Yeah, so it would seem. Any objections if I tell the lady everything's under control now and she can go home? I don't think the ambulance will take long to get here. This is not such a huge place.'

'Yeah, good idea. Will you go with him in the ambulance, Roy? He speaks a little German but that's all and he's only thirteen. He'll get a shock when he comes to and finds himself in a German hospital.'

217

'Yes, of course I will. Want me to send someone to get you out of the bathroom?'

'No, no,' Patrick said quickly. 'That will do more harm than good. I told you it's a complicated situation. Just do everything you can to help Nat.'

'Okay. What's his full name?'

'Nathaniel Glison and he's from Norfolk, like I said. That's pretty much all I know about him.'

'What's he doing in Potsdam; who's he staying with here?'

Patrick thought quickly. *Name, rank and serial number, seems the best way to go. If I tell him about Philippe Maigret and the train from Paris and everything else it's really going to foul things up!*

'Er... his granny who lives in Paris.'

'And where's she now?'

'Er... out shopping. She'll be back soon.'

The elderly German lady went home to make herself a cup of tea while Patrick backed away from the window as the ambulance arrived. A brace was put around Nat's neck, an oxygen mask fitted, and then he was lifted carefully on to a stretcher.

'I'm coming with him,' Roy said.

'You a relative?'

'Yes,' he replied without hesitation. *Not a lie,* he thought – *six degrees of separation and all that existential guff.*

'*Bon chance,*' he called in the direction of the upstairs window where he knew Patrick would be listening.

Halfway along the route to the hospital, Nat's eyes

flickered and he regained consciousness. He looked at Roy in bewilderment.

'Everything's okay, Nat – it's me, Roy. Don't you remember me? You're on your way to a hospital in Potsdam. You've had a fall. Remember?'

Nathaniel remembered alright: he remembered very *well*, and he knew he'd never seen Roy before. *But that's not important now,* he thought.

'Please… Roy. Phone the British Embassy in Berlin. Ask them to tell Chief Inspector Scott where I am. He's looking for me and Megs.'

'Megs?'

'My gran, she's married to Philippe Maigret. He'll be looking for us, too.'

'He a cop?'

Nat nodded.

What kind of unholy mess have I stumbled on here, Roy thought. But before he could ask Nat any more questions he lost consciousness again and he stayed that way until long after they reached the hospital.

TWENTY-THREE

Megan and David Quinn returned to the apartment building fifty minutes later. When Quinn discovered that Nat was missing he let rip with a torrent of expletives and threw a series of hefty punches at Patrick, who attempted to defend himself. Despite his efforts, Quinn landed a direct blow to his chin which sent him reeling backwards, almost into the bath, another to his nose and lip, both of which began gushing blood. But then came the final clout: that one was the most serious. It hit him just below his right eye with an impact that made him fear his cheekbone had been shattered. The dreadful searing pain from that blow would last a long time in his memory.

Megan had been inclined to thump Patrick herself – although she usually avoided violence apart from the occasional pillow aimed at Philippe – but Quinn's attack left him so dazed and shaken that she immediately went to his aid.

'Look at him, David Quinn, so-called man of peace! See how he's bleeding. *You* did that! You should be ashamed of yourself. You're a grown man and he's not much more than a lad. Apologise to him immediately, then find something to stop the bleeding.'

'Er... sorry Pat mate. Heat of the moment, and all that kind of...' Quinn mumbled before he shuffled, red-faced, out of the bathroom.

'And see if you can't find some painkillers and maybe some brandy,' Megan called after him while continuing in her attempt to staunch the flow of blood on Patrick's face with some tissues. *Poor lad, his eye's already beginning to close up,* she thought, *but he shouldn't have let Nat risk his life that way. I'll deal with him later; now's not the right time.*

She led Patrick into the sitting room and sat him down in what looked like the most comfortable chair. 'Lean your head back,' she advised, 'that might help slow the blood flow.'

Quinn lumbered in from the kitchen, still shame-faced, but with a glass of water and some aspirin in his hands.

'Sorry, Pat – couldn't find any alcohol, my mates must have finished the whisky before they left.'

His mates, Megan thought, studying him. *That's why he's been so aggressive lately, that's what the violence has been about. He lost control because his friends are dead and now it's only him to stop whatever he fears will happen in Berlin tomorrow. I was wrong before; Patrick and I must help him.*
Don't try to con us, or kid yourself, her conscience warned. *You can't wait to see Tom Aitkers again – can you? There's nothing wrong with being a little curious, is there,* she countered. *As long as that's all it is,* her conscience insisted. *But it's not, is it? Maybe,* she replied. *And that's good enough for now.*

Quinn slumped down in a chair next to Patrick and closed his eyes. Megan allowed him remain silent for a few minutes then she said, 'Are you just going to sit there for the rest of the day without saying or doing anything?'

'Probably. What's the bloody point anyway? My mates are dead and it's too late for us to do anything now.'

'The *point* is, that if you don't want to spend the next twenty-four hours answering questions from the Potsdam police, we should all leave immediately.'

'What?'

'This Roy, the Good Samaritan who called the ambulance and went with Nat, will tell the hospital people everything and then they'll be obliged to call the police. That's what will happen. Isn't that right, Patrick?'

'Yes, it's standard procedure in cases of assault.'

'What assault? I've only just hit you!'

'Not *that* episode! Roy asked why I didn't come downstairs to help Nat and I told him that I was locked in the bathroom. So that's assault and probably false imprisonment as well.'

'Bugger,' Quinn said. 'We've got to vamoose before this Roy character tells everyone everything.'

'Yes, that's what I've been trying to tell you,' Megan said patiently, 'but first we have to find out how Nat is doing and *where* he is – what hospital, I mean.'

'And we will, Megan,' Quinn said, 'but not now. First we have to leave because…'

'Listen, David. I *will* help you despite what you did to Patrick and despite what I said before about you having a touch of Walter Mitty in your character, but before we go anywhere we have to lay down some ground rules.'

'No time,' Quinn said, assuming command again. 'We go first *then* we talk.'

'No. Either we talk now or I go nowhere.'

'Okay, but make it snappy.'

'First rule: no more violence. Second rule: no more aggression. Third rule: all cards on the table as soon as possible. And the final rule is the same as the first,' Megan said. 'Agreed?'

'Agreed – now let's get the hell out of here.'

'To where, exactly?' Patrick asked, grateful that the aspirin was starting to kick in.

'We'll find a hotel or guest house on the outskirts of town. I've been in that area with my friends so I have some idea of what's on offer around there.'

They packed up as much useful gear as they could find, stowed it in a sports bag then left the apartment, replacing the key under the door mat.

'Shouldn't we remove any evidence that we were ever here?' Patrick, who had already been accepted for graduate entry to the Metropolitan police in London, asked, polishing his fledgling credentials.

'Nah will take too long. But don't worry – it will probably take the local cops even longer to get their act together, even if they come right away!'

What a strange trio we must seem, Megan thought as they drove towards the suburb of Potsdam where she and Quinn had been shopping earlier: *a middle-aged woman, a younger man with the whiff of the swashbuckler about him, and a young, good-looking chap whose appearance suggests he's been out-punched in a street fight. I doubt even a Salvation Army doss house would accept us!*

However the Potsdam guest house owner, who fortunately spoke English, would. But she did look them up and down very carefully before she made her decision. *The lady must be the aunt of the older man,* she concluded. *I can see the family resemblance – I have a gift for that, everyone says so. But the younger man, where does he fit in? And what's happened to him?*

As though reading her mind, Quinn said, quite formally, 'Allow me to introduce my aunt, Madame. Her name is... er Megan er Brown and I'm David Brown.'

Megan raised her eyebrows but said nothing. *At least he didn't say Smith,* she thought.

'And who is this?' she asked, with a nod in Patrick's direction.

'Er... a friend of the family. His name is Patrick... White.'

Great! Now we have two Browns and a White, Patrick thought, groaning inwardly. *I'd have supposed that an ex-GCHQ officer could come up with something better than that!*

Let's hope the frau doesn't read Australian literature, Megan was thinking, *otherwise she'll know who the real Patrick White was!*

Bollocks, thought Quinn, *why the hell did I come up with two poxy names like Brown and White?*

However, much to their surprise, Madame-the-guesthouse-owner accepted all of this twaddle at face value, but that might have been because she was curious as to what had befallen Patrick.

'What happened to the young man?' she asked. 'Does he need a doctor to look at him? I could arrange if you wish.'

'No,' Quinn said, at exactly the same time as Megan said 'Yes.'

'Which shall it be?' she asked, glancing from Megan to Quinn. 'Yes or no?'

'Yes, most definitely,' Megan replied quickly, shooting a furious look at Quinn.

'Yes,' Quinn conceded.

'Yes,' agreed Patrick. *And thank God for that.*

'Why?' Quinn whispered to Megan as they followed the *frau* up the stairs to their room.

'What better way to discover the name of the most likely hospital to which Nat would have been taken? It saves us having to phone every hospital in Potsdam to find him.'

'Good thinking,' Quinn said, 'but what if the doctor reports Pat's injuries to the police?'

'He won't. We'll think up a plausible story to explain his injuries before he gets here.'

And they did.

'What has happened to you, young man?' the genial doctor asked when he arrived twenty minutes later.

'I tripped and fell down some stairs,' Patrick replied, hoping he sounded convincing.

He didn't, but it didn't seem to matter to the doctor. *If I had a euro for every time I've heard the old tripping and falling down the stairs story I'd have been able to retire long ago. And both the patient and the older man have abrasions on their knuckles. Those two have had a fight over something but they're calm now and it's not my business to interfere. Nor are the injuries serious. Most of them will heal in a few days. Of course the lad's black eye will last at least a week and visit all the colours of the rainbow before it heals, but he'll survive and I'm no longer young and I've had a long day.*

'Er, Doctor, I'm sorry I don't know your name,' Megan said.

'Franz Josef Richter at your service, Madame,' he said with a courtly little bow.

'Like the Richter who invented the scale for measuring earthquakes?'

'Yes, just like him, although he was born in Ohio, not Germany as I was. But he had German heritage; his great-grandfather came from Baden-Baden, I believe.'

'Is he a relative of yours?' Patrick asked, joining in the conversation.

'Maybe. But a very distant one, if he is,' the doctor chuckled.

Well isn't this all just peachy? Quinn thought. *Any moment now the frau downstairs is going to invite us into the parlour for afternoon tea and it will be fairy cakes all round.*

Get a move on, he signalled to Megan, who gave a quick nod.

'Well, I suppose we must not detain you any longer, Dr Richter,' she said. 'You've been very kind, and we thank you. Now about your account?'

The doctor tutted dismissively. '*Nein, nein,* Madame. What did I do? So little – just a touch of the hand here and there and a little antiseptic. How do you say in England? It's on the…'

'House,' Quinn said quickly. 'And my thanks to you too.'

'And mine,' Patrick said.

Doctor Richter bowed again, shook hands with everyone, and prepared to leave, pleased that he would have an interesting story to relate to his wife over dinner.

'Oh, Dr Richter, there's just one more thing,' Megan said. 'If Patrick needs a hospital where should we take him?'

'Ah, *nein,* my dear. Set your mind at rest, he will not need a hospital. He should just take the painkillers I've given him every four hours. And he should rest, that's all the treatment required.'

'But in case of the unexpected, Doctor – please.'

'Oh well, if it will allow you to sleep more peacefully in your bed I would suggest St Josefs-Krankenhaus Hospital, but I'm sure you won't need it.'

'Even so, would you please write down the address and phone number, Doctor,' Megan persisted.

'Very well.' And he did.

As soon as Doctor Richter had left, Quinn handed his mobile to Megan and she phoned the hospital.

'I'm concerned about my grandson, Nathaniel Glison,' she said to the woman who answered the phone. 'Apparently he's had a fall and I'm wondering if the ambulance took him to your hospital. He's thirteen and lives in England.'

'One moment, please,' the woman said pleasantly in excellent English.

After what seemed like a very long time, the woman picked up the phone again.

'Yes,' she said, 'I can confirm that the young man was admitted earlier this afternoon.'

'And what can you tell me about his condition? Please can I see him now?'

'No, not tonight, but tomorrow morning at about 10am. Then you may see him.'

'And his condition?'

'He's had a shock, but no bones have been broken although he does have some nasty bruises. He had a little supper earlier and now he's sedated. The doctor wants him to sleep well tonight.'

'Ask about Roy,' Patrick whispered tugging at her sleeve.

'And the young man who came with my grandson in the ambulance? Roy is his name, I believe.'

'Oh, he's gone home now, Miss,' the nurse said. 'But he left his phone number. Would you like me to give it to you?'

'Yes, please, I'd like to thank him.' Megan repeated the numbers as the nurse gave them, and Patrick wrote them down.

As Megan finished the call, Quinn said, 'It's time, Megan.'

'Time?'

'To get ready for your big date tonight,' he said in a business-like voice. 'Mustn't keep your boyfriend waiting. That wouldn't do at all.'

'Listen here, Quinn; if you refer to this... *event*

tonight as a *date,* or Tom Aitkens as my *boyfriend* one more time – just one more time – I will not be responsible for my actions!'

'And the same goes for me if you call me Pat again,' Patrick added.

They both looked like they meant it. And they did.

TWENTY-FOUR

Tuesday 14th March (early evening).
Potsdam. Germany.

Roy tried twice to contact the British Embassy in Berlin. Once while Nat was in X-ray, and again while he was being examined by a neurosurgeon who had been called in on his day off to assess whether Nat's brain and spine had suffered any trauma.

The first time the phone operator told him, in a barely civil tone, that there was no one by the name of Chief Inspector Scott working at the embassy. Then, as he was halfway through his convoluted tale, she asked him if he'd been drinking or whether this was a student prank.

'He's probably just visiting,' Roy persisted, ignoring the character slur.

'No. There's no one here by that name, nor is anyone of that name expected,' she replied.

And that seems to be that, Roy thought wryly, *and a clearer example of being given the bum's rush would be hard to find!*

He bought himself a cup of indifferent coffee from a machine in the lobby, drank most of it, and decided to try the embassy again.

This time a different voice, young-sounding and male, answered the phone. Roy could picture him: a gawky kid doing work experience because his father held a senior position at the embassy. He wasn't entirely wrong.

'I'm so sorry, sir,' he said, 'but I've checked the staff list and there's no one here by that name. And by the look of things no one by that name is expected.'

'What about Philippe Maigret?'

'French?'

'Yes.'

'We're not expecting him either,' the eager-beaver said after a short delay.

'Would you take a message in case either of them should turn up in the next twenty-four hours?' Roy asked.

'Er, well... I can only take brief messages.'

'That's fine by me. Write this down please: a lad of about thirteen, British from Norfolk fell from a third floor window in Potsdam this afternoon. His name's Nat Glison and he's in the St Josefs-Krankenhaus Hospital...'

'Please slow down, sir – I'm writing this in longhand!'

'Will do.' Roy waited a few moments then continued, 'He's in the St Josefs-Krankenhaus Hospital...'

'Could you spell that for me please, sir?'

Roy did. 'In Potsdam. He seemed anxious that a

Chief Inspector Scott be informed, through the Berlin Embassy, as soon as possible. Or Philippe Maigret, I believe he's a police officer too, or both. Now have you got all that?'

'Just about, sir,' the trainee replied. 'And might I ask your name, sir?'

'It's Roy. R o y.'

'And your surname, sir?'

'Natiramas. Do you want me to spell that for you too?'

'If you wouldn't mind, sir.'

'It's very easy. Just spell Samaritan backwards and you'll have it.'

'Oh, I see! Many thanks, sir.'

But already Roy had pressed the end call on his phone. *At least I didn't send him to the hardware shop to buy a tin of striped paint, as my grandfather did to me once! And I've done my best,* he thought, *much good it will do poor Nat.* He was wrong: the conscientious kid had carefully written out the note again and left it propped in a prominent place on his work station. And before too long someone would notice it and that someone knew all about Chief Inspector Scott and Philippe Maigret because he'd been the person fielding the requests for information that Clive Scott had made during the drive to Berlin. And what's more, he knew *exactly* where both Scott and Maigret would be at seven o'clock that night.

Roy said goodbye to Nat just before he was sedated.

'Did you phone the embassy, Roy?' Nat whispered.

'Yes, I did, my young friend.'

'And?'

'Everything's okay so there's no need for you to worry. Have a good sleep now, Chief Inspector Scott will be here in the morning,' he lied. *Needs must,* he told himself, *no sense in worrying the poor kid any more than necessary.*

'And Philippe too?'

'Yes, both of them. In the morning. Now sleep well. And happy dreams.'

It wasn't until he left the hospital that Roy remembered his bike was still at the apartment building. *Fishcakes,* he said to himself. *Now I'll have to either walk or take a bus. Hope no one's nicked it. And I suppose I'd better find out how Patrick's doing in the locked bathroom.*

His bike had not been stolen, nor had he really thought it would have been, but Patrick's fate was a different matter.

He hovered around the entrance to the building waiting for someone to let him in, hopping from foot to foot to keep warm. When at last, a young couple arrived, he spun them a story about visiting a friend and being locked out, which they readily believed. He rode in the elevator with them to the third floor where he left them with a quick "bye now".

There were three different doors located in the lobby area. He rang all of them The first door was opened by a young woman carrying a fractious baby. A dishevelled older man, who looked like he had lost his shaving razor and had been asleep, opened the second door. No one answered the third door even though he rang the bell loudly several times. He looked carefully around the lobby then lifted the doormat. *Why do people always hide the key under the mat,* he asked himself for the hundredth time; *it's the first place any self-respecting burglar would look!*

He walked carefully around the small apartment; two bedrooms, a kitchen, a living room-cum-dining room, and a bathroom. That was it. But now the bathroom door was wide open and there was no sign of Patrick. He found the bloodied tissues discarded in the bathroom bin, and some matching ones in the kitchen. *Someone's obviously left in a hurry,* he thought, *but the place seems reasonably clean and tidy. What went on here?*

While Roy was searching in Potsdam, Clive Scott was giving a rousing rendition of *Scotland the Brave* to an imaginary but never-the-less appreciative audience in the shower in the guest quarters of the British Embassy. The young telephone operator's meticulous note had not yet been read.

By the time it had been, Clive Scott would have taken a leisurely stroll in the early spring evening across *Pariser Platz* which is considered the best real estate space and arguably the most beautiful place in Berlin: around *Pariser Platz,* which lies on the eastern or *Unter den Linden* side of the Brandenburg Gate, elegant town houses, embassies and the luxurious Adlon Hotel were built in times long past.

During the division of Berlin the Square was on the East Berlin side of the sector border, while between 1961 and 1989 it lay between the inner and outer sections of the Berlin wall. It was, therefore inaccessible to Berliners and visitors. The buildings surrounding the Square were badly damaged during World War Two, and virtually everything, except the Brandenburg Gate, had to be demolished.

Since the reunification *Pariser Platz* had gradually been restored to its former splendour as one of Berlin's central plazas with the last remaining building, the new United States Embassy, having been completed in 2008. Unfortunately the building's design, with its emphasis on security, had been derided by German architectural critics who called it a 'triumph of banality' that would look more at home in Baghdad than Berlin.

Clive Scott, with his sister married to a German professor and living in Freiberg in the south-west of the country, was aware of the criticism. Consequently he ran a careful eye over the embassy on the south-west corner as he ambled by permitting himself a small shudder as he did. *If there's an architectural prize for the ugliest embassy in Europe this one has to be the front-runner,* he thought.

As he was in good time to meet the French detectives he strolled around to the north side of the Square which was dominated by the French Embassy. *Marginally better,* was his judgement, *but not in the same league as the old embassy destroyed in the war. Architects,* he thought, sighing as he did, *should damn well be made to live for a time in the monstrosities they design, that would refine their skills and concentrate their minds. And the world would be a better place – at least as far as our eyes are concerned!*

Clive's destination that evening was, in fact, the Hotel Adlon, which had suffered heavy damage during the war but was left in repairable condition. However, in the weeks following the German surrender it mysteriously burnt down, the story being that this occurred during a particularly raucous party being celebrated by Soviet army officers.

Clive knew that story too, and being a self-admitted 'army brat' was inclined to believe it! However a faithful copy of the hotel was subsequently built and it is now one of the most prominent buildings on the Square.

And it was the Hotel Adlon, with all its history and grandeur, in which Tom Aitkens always chose to stay when in Berlin.

At Philippe's insistence, Clive was due to meet them at 6.45pm, even though the drinks with Tom Aitkens had not been scheduled until 7pm.

Philippe wants to get the drop on him, Clive thought, *like some old gunslinger in an American western from the sixties. He knows Aitkens will have the home advantage and he wants to familiarise himself with the locale before he arrives.*

As Clive Scott reached the Hotel Adlon he glanced at his phone then switched it off. Not more than a few minutes later the carefully penned note written by the young eager-beaver at the British Embassy was found and read and a text was immediately sent to the chief inspector.

Clive was not surprised to find Philippe Maigret and Georges Martin already lingering in the bar area. *Philippe's been a bundle of nervous energy ever since Aitkens accepted our invitation. He just can't wait to see the man with whom Megan fell in love when she was a young girl. For his sake I hope he's fat, bald, and has been cruelly treated by Old Father*

Time. But, of course, Tom Aitkens had not suffered any of those misfortunes.

'Let's be quite clear about one thing,' Maigret said as they sat down at a table in a quiet corner of the bar. 'We're paying for the drinks. Or, at least, *I* am. There's no way I want to be beholden to this man for anything – not even the damn peanuts and olives that they'll probably bring us.'

'Fair enough, Philippe,' Scott said before Georges could speak. 'I quite understand. However, since you've started down this particular path, what's our position regarding the shaking of hands or not, as the case may be?'

'Of course we'll shake his hand. We're civilised men, aren't we?'

'Hmm, yes we are, but I'm not sure I would be quite so civilised if I were wearing your shoes.'

'Well you're not, and they wouldn't fit your big feet anyway,' Maigret said, attempting to relax.

As the waiter glided over to take their drink order, Thomas Jefferson Aitkens arrived. No gliding for him: he bounded in like an enthusiastic puppy.

The three detectives immediately stood to greet him. *I know which one of you is Philippe Maigret,* Tom Aitkens thought before anyone spoke. *And you are exactly as I'd imagined you. But then I did have an advantage: I've known about you for some considerable time.*

And Tom Aitkens had another advantage besides the familiar locale. He also had a fairly good idea why Philippe Maigret had asked to meet him that night.

TWENTY-FIVE

*Tuesday 14th March
(early evening.) Berlin.*

And Thomas Aitkens was very nearly as Philippe Maigret had imagined *him* – except better, much better, on all fronts. More polished, better-looking, more assured – and better-off. *I'm comfortably wealthy thanks to my father's estate,* Maigret thought, *but he could buy and sell me many times over. Maybe he's not quite reached Master-of-the-Universe status yet but he's not far from it. And I can't compete.*

The gliding waiter returned to their table and they ordered their drinks. The three Europeans chose Scotch; straight and neat for Clive and with a splash of mineral water for Philippe and Georges. The American chose Jack Daniels on the rocks. *Lolly-water for adults,* Clive Scott thought scornfully, *and certainly not a man's drink.*

'Now, gentlemen, to what do I owe this pleasure?' His voice was pleasant; moderated. *More mid-Atlantic than American,* Maigret thought, *and definitely achieved by intervention. But for what purpose: artifice or vanity?*

'I wonder if you would tell us what brings you to Berlin at this time, Mr Aitkens,' Philippe Maigret said.

'A question I might well ask of all three of you, Chief Inspector Maigret,' he replied. It was an easy, smooth reply, but his eyes were cold. 'You seem to have strayed a long way from your *usual* territory.' It was the way that he emphasised the word 'usual' that made Maigret's brain snap to full-focus.

'Have we met before, Mr Aitkens?' he asked, although he knew they had not. *Not in this or any other Universe,* he thought, *and never again if I have any say in the matter!*

'I don't believe so, Chief Inspector,' Aitkens replied. 'But then I have met a great many people over the years.'

'We're in Berlin on police business,' Clive Scott said gruffly, determined to break through the useless chit-chat as he saw it. 'And I'm even further from my natural habitat.'

Both Philippe and Georges looked at Clive in alarm. *Keep your hair on,* his eyes signalled back to them, *I have no intention of mentioning Madame Maigret.*

'Oh?'

'Yes, we're looking for three passengers who went missing from the Paris to Berlin train on Monday night.'

'And you think I might know something about this?' Aitkens asked. 'How could I? I only arrived in Berlin this afternoon.'

'Yes, we know that,' Georges Martin said without thinking. That comment earned him a withering look from his boss.

'How?' Tom Aitkens asked. It was a reasonable question. 'Has someone been checking on me?'

'Now how could we do that?' Clive Scott said affably. 'We're not James Bond.'

Tom Aitkens glanced pointedly at his watch. 'Look, I have somewhere to be before 8pm so can we move this conversation on please?'

'That's rather up to you, Mr Aitkens,' Philippe Maigret said. 'I'd like to ask you again – what is the purpose of your visit to Berlin?'

'And, at the risk of appearing rude, I'd like to tell you that it's none of your damn business.'

'Well, you'd be wrong then,' Clive Scott said. 'Because we think it might be very much our damn business.'

'Are you here for the Simon and Garfunkel concert tomorrow night?' Georges asked in a further verbal intrusion which provoked an even more crushing look from his chief. But to the police officers' surprise it proved useful.

'What?' Tom Aitkens said. 'Is this some kind of joke?'

'No joke, I assure you,' Philippe Maigret replied.

'Then let me tell you, gentlemen that I am the CEO of a multi-national company and I am not in the habit of flying from one continent to another in order to attend concerts about which I know absolutely nothing!'

'You didn't organise the concert here tomorrow night?'

'Let me say this as clearly as I can. I do not know

anything about a concert here in Berlin tomorrow night…'

'But isn't the name of your company *Scarborough Fair Inc.?*'

'Yes it is, Chief Inspector Scott. But so what?'

'You didn't know anything about the concert even though your company is sponsoring it?'

'*My* company? Gentlemen, let me explain how the corporate world works. *Scarborough Fair Inc.* has a German subsidiary, based in Berlin, the name of which is also Scarborough Fair – but minus the *incorporated* part. The Berlin subsidiary has its own employees, its own budgets, and its own publicity machine. And it is obviously these people who have arranged this event. They haven't consulted me about it – hell, I'm not even *going* as far as I'm aware! And in the interest of saving time, I'm here for a series of business meetings and other er… events, *excluding pop concerts,* over the next three days. Now if you will excuse me I have a car coming to take me to dinner.'

'Wait!' Chief Inspector Maigret said. 'Do you know a man by the name of David Quinn?'

'I told you before, Chief Inspector, I meet many people during the course of my business life, however I do not believe I know anyone by that name. Who is he?'

'He's ex-British security service,' Clive Scott said, risking his pension instead of allowing Philippe to jeopardise his. 'And he seems to have gone walkabout.'

'So it would seem you *have* ventured into the realm of James Bond after all, Chief Inspector Scott. But I still don't know him.'

'And yet he appears to know you, sir,' Georges Martin said. 'And he says that you are involved in something er... very *unpleasant* that is expected to happen in Berlin tomorrow.'

'*Baloney* – total rubbish! Where's his proof – and where's yours for that matter?' Tom Aitkens said angrily. 'And I've had more than enough of this interrogation now, so please excuse me, *officers*.' He paused long enough to throw two fifty euro notes on the table and then stormed out of the bar.

'That went well, didn't it?' Clive Scott commented as they watched the departing figure of Aitkens. 'So where do we go from here?'

'Did you notice how often he glanced at his watch?' Georges Martin asked. 'He had trouble staying still at times...'

'He had somewhere he needed to be. He told us – a dinner engagement,' Clive Scott said.

'Yes, but what *kind* of a dinner engagement?'

'You're thinking *cherchez la femme,* Georges?'

'Yes, sir.'

'I didn't appreciate the full extent of your French language ability, Clive,' Philippe said. 'I'm quite impressed.'

'You know my limitations all too well! But I know that phrase alright, as does half the world – *look for the woman.*'

'Yes, *or find the woman.* I think Mr Aitkens had a romantic dinner planned for tonight and that's why he couldn't wait to get away from us,' Georges replied.

'But what woman?'

'Exactly, Chief. What woman, and where?'

They sat in silence for a few moments pondering the question. The floating waiter kept an eye on them but didn't intrude.

'I feel like getting drunk,' Philippe Maigret said.

'Well, we've got plenty of Aitkens' money with which to do it,' Clive Scott said.

'No, that goes in the nearest charity box!'

'Agreed. But getting drunk's not a good idea, my friend, nor will it solve anything.'

'You're right, Clive.'

'However, another dram or two won't hurt us – will it?' Clive said, signalling the waiter. 'Then I'd like to head for the best curry joint in town!'

They enjoyed their next dram, as Clive insisted on calling their drinks, and then, halfway through their third dram came another intervention from Georges Martin.

'Let's retrace our steps a little,' he said. 'I think it's time for a review.'

'Of what?'

'Of why we went down this Simon and Garfunkel route in the beginning.'

'Well it was because…'

'It was because of the name of Thomas Aitkens' company,' Georges said, interrupting Clive Scott, 'and the connection with the English folk song.'

'Who gave us the name of the company?'

'Er… the British Embassy in Berlin,' Maigret said.

'Wasn't it Quinn?' Scott asked.

'No, he only *mentioned* Aitkens, and the... er... New York context,' Georges said, choosing his words carefully.

'The embassy told us,' Maigret insisted.

'Yes, but that was only because we asked questions about Thomas Aitkens. We've been going in circles, haven't we?' Georges said.

'Or we're being played. But if we are, how far back did the playing start?'

'If memory serves me correctly,' Clive said drily, 'it was the Mesdames Maigret, both senior and junior, who started the whole shebang.'

'What?' Maigret exclaimed.

'*Shebang?*' Georges Martin queried.

'Operation, shemozzle... er... *kerfuffle!*'

'Leave my wife and mother out of this, Clive,' Philippe said. 'It was your old Jordanian friend, Akram, who started everything.'

'Yes, that's exactly what I'm saying, Philippe! And who put us on to him in the first place – your wife and your mother!'

'*Merde!* So they did,' Maigret conceded.

'An unlikely pair of Mata Haris, I grant you, but there it is.'

'Wait a minute though, Clive. How sure are you that Akram's days with the Jordanian security service are really over? Why should we trust him? He *was* following my wife.'

'No, Philippe, he was following *Quinn*. And, to answer your question, I'd trust Akram with my life.

Have done so in the past and would not hesitate to do again. Akram's as true blue as they come.'

'Maybe, but what do we know about Jamal?'

'We know his mobile seems to be permanently switched off,' Georges replied.

'Yes, and in fact we've never questioned him about the massacre in the *10ᵉ*. Not in person, I mean. Not real, *forensic* questioning under caution,' Maigret said thoughtfully.

'But Ibrahim was his uncle and he was murdered too.'

'Was he?'

'You know he was Chief; we identified his body.'

'No, I mean was Ibrahim really Jamal's uncle? Who told us he was?'

'Jamal did, boss. At least I think he did. Or was it Akram?'

'And it was Jamal who mentioned the Simon and Garfunkel concert to Akram who then passed that information on to us.' Clive said.

'And that's where the wild goose chase started,' Philippe Maigret said, leaning back against his chair, taking a large slurp of his scotch and finally looking satisfied.

'Want me to phone old Akram again and see what he knows?'

'Yes, good idea, Clive. Let's see if Akram can really vouch for Jamal.'

Clive Scott took out his phone, switched it on ready to make the call, and read the text from the embassy.

'Shite!' he exclaimed, immediately passing the phone to Philippe Maigret without a further word. He read it several times to make sure he could trust the message his eyes were sending to his brain.

'But if Nat's in a Potsdam hospital,' he said, his voice as plaintive as a child's, 'where's Megan and what's happened to her?'

★

'You're not intending to do anything rash or stupid, like making a run for it, or contacting the police while we're gone, are you Pat... Patrick?' Quinn asked as he and Megan were about to leave.

'How many more times are you planning to go over this?' Patrick asked angrily. 'I've given you my word that all I intend to do is find somewhere to have a quick meal, then come back to get an early night.'

'You sure – totally sure?'

'Ask him one more time and I'll thump you myself,' Megan said. 'Isn't Patrick's word good enough for you? It certainly is for me, especially since you swear you've now told us everything you know about what might happen tomorrow.'

'Yes. Sorry mate. Sorry Megan, it's just that there's so much depending on what we do between now and 3pm tomorrow.'

'Haven't your colleagues in Berlin been able to give you any further information?'

'Yes, but they're still saying Aitkens is what they

keep hearing on the street. Aitkens is in it – up to the hilt.'

Or he's the target, his friends had said. *But don't let Megan and Patrick know that or you'll spook them.*

★

'There's no need for either of you to come to Potsdam with me,' Philippe said, as they left the hotel. 'Nat is my responsibility: I'll wait at the hospital until Megan… until Megan ..'

If she comes. If she's in any position to come, Clive Scott and Georges were thinking.

'I know what the two of you are thinking, but you're wrong. Megan is not dead: if she were I'd know it. I'd *feel* it – in here,' Philippe said, tapping over his heart.

'I'm sure you're right, Philippe. She's probably at the hospital already, waiting for you. But have you forgotten that Nathaniel is a British citizen? That makes him *my responsibility* too.'

'Your embassy will take care of that side of things, Clive.'

'Maybe. But it's academic anyway because I'm going with you and so is the diplomatic car. I'll nip back and pick it up now.'

'And I'm coming too, Chief,' Georges Martin said.

'I can't wait! I'm getting a taxi now!' Philippe said impatiently.

'Mate, it is 24 km to Potsdam, and I think you might find a German speaker useful, as has happened before on this little road trip!' And with those words Clive Scott jogged off surprisingly speedily for a man of his size with three drams of Scotland's finest inside of him.

'He's right, sir,' Georges said. 'But we can't let him drive; he'd be over the limit.'

'And so would you! But I'm sure he's had more drams of scotch than either of us put together: he was probably weaned on it so if he wants to drive we'll let him. I'm sure he'll be safe.'

'And I suppose no German police officer is going to stop a British car with diplomatic plates,' Georges said. 'Now excuse me, Chief, I need a quick trip to the bathroom. Won't be long.'

Something Georges just said is significant, Philippe thought as his colleague dashed back into the hotel. *But what was it. Think man: what did Georges just say, word for word?* He re-ran their last conversation in his mind. *The car – it was the car that was important. But why?* Then finally his brain supplied the answer, *because Aitkens had a car coming to take him to dinner. Why a car? He could have taken a taxi from the rank opposite the hotel. That's what I was planning to do. Don't be ridiculous! Men like Aitkens don't take taxis! They have chauffeurs, and limousines and private bloody jets!*

Philippe Maigret strolled casually into the hotel, meeting Georges as he did.

'Going somewhere, boss?'

'Come with me, *mon ami*.'

Maigret walked up to the concierge desk.

'Good evening, sir,' the young man said in German.

'Leave this to me, Chief,' Georges whispered, but the man heard him.

'*En Français?*' he asked.

'*Oui – ou en Anglais, si vous* préférez.'

'English is fine,' Philippe said.

'Thank you, sir. Now how may I help you?'

'My friend and I had drinks in the hotel's bar with one of your guests earlier this evening. An American, Thomas Aitkens.'

'Oh, yes, sir, Mr Aitkens is one of our *favourite* guests.'

I'll just bet he is, Philippe thought, *and very generous with his tips too!*

'Mr Aitkens unfortunately left his wallet behind,' Philippe said, 'and I'd like to return it to him if possible.'

'You could leave it with us, sir. It will be quite safe.'

'I'm sure it would be, but Mr Aitkens mentioned that he had a dinner engagement at 8pm tonight. If he's the host he'll be embarrassed when he finds his wallet's missing.'

'Oh, I see – yes, that could be a problem. Do you want me to try to contact him, sir?'

'No, that won't be necessary. He had a car coming for him; did he arrange that through you?'

'Not me, sir, I've not long come on duty. But let me check my book.' He opened a leather-bound journal and scanned it quickly.

'Ah yes, here it is. My colleague arranged the car for him. Mr Aitkens wanted it for 7.30pm.'

'And where was he going?'

'Potsdam, sir.'

'And the name of the restaurant?'

'No restaurant was mentioned sir, just that he was going to Potsdam.'

As they left the concierge desk Georges Martin said, 'We don't believe in coincidences, do we, Chief?'

'No we don't, *mon ami*. And even if we did, we'd never be duped by a coincidence as massive as this one!'

TWENTY-SIX

Tuesday 14th March. Potsdam. 8pm

Tom Aitkens had chosen *Quintessenz,* an intimate, softly-lit restaurant a block or two away from the main streets of the old town, for his rendezvous with Megan. From past experience he knew that very few of his fellow Americans frequented this restaurant. He also knew that is was unlikely that any tourist would wander this far from the bright lights. He knew *Quintessenz* well; it was a favourite of his, and he had made his preparations with care. The best French champagne – perfectly chilled – accompanied by Beluga caviar with freshly made blinis was to be awaiting his guest's arrival. Caviar was not readily available in Potsdam but the owner, knowing that Mr Aitkens was a man used to getting what he wanted, had procured some of the finest caviar from a contact in Berlin. At a considerable cost, of course, but Mr Aitkens was a man with very deep pockets!

'Wish me luck,' Megan said to Patrick as she and Quinn left their room to go to her dinner engagement.

'You look lovely, Megan,' he said, 'blue really suits you. Tom will be blown away when he sees you.'

'That's not really the effect I'm looking for, Patrick but thanks for the vote of confidence.'

Tom always loved you in blue, didn't he, her conscience remarked. *Isn't that exactly why you chose this dress? Shut up – I know what I'm doing,* she replied. *Just as long as you do,* her conscience countered, determined to have the last word, *because we've just taken a vote and you wouldn't like the results if we told you!*

'Now, at the risk of getting walloped, let's go through this scenario one more time,' Quinn said as they drove towards Potsdam old town.

Megan sighed. 'Must we, David?'

'Yes, we must. Plan A, if you spend the night with him I'll pick you…'

'That's not Plan A – that's Plan Never-going-to-happen,' she interrupted. 'And you know it. Now give me some money so I can take a taxi back to the guest house after we've finished dinner.'

'Hmm, we'll see. Plan B, if he drives you home, which I expect he will, you pretend that you're staying at that small hotel two blocks away that I pointed out to you earlier. You don't, under any circumstances, let him bring you back to the guest house. Agreed?'

'Agreed. And then first thing tomorrow morning you take me to the hospital to see Nat. Yes?'

'Yes.'

Shortly after this conversation took place the three detectives arrived at the St Josefs-Krankenhaus Hospital. Philippe Maigret strode quickly into the hospital, barely waiting for the car to stop, approaching the first nurses' station he encountered. The nurse to whom he spoke had only a rudimentary knowledge of English, and none at all of French. She shook her head and said '*Nein, nein – am morgen,*' very loudly.

'No – not in the morning – now!' Philippe insisted.

'Leave this to me, mate,' Clive Scott said as he joined him.

Then followed an animated conversation in German which ended with the nurse shouting that no one – *no one at all* – would be permitted to see the patient before the morning. Nor did it matter if the French gentleman *was* the boy's grandfather; he would most certainly *not* see the lad that night. And those were the doctor's orders.

'Oh, but I think he most certainly can,' Clive said calmly, producing his Scotland Yard ID. 'For the love of God, Philippe show her your ID too before I strangle this stupid… *frau.*' Both Philippe and Georges did as Clive had suggested.

'Even if you are the police,' the *frau* said frostily, not happy to have been outplayed, 'only the grandfather may see the lad and only for a short time.'

'Listen to me, sister,' Clive said in German, 'you are to give this man who, if you had any shred of humanity left, you would see is totally exhausted, a comfortable chair in which to sleep for the entire night, if that's what he chooses, and…'

'What's going on here, and what's all the noise about?' It was the neurosurgeon who had been brought in earlier to examine Nat and who was now on his way home.

The nurse and Clive competed to tell the consultant their side of the argument. Clive won.

'Chief Inspector Maigret, please follow me,' the consultant said. 'And nurse, arrange for whatever the chief inspector needs, including *hot* food, to be sent to his grandson's room as soon as possible.'

'Thank you and God bless you, sir,' Scott said, shaking the consultant's hand.

The consultant shrugged. 'Jobsworth,' he whispered in English, shooting a quick glance in the nurse's direction.

'Jobsworth?' Clive Scott repeated, greatly amused. 'I take it you've worked in the NHS in England then – have you Doctor?'

The consultant laughed. 'Yes. Now is there anything more you need, Chief Inspector Scott?'

'Yes, I need to contact the person who came with Nathaniel in the ambulance. I understand his name is Roy and I hope you have his number,' Scott said in German.

'Leave it with me. I'll come back as soon as I've taken Chief Inspector Maigret to see his grandson.'

And, not more than ten minutes later, the consultant returned with the information.

'German efficiency at its best,' Clive said, as he was handed the neat note on which the number had been written.

'Works sometimes,' the consultant chuckled, 'but we can't always count on it.'

'Is Nathaniel still asleep?' Clive asked.

'Yes, and he will be until tomorrow morning. He's had an eventful day followed by a number of tests, followed by some food and then a strong sedative. Sleep's the best thing for him right now; the body knows how to heal itself.'

'Will he be discharged in the morning?'

'Doubtful, I'd say. We may keep him in for another couple of days just to be sure. We'll see how he's doing in the morning.'

'Thanks, Doctor,' Scott said, shaking the neurosurgeon's hand again.

After the doctor left, Clive and Georges Martin walked back to the lobby and sat down while Clive made his phone call. Roy answered almost immediately.

'So the young kid at the embassy actually did leave a note,' he said after Scott told him who he was. 'I'm impressed.'

'Yes, he did. Now what can you tell me about how Nathaniel from Norfolk ended up in a Potsdam hospital?'

Roy did.

'How far away from the hospital is this apartment building?' Clive asked.

'About ten minutes or so. Want me to meet you there?'

'Would you?'

'Yes, of course. It's only a couple of streets away

from where I'm staying,' Roy said, giving Clive the address.

'Good man – see you soon.'

'Got a satnav?' Roy asked.

'Wait until you see the Jag I'm driving, Roy. It's got satnav to burn and so much other stuff that I'm terrified to touch because I don't know what it might be capable of. Could have an ejector seat for all I know.'

Roy met them at the apartment building fifteen minutes later. This time there was no need for them to loiter for a resident to let them in.

'Look the other way for a moment,' Clive Scott told Roy. He did and – hey presto! The door was open.

'How'd you do that? Was it even legal?'

'Ask me no questions and I'll tell you no lies,' Clive said.

When they reached the third floor Roy collected the key from under the door mat as he had done before.

'Touch nothing,' Clive Scott instructed, pulling on his forensic gloves and handing Georges Martin a pair to do the same.

'Too late – I touched stuff when I was here before.'

'Like what?'

'I'll show you.'

Roy took Clive into the bathroom and pointed out the bloodied tissues in the waste bin.

'And there are more in the kitchen bin,' he said. 'Some of these in the bathroom look like they've been used for a nose bleed because the blood's bright red.'

'Know about blood, do you, Roy? You an axe murderer or something?'

'Second year med student; it's Haematology 101,' Roy laughed. 'Where's the French officer?'

'Taking photographs of everything, as per his chief's orders. Chief Inspector Maigret stayed at the hospital; Nathaniel's his grandson. Hello, what do we have here?' Clive said, lifting out the pieces of clothes line rope that had been used to tie Nat and Patrick.

'Restraints?'

'Looks like it. Get Georges for me will you? We need to photograph these in situ then we'll take them away with us.'

They stayed in the apartment for half an hour, then left, taking away all the evidence they could find.

'Had any dinner yet?' Scott asked Roy as they walked out on to the darkened street.

'Not yet, and I'm absolutely starving!'

'Me too,' Clive said. 'Know any good curry places in Potsdam?'

'Yeah, I do, Clive. In fact I know the best, the very best, curry establishment in town. It's a bit of a drive, but it will be worth it.'

'No probs take us there, and it's my treat!'

'Really?'

'Yes.'

The smell – the delicious Indian spice aromas – caressed their noses before they even left the car. Clive Scott stopped in his tracks and breathed deeply.

'Oxygen of the gods,' he said.

'So Mount Olympus was actually located somewhere in the Punjab, Clive?' Roy asked.

'Yep, somewhere around that region!'

As they walked into the *Shahbag* restaurant, Georges Martin collided with Patrick Evremond, who was on his way out.

'Why don't you watch where you're going, man?' Patrick said irritably. Then he did a double-take. 'Georges Martin! Is that really you? What are you doing here?'

'Cripes, mate – what happened to you?' Roy said, peering closely at Patrick's facial injuries. 'Run into the back of a bus?'

'Something that felt like that,' Patrick muttered, anxious to be on his way before too many questions were asked. There was no chance of that!

'Not so fast, Sonny-Jim,' Clive Scott said. 'You're going nowhere until I say so. Now, what happened to your face?'

'Quinn happened.'

'He did this to you? Why?'

Patrick thought quickly. *What's safe to tell him and what's not – that's the question? If he's with Roy he knows about Nat falling out of the window. So I can tell him that's why Quinn attacked me. But not much more. And certainly not where he and Megan are, nor where we're staying.*

'Er he lost his rag when he discovered that Nat had gone.'

'Right – get back inside the restaurant. I have a few important questions to ask you.'

'I've already eaten, Chief Inspector. Now all I want is to go home to…'

'And that's question number one,' Clive said. 'Where are you staying and where are Megan and Quinn?'

'Sorry, can't tell you.'

'Oh, you'll tell me alright,' Clive Scott said. 'Or what Quinn did to you will be nothing compared with what Philippe Maigret and I will do.'

'Now hold on a mo,' Roy said. 'There'll be no police brutality while I'm around.'

'Feel free to leave anytime you like, Roy!'

'I'm not going anywhere, Chief Inspector Scott.'

'Look, I'll tell you as much as I can. Okay?'

'We'll see. Get on with it!'

'Megan and Quinn are er *around*. And we're er also *staying* er around.'

'Keep score, Georges. Nothing and nothing, so far,' Clive Scott said.

'Quinn's been in touch with some er… *colleagues* in Berlin, and their latest information is that kick off is supposed to be around three o'clock tomorrow.'

'Where?'

'Berlin, as far as I know. And Quinn's promised Megan and me that's all he knows too.'

'And you believe him?' Georges Martin asked sceptically.

'Yes, we both do. And that's why we've said we'll help him.'

'What can the two of *you* do?' Scott asked quickly.

'I can't tell you that. But all Quinn needs is

twenty-four hours and that's what we've decided to give him.'

'Tomorrow's 15th March; one way or another it will be all over in twenty-four hours. Are you happy to be an accessory to carnage, Patrick?'

'Of course I'm not! Quinn's trying to stop that from happening!'

'Sure?'

'Yes. I'm sure.'

'The 15th March; now there's a memorable date for you,' Roy said quietly.

'What?'

'Yes. That's the date the Boche marched into Czechoslovakia in 1939. Then they took over Bohemia and founded a protectorate over Slovakia. And that was the end of appeasement because it proved that Hitler had lied at Munich.'

'How old are you, Roy?' Scott asked. 'And how could you possibly know all that?'

'I'm twenty-four and my grandparents were born in Czechoslovakia, that's how,' Roy said. 'My surname's Havel.'

'Want me to follow him, Chief Inspector?' Georges Martin asked after Scott had finally decided that Patrick could leave.

'No,' Clive said thoughtfully, rubbing his ample chin. 'Let's give Quinn time to do whatever he's planning to do.'

'That's taking a risk, sir.'

'Yes, and don't I know it! But it feels right to me.'

★

Quinn stopped the car around the corner from the *Quintessenz* restaurant and Megan climbed out.

'Remember – find out as much as you can about why he's in Berlin and his movements over the next couple of days. And particularly his movements tomorrow. Tomorrow's the Ides and that's the critical time for us.'

'I know, I know. I'll do my best David. I promise you I will.'

'If you really meant that you would give him what he wants. Do you need to read his text again so you'll know exactly what that is?'

Megan glared at Quinn but said nothing. Then she turned on her heel and walked towards the restaurant with head held high.

Tom Aitkens, anxiously watching the door, saw her come in. He immediately got to his feet and walked towards her, his heart turning cartwheels.

Yes, he told his heart, *this is the girl. This is that Megan Ross girl from long ago. We won't let her get away for a second time, will we,* his heart fretted. *We'd break forever if that happened. Trust me,* he replied. *This time we're keeping her!*

TWENTY-SEVEN

*Tuesday 14th March. Potsdam.
later in the evening*

After their meal at *Shahbag,* which exceeded Roy's recommendation, Clive and Georges drove Roy home. As soon as he left the car they detoured to the St Josefs-Krankenhaus Hospital to check on Philippe Maigret. They were relieved to discover that *Brünnhilde the nurse,* as Clive referred to her, had left and in her place was a SYT[1] (also Clive's description!), a petite blonde in her late twenties whose name was Gabriela and whose English was good. *Just my type,* Georges Martin thought wistfully, *and we're ships passing in the night, as usual!*

Gabriela led the way to Nat's room where they stood together in the doorway, charmed by the scene in front of them. Philippe was stretched out, *to his impressive extent* (another of Clive's descriptions) fast asleep in an armchair with pillows behind his head, his lean body partly covered by a mohair rug which was clearly not standard hospital issue. Before settling down for the

---

[1] Sweet young thing

night he had moved his chair as close as possible to Nat's bed, and now, in untroubled rest, his left arm lay outstretched on the bed. And on that protective arm rested the sleeping Nat's head and shoulders. The nurse and two detectives looked at each other and smiled: there was no need for words.

They left the hospital each with that reassuring image in their mind's eye to return to Berlin. Georges insisted on driving while Clive, with his appetite for curry gratified and a couple of glasses of German beer inside of him, was nodding off. The vibrating of his phone brought that to an end. It was the British Embassy. He listened without speaking apart from the occasional *when, how,* followed by *we're on our way, thirty minutes,* and *we'll meet you there.*

'Change of plans, Georges,' he said. 'We've got a body.'

'Who?'

'Apparently it's the elusive Jamal; he who never answers his phone. I guess we can't blame him for that if he's dead.'

'Where is he, sir?'

'In the morgue. I know where that is, I've done liaison work in Berlin before. It's more or less under the same roof as the main police nick. I'll direct you.'

Two embassy officials met them at the morgue. This was standard procedure as Jamal was a British citizen. Clive and Georges ran an experienced eye over him. He'd been shot in exactly the same way as the victims in both the *10th arrondissement* in Paris, and the undercover agents in Neuwied: one shot to the head, one to the heart. Not long dead, body dumped in an alley where it would be discovered sooner rather than later.

Same method, same weapon, therefore the same killer? Maybe.

What will we tell London, the embassy officers wanted to know. 'Say nothing, at least not yet,' Clive Scott said. 'I'm taking charge and I'll take responsibility. Anyone asks questions tell them to call me in the morning. I'm off to my bed now.'

As Clive and Georges walked towards the Jag Clive said, 'Keep this under your hat, Georges – we've got another problem now.'

'Sir?'

'That man in the morgue is *not* Jamal Ahmadi.'

'What? But your embassy people said it was; he had identification on him that proved that.'

'Yes, but no passport.'

'Well, it's probably back wherever he was staying, I suppose. And why does that matter anyway?'

'This is why,' Clive Scott said, as they reached the car. He scrolled through his phone until he found what he was looking for. 'See this? This is Jamal Ahmadi's passport photograph which I had sent to me from London this morning. Tell me, Georges, does that look like the man we've just seen?'

'Yes, it does *look* like him. A little like him, at least.'

'Yes, similar, but not the same. That unfortunate man in the morgue, whoever he might be, is a decoy, the proverbial red herring. And why?'

'Because... because Jamal Ahmadi is our killer?'

'Yes, and it's probable that he's also planning the atrocity here tomorrow.'

'But he couldn't have been responsible for the murdered agents in Neuwied could he? The timing's wrong.'

'Not completely impossible,' Clive said. 'They weren't exactly... *fresh*, were they? How did he seem when you interviewed him after the murders in the 10th?'

'That's just it, Chief Inspector Scott – we didn't!'

'Didn't what?'

'Didn't interview him before. I've never even *seen* a photograph of him until the one you just showed me.'

'But how could you *not* interview him? Isn't the last man still standing always the obvious suspect?'

'We couldn't find him. Then Quinn disappeared from the hospital and we...'

'Took your eyes off the ball. Didn't you?

'No, we were dealing with more urgent concerns,' Georges replied, looking uncomfortable. 'And Jamal wasn't considered a suspect. Nor was he the only man left standing. Your friend Ahmed fits that description too.'

'Ahmed had nothing to do with the killings! We know that because he received a call on his mobile from Ibrahim as he lay dying! I don't know about you, but in my opinion that puts him in the clear.'

Georges said nothing. What was there for him to say?

'And I tell you another thing laddie, if Jamal, the *real* Jamal, should commit bloody massacre in this town tomorrow, I wouldn't want to be wearing your skin or Philippe Maigret's either!'

Tom Aitkens seated Megan comfortably at the best table *Quintessenz* could offer, then sat down opposite her. He smiled and reached for her hand. Then he nodded to the waiter, which was the signal for him to pour the champagne.

'I couldn't believe my eyes when I read your text,' he said after their glasses had been filled. 'It seemed too good to be true and…'

'And it was, Tom. I didn't send that text.'

'You didn't? Then who did?'

'Someone not me, obviously!'

'Don't play games with me, Megan,' he said, abruptly releasing her hand. 'That's not your style, nor mine either.'

'I'd tell you more if I could.'

'And yet here you are,' he said, smiling again. 'And you've hardly changed at all.'

'Take it down a notch or two, Tom,' she said.

'What?'

'The charm offensive. Whatever you're selling, I'm not in the market to buy.'

'Then why are you here? Unless – oh I see! Someone *told* you to come, didn't they?'

'Yes.'

'Who was it, the… er *elegant* French cop you married or…'

'How did you…? No, it wasn't him; he doesn't even

know I'm here. And I don't like your emphasis on the word elegant, nor the implication. There's nothing remotely effeminate about my husband. I can vouch for that.'

'Did I say there was?'

'Yes, I believe you just did.'

'Are you surprised that I know about him?'

'Yes.'

'Then let me surprise you further, my dear. At seven o'clock this evening I had drinks with him in my hotel in Berlin. And not just him – the impeccable Philippe Maigret – but also two of his cohorts: a young inspector – Martin, I believe his name was, and a bully-boy chief inspector from Scotland Yard.'

'Clive Scott.'

'The very same. It's a pity you couldn't have witnessed the event. You'd have found it as amusing as I did. We danced around each other like a couple of ballet dancers deciding whether to attempt a *pas de deux*. Of course, he'd have had to dance the prima ballerina's role if we had!'

Megan kicked him under the table.

'Ouch! What was that for?'

'You know very well. And the next time you cast doubt, no matter how slight, on Philippe's masculinity, I'm leaving.'

'You look like you mean that.'

And she did.

'But to continue with my story: we... er *skipped* around each other. I knew who he was, and I had the feeling he knew who I was, but neither of us said anything. Amusing – as I said earlier.'

'But how could you know about Philippe?'

'I know a great deal about you and your life, Megan, and have done for years. Did you get the flowers I sent when Michael Lisle died?'

'Yes, thank you, it was a kind thought and they were beautiful. I hope you received my note.'

Tom Aitkens reached into the inside pocket of his suit coat and took out his wallet. From it he removed a neatly folded note which he opened, smoothed out and then passed to Megan.

'You carry my note in your wallet?'

'Yes, of course. Where I go, it goes.'

'Isn't that a little creepy?'

'No, why should it be?'

'Because the world moved on a long time ago and so have we.'

'I haven't. Nor can I believe that you'd rather live in some flea-bitten dump in Paris with a *fancy-pants* French cop who wouldn't know his ar... *arm* from his elbow than live with me in luxury in Connecticut or wherever else you preferred.'

'Tom, I'm not the Megan who fell in love with you during that wonderful New York summer over thirty years ago. That girl has gone and she's not coming back. Not ever.'

'Why did you leave me?'

'You know why. *You were not worthy.*'

'And there it is – finally! A youthful... *transgression* all that time ago and still you haven't forgiven me.'

'Youthful transgression?'

'Misjudgement, then.'

'You were twenty-seven years old and you had plans. You thought I was trying to trick you into an early marriage and you told me so – most eloquently, as I recall. But I forgave you a long time ago when I realised you were never going to be husband material; at least not for me.'

'And after all that trouble it turned out to be a false alarm because there never *was* a pregnancy.'

'No, there wasn't. The babies came later with Michael. And he was a lovely father.'

For the next few minutes they both gave excessive attention to their food, not saying anything.

I don't think this evening is going entirely to Mr Aitkens' plan, the shrewd restauranteur thought, watching them carefully. *And that's bad news for us because if this dinner doesn't live up to his expectations he probably won't leave his usual generous tip!*

'Everything good with your food, Megan?'

'Yes, it's lovely. Really delicious, thank you.'

'Does the name David Quinn mean anything to you, my dear?' he asked. Her start of surprise and the look on her face gave him his answer. 'I see that it does. So how did you get mixed up with a British spy?'

'He's not a spy – he's... he's a... *peace advocate.*'

'Oh really? If he is then I'm a horse's ass.'

'And that's pretty much how he described you!'

'Did he now? And how would he know anything about me. Oh, – because he's a spy! What else did he tell you, I wonder?'

'It's a long story, and I'm not sure I know where to start.'

'We're in no rush, are we? Start wherever you like, I'm a quick study.'

'Okay. He said that you were *never* an art critic, in fact he found the suggestion very funny.'

'But you know I was, Megan. We used to lie in bed on Sunday mornings while I read you my latest pithy comments on the New York art scene and then we'd...'

'If you keep interrupting I'll never get to the end of the story,' she said quickly.

'Okay. I'll shut up now.'

Megan began her story: '*Are you going to Scarborough Fair* was what Quinn said to me at Les Invalides when I was there with Nat, my grandson.' On hearing Quinn's opening gambit Tom Aitkens raised his eyebrows but said nothing.

'Of course I replied with *Parsley, sage, rosemary and thyme.*' More raised eyebrows from Tom, but nothing said.

'After our... er *impromptu* meeting he was deliberately run down by a car and taken to hospital in a very bad state. While he was there someone tried to kill him.' She could see that Tom was itching to say something so she quickly added – 'And all of that can be verified by my *non-ballet dancing, fancy-pants* husband the detective!' Tom stifled a laugh but remained silent.

'On Monday night Nat and I took the train from Paris to Berlin. David Quinn, having escaped from hospital, to cut a long story short,' she added, seeing a look of incredulity appearing on Tom's face. *Too late,* he mouthed, grinning. *Cut to the chase, I'm losing the will to survive,* he mouthed again.

Megan took a deep breath, followed by a swig of champagne and continued with her story.

'Without my knowledge, Quinn had stowed away on the train. He came to our compartment in a very bad physical state and I knew I must help him.' She glanced at Tom who was now affecting a yawn. She ignored him and went on with her monologue. 'He told us – *stuff* – alarming *stuff,* and asked us to leave the train with him when the Munich uncoupling took place at half-past midnight.' By now Tom's eyes were rolling and he slumped back in his seat feigning drunkenness, or maybe death.

The restauranteur, still carefully observing the two of them, was alarmed. Megan caught his eye, smiled and indicated that all was well.

Then she pressed on with her tale. 'Quinn said, or at the least implied, that you were some kind of stooge for the US government – or the CIA – or whatever. He told me about his friend, Major Simon Pascoe, who was killed in Afghanistan by a sniper using a British-made rifle loaded with British ammunition. He said that peace was bad for the arms trade so when things got too quiet and peaceful in the world there were people who would whisper things in the wrong ears to stir up trouble. He called them *facilitators* – or agitators – and he said you were one of these people: a puppet of the US government and that you always had been, which made you the worst kind of *dratsab!*

And since the time we left the train we've discovered three dead bodies in an isolated cottage in Neuwied – two of whom were friends of Quinn's – and now we're here with him. And he's desperate to prevent mass murder tomorrow in Berlin.' *You're in Potsdam;* Tom mouthed, miming the slitting of his wrists with the blunt side of the butter knife.

'May I speak now?' Tom said when she finally stopped to draw breath.

'If you must.'

'Not one word of what he told you about me is true.'

'Then prove it!'

'How? It's not possible to prove a negative.'

'Then tell me why you're in Berlin at this particular time. And tell me if you were ever an art critic. And why did you name your company Scarborough Fair Inc.?'

'I'll answer the last question first. You *know* why I chose the name I did for my company, it's as obvious to you as it was to me: wasn't *Scarborough Fair our song?* And yes, I was at one time an art critic. And a damn good one at that! Finally, I'm in Berlin for some business meetings and some er… trials of new er… products.'

'And you're not a stooge for the US government?'

'No. However,' he paused for effect, 'however, since 9/11 happened, and the world changed forever, I have done *some* work for the US Government.'

'What kind of work?'

He sighed. Not quite as long or as deep as Philippe would have sighed, but it was still a credible sigh.

'After you abandoned me…'

'I did not abandon you, Tom. I left New York, that's all.'

'Well it certainly felt like abandonment to me. So after you left New York, and when you wouldn't answer my letters or my phone calls, I went off the rails for a time.'

'This is emotional blackmail. And it won't work.'

'After a year or so, and some expensive rehab,' he said, ignoring her comment, 'I came to my senses, with the help of a number of good friends and eventually I enrolled as a post grad student at MIT in Boston. There I met a brilliant young guy, Owen Griffiths, an electronics whiz kid: a natural born genius and we hit it off in a big way! After we graduated from MIT we left Boston and set up our own electronics company in Connecticut, my home state. He was the innovative brainbox and I was the business impresario. And to our surprise that proved a winning combination. More by luck than strategy we tapped into a market that Silicon Valley had overlooked and we made money hand over fist.'

'Good for you, Tom. And after 9/11?'

'After 9/11 the kid gloves came off as far as I was concerned. So when I was approached by er… a branch of the US Defense Agencies…'

'FBI? CIA? Department of Defense? Homeland Security?' Megan interjected.

'Not the FBI and not the CIA…'

'So the D.O.D or Homeland Security…'

'As I said, *not* the FBI and *not* the CIA…'

'And what did they want you to do for the… *cause?*'

'They wanted us to develop and make… *products* for the protection of our country. And we agreed to do this and to work almost exclusively for the US Government. But I do not travel around the world starting wars, or skirmishes or anything of that nature, nor am I a spy. I am a patriot.'

'*And patriotism is the last refuge of a scoundrel,*' Megan said.

'When Samuel Johnson said that – way back in 1775, if I remember correctly – the world was a very different place. I doubt that he would feel the same way now. And if he did, he'd be considered a fool; either that or a pontificating old windbag! And for all we know that's exactly what people thought of Dr Johnson when he actually did say it! Did you really expect that I'd stand by and do nothing while a bunch of medieval blood-hungry maniacs tried to destroy my country?'

TWENTY-EIGHT

Tuesday 14th March. Potsdam. 9pm

Tom's question hung in their air between them while they again paid excessive attention to their food.

By now the waiters and their boss – experts all in body language – were taking wagers as to which way this bizarre dinner might proceed. Would the lady throw something liquid over Mr Aitkens – champagne or water not specified both acceptable – that was Option A. Option B anticipated that she would dissolve into tears before the meal was finished and run out of the restaurant – and Option C was that she would succumb to Mr Aitkens' seduction, they would kiss passionately then leave arm-in-arm. There were very few takers for Option C but a sizeable number was currently lining up behind Option B! There was another option: Option D which comprised a number of elements of previous options. This option suggested that the lady would burst into tears, throw a liquid of some kind over Mr Aitkens, then run out of the restaurant alone. This option seemed to be gathering traction as time passed.

'Do you know what a drone is, Megan?' Tom asked, finally breaking the silence.

'Of course; did you forget that my father kept bees? A drone is a male honeybee which is the product of an unfertilized egg and its primary role is to mate with a fertile queen bee, after which it dies.'

'Yes, I did forget about your father's hobby. I'd like to declare solidarity with the poor damn drone! Not only did he get short-changed by evolution but I know how he feels! *Fleeting moments of ecstasy followed by a lifetime of death!*'

Megan laughed. 'How can anyone have a lifetime of death? It's not possible!'

'Don't you believe it – I'm living proof that it is!'

Tom took hold of her hand, raised it to his lips, and kissed it tenderly.

At this point the waiters shook their heads and threw in the towel or the sponge, or whatever prize fighters use to concede defeat, in disgust and all bets were declared off. It was probably a wise move.

'You weren't talking about bees, were you? I read the papers; you meant drones in warfare, didn't you?'

'Yes. But drones can be, and are, used both for defence and attack, which is something the media is not always interested in reporting.'

'And you make these things?'

'Yes, amongst many other projects. And that's really why I'm in Berlin. We're testing a new prototype tomorrow, but you didn't hear that from me.'

'But I did! And you shouldn't have told me.'

'And yet I did. And do you know why?'

She shook her head.

'Life's a funny old thing, isn't it?' Tom said, reaching for his champagne glass again.

'If you need Dutch courage before you can tell me then maybe you shouldn't say anything more.'

'Stay with me tonight, Megan,' he said earnestly. 'All I want is to feel you close to me again. I promise that nothing else will happen unless you want it to.'

'That's exactly what I'd be afraid of! I'd never risk my relationship with Philippe like that, even if the night *were* totally innocent.'

'And yet I can't help feeling that there's a little corner of your heart that still belongs to me. Why would I feel that way if it wasn't true?'

'Hearts don't have corners, they have ventricles,' she said.

'Well, a little section of the ventricle of your heart with my name on it then, Ms Pedantic!'

'Large ventricle or small?'

'Aren't they both the same size?'

'No, the muscle of the left ventricle is two or three times thicker than the right, although the size of the cavity itself is about the same as the right.'

'How do you know that?'

'I don't know – must have read it somewhere.'

'I'll settle for whatever little piece of whatever damn ventricle you choose,' he said.

'Then tell me where you're testing the drone tomorrow.'

'And for that... *treason* against my country I'd get what in return?'

'Oh, how about a quarter of my left ventricle, engraved with your name? And...'

'And what?'

'When we leave the restaurant I'll show you where we're staying in Potsdam, which Quinn specifically said I must not. And that's my *disloyalty* – to my husband, to Quinn and everyone else.'

'No. That's a sucker bet. I stand to lose far more than I'd collect. I'm no Edward Snowden, Megan!'

'Then call off the test or postpone it, but please, I beg you, don't do it tomorrow.'

'Can't do that either. We have top Air Force brass and other big-wigs coming to watch it: we must go ahead.'

'Why test in Germany? Why didn't you do it in your own country?'

'Two reasons: it's important, politically, that the US keeps the Europeans onside, and we get far less media scrutiny here than in the US where our testing sites are fairly well known. We're not ready to go public with this clever gizmo and what it can do yet.'

'Will the German Chancellor be there?'

'I'll pass on that one, Megan.'

'Will your drone be carrying weapons?'

'And I'll pass on that too.'

Megan said nothing for a few minutes, then she asked, 'Do you have anything I could write on, Tom, and a pen I could use?'

'Would the back of my business card be big enough?'

She nodded. He passed over the writing materials and she wrote quickly.

'This is all I know about tomorrow's events,' she said, pushing the card towards him face down, 'and it came from David Quinn via his colleagues in Berlin. Depending on how accurate it is, perhaps you'll change your mind.'

Tom Aitkens turned the card over and looked down at what she'd written. *Railway line nearby, 3pm Wednesday 15th.*

'Oh my God!' Tom Aitkens said. And that was *all* he said.

★

When Clive Scott arrived back in the British Embassy that night he sat down to make a list of Knowns, Unknowns and Each-way bets. Three columns and one name appeared in all of them. He reached for his phone then looked at his watch. *Too late to call Akram,* he thought, *bakers start work at sparrow's fart. I'll call him in the morning – first thing.*

Clive undressed, went through his usual night time rituals, then fell gratefully into bed and switched off the light. Just as he was drifting into sleep, two things happened. First came the signal that a text had been received, followed swiftly by his phone buzzing. *Bugger,* he thought, tempted to ignore both; but he could not. The phone call was from Akram in Paris.

'Must be mental telepathy, old son,' Clive said. 'I was

about to phone you then I remembered that you bakers have an early start, so I put it off until the morning. But you're up late, aren't you?'

'Don't sleep so well these days, Clive. Not since my wife died and I sleep alone – can't get used to it.'

'I understand. What can I do for you, my friend?'

'I'm worried because I haven't been able to contact Jamal since that call after he arrived in Berlin. His phone seems always to be switched off.'

'I haven't had any luck with him, either.'

'Do you think he's alright? What should I do?'

This is it now, Clive thought. *How much do I tell the old boy? The whole truth or a sanitised version.* He settled for neither.

'Before I answer your question, Akram, I have one of my own for you. How do you know that Jamal was Ibrahim's nephew?'

'He told me!'

'Who? Ibrahim or Jamal?'

'They both did, at different times. But what is this, Clive? What's going on?'

'Are you sure about that?'

'Yes, I'm sure. Now tell me what this is all about,' Akram said, losing patience with Clive's questions.

'There's been a development tonight, here in Berlin. We've found a body and...'

'For the sake of our friendship tell me it's not Jamal's body, Clive!'

'It's not Jamal.'

'Thank Allah!'

'However, and this is where the waters become a little muddy, the dead man bears more than a passing resemblance to Jamal, and he was carrying various items of ID which were all in Jamal's name. Why would that be, do you suppose?'

Akram said nothing. Clive could almost hear the cogs of his brain searching for the answer. *Once Jordanian Intelligence always will be,* Clive thought, *there's no such thing as retirement from a country's security service.*

'Do you think the real Jamal killed this... this *imposter*, Clive?'

'It's on the cards, mate.'

'I hope you're not right.'

'But if I am, then why would he do it?'

'I've heard that some...predatory animals lay... false trails to confuse the enemy, Clive,' Akram said carefully. 'And I've also heard that man is the most predatory animal of all.'

'You're not wrong there, mate! So Jamal's predatory, is he?'

'Maybe. He's a clever young man; maybe too clever, if you know what I mean. And ambitious.'

'Ruthless?'

'It grieves me to say it, but yes. He could probably be ruthless.'

'And the massacre in the 10th in Paris, old friend. Is he capable of that too? Could he have killed his uncle and everyone else in that upstairs room?' Clive heard the gasp from Akram that followed his words.

'If he could... commit that *abomination* then...'

he paused, unable to continue for a time. 'If Jamal could do that, Clive, I think I've lived too long on this earth…'

And then Akram broke down completely unable to continue. Clive waited a few minutes before he asked his next question.

'What work did Jamal do?'

Akram blew his nose loudly, sniffed a couple of times, and replied, 'He's very well informed about modern technology, but I don't know if he had employment in that area.'

'Computers?'

'Oh yes, I think he's good with computers and programming or something like that. I remember Ibrahim mentioned that once; he was very proud of his nephew. But that's really all I can tell you.'

I think that's more than enough to guarantee a fairly sleepless night, Clive thought ruefully.

'Thanks, Akram. I'll be in touch if I learn anything more about Jamal's whereabouts.'

After finishing his conversation with Akram, Clive turned his attention to the text message. And that was even more alarming than his phone call had been: it was the answer to a call he'd made to an MI5 contact in London before he joined Philippe and Georges for their drinks with Thomas Aitkens.

Jamal Ahmadi has 2.1 degree in Computer Sciences from Manchester. No real red flags raised this side of pond but some unease about the company he sometimes keeps. Possible radicalised recently. Yanks have him on no fly list but we don't know why and they won't tell. If located apprehend. We'll do the rest. But mind how you go, Clive. Will send further info as and when.

★

Tom and Megan finished their meal, with no liquid thrown and no one storming out of the restaurant, and he asked for the check. When Megan made a visit to the bathroom, Tom signalled Gustav, the restauranteur and asked for one of *Quintessenz's* business cards. He wrote quickly on the back of the card then slipped it into his pocket. As he helped Megan with her coat he whispered 'check your pocket later.'

'When will I see you again?' he asked as he walked her to the door of the guest house.

'I don't know, Tom. I'm not exactly a free agent, you know.'

'I think you'll have considerably more freedom after Quinn reads what I've written on the card in your pocket – *don't look now!* And tell him to phone me in the morning. I've written my private number on the card.'

Then he kissed her goodnight – a fleeting kiss on the lips – and walked slowly back to the car alone.

Quinn was waiting for her just inside the front door.

'Why did you bring him back here?' he demanded. 'I told you not to!'

'Things have changed, and I've something for you from Tom.'

'What?'

'When we're upstairs.'

'Can't talk there, Patrick's asleep. Show me what he gave you.'

Megan handed him the business card. On it Tom had written – in addition to his private mobile number – *Listen to what Megan tells you Quinn then connect the dots.*

'What does it mean?'

'I don't know, but I think you and I have a lot to discuss before we get any sleep tonight!'

★

When Thomas Jefferson Aitkens arrived back at the Hotel Adlon in Berlin he did a number of things in quick succession. Firstly he spoke to the concierge, who nodded and said, 'It will be done, Mr Aitkens, first thing tomorrow morning.' Tom thanked him and, as he shook his hand, slipped a twenty euro note into his palm. 'Thank you, sir; rest assured I will see that everything's done as you wish.'

Secondly, he went upstairs to his room, threw off his coat and tie removed his shoes, and made a call to the US Embassy using the hotel's landline. The man who answered grunted, 'Do you know what time it is, Tom? Couldn't this have waited until the morning?'

'No, it couldn't. The… er *function* we have coming up…'

'You on a secure line, buddy? If you're not, don't go any further.'

'I don't have a personal *Cone of Silence* if that's what you mean…'

'Say what?'

'Sorry, I forgot you're too young to remember *Get Smart* but I'm not. I'm using the hotel's phone system, not my cell.'

'Not good enough,' the voice on the other end said. 'Go into the bathroom, close the door, and turn on the shower. And after you've done all that, still choose your words carefully. I mean, *very* carefully.'

Tom did as instructed.

'I need to know about the guest list for the… party.'

'Why?'

'Because there's been a leak, and it didn't come from me. You either need to pull the plug or beef up security in a big way!'

'What? No! Who knows?'

'A Brit intelligence officer from GCHQ Cheltenham who went… *native* some time ago.'

'Brits in the know too?'

'About what?'

'The AWOL officer, the leak or the… party.'

'Are you telling me the Brits haven't been invited?' Aitkens asked incredulously.

'Answer my question first, bud – that's the way this security business works.'

'They know their guy is missing and it's possible they know about the leak but I can't confirm that. Now answer my question.'

There was silence on the other end of the line.

'I said answer me – dammit!' Aitkens shouted.

'They're not invited. The State Department thinks

the Brits are too liberal and woolly these days – they want everyone to love them. And their ship of state leaks.'

'Well you can't blame them for this leak if they haven't been sent an invitation,' Tom fumed. 'Now can you?'

More silence on the other end.

'So if the Brits are not coming, tell me who is.'

'The usual NATO lot.'

'What, *all* 28 or whatever the number is up to now?'

'Don't be stupid. We wouldn't trust some of them as far as we could throw them! No, I mean the original members, the 1949 alumni.'

'Of which the United Kingdom was one,' Tom said. 'So why the snub? Why spit in their faces?'

'We'll tell them afterwards and give them a few treats from the cookie jar to ease the hurt pride. They'll get over it – the State Department will spin them a yarn and everything will be fine and dandy. Trust us; we know what we're doing.'

'Do you? Do you really? So let me check the list with you: Belgium, Canada, Denmark, France, Iceland, Italy, Luxembourg, the Netherlands, Norway, Portugal, and the United States but not the Brits. Anyone else – like Israel?'

'No, no, not them! The President's tired of their endless kvetching!'

'So who's taking the Brits' place?'

'It's on a need-to-know basis, Tom, can't tell you anything more.'

'Tell me now, right now, otherwise I'll pull the plug on the spectacular…'

'You're bluffing…'

'I'm not! Do you think I don't know how to disable something I've worked on for years? And if I didn't know I'd rather smash the bloody thing to smithereens than…'

'Saudi Arabia,' the voice said.

'Saudi Arabia? So you turn your back on your oldest ally while at the same time sucking up to a bunch of…'

'The President calls it *reaching out the hand of friendship…*'

'Yet only a couple of months ago the State Department was convinced that the Saudis were bankrolling IS – *Daesh* – might even have *instigated* the whole damn thing, and now you want to sell our game-changing aircraft to them? You're unbelievable, and so is our foreign policy.'

'I reiterate: the President calls it *offering the hand of friendship*. He thinks it is probably better to have them *inside* the tent er… *hissing* out than outside *hissing* in – and he wants peace-making in the region to be his legacy for his term in office.'

'If that's true then the President is either being badly advised or he's a fool or both: in which case I'd regret ever voting for him.'

'I had a Mr Moneybags like you tagged as a Republican, Tom.'

'What me, never! Always voted Democrat. Is Merkel coming tomorrow?'

'No, no civilians at all. Just the top defence people, or as we like to think of them, our client base: our preferred customers.'

'Including Saudi Arabia?'

'Including them – their money's as good as anyone else's. And they've got lots of it!'

'You'd actually take the offspring of Owen Griffiths' genius, developed for the defence of the country he loves, and throw it into a stinking sewer like that?'

'Why not? It's business, Tom.'

'Well it's not any business I want to be involved with any longer. All bets are off! You'll hear from our lawyers in the morning.'

'You break your contract and we'll break you financially, Aitkens!'

'Don't threaten me! I don't give a damn about the money. I've more than enough for the rest of my life anyway.'

'Then think about your reputation. There are many ways we could break you; finish you for good. Want your kids to think their father's a traitor? Or a paedophile? Want that splashed all over the media?'

'Do your worst and to hell with the lot of you!' he said, slamming down the phone.

Still shaking with anger he turned off the shower, left the bathroom and stripped off ready for bed. Then he picked up his cell and called the British Embassy.

'I'm afraid Chief Inspector Scott has retired for the evening, sir,' the pleasant female voice on the other end said. 'May I have him call you in the morning?'

'Sorry ma'am, but the matter is very urgent. I need to speak to him tonight.'

'I don't believe he would wish to be disturbed this late,' she said politely.

'Tell him it's Tom Aitkens. I think he'll want to speak to me now.'

And he did.

TWENTY-NINE

*Tuesday 14th March. Berlin.
Almost midnight*

Clive had finally drifted off when the call from Tom Aitkens was transferred via the embassy switchboard. Sensing, quite correctly, that she was about to receive the sharp end of his tongue, the operator quickly said who was calling; he underwent an immediate mood change and his brain snapped to full alert.

'Put him through, please, Janet,' he said. 'And just so you know for future reference, I will *always* want to take calls from Mr Aitkens, whenever and wherever. Pass that on to the rest of the troops too, please.'

'Yes, of course, Chief Inspector,' she said, 'and goodnight.'

Clive Scott listened in silence while Tom Aitkens related the information Megan had given him during their dinner, and his subsequent conversation with his US Embassy contact. But although he said nothing his heart was pounding and his mind was racing. He tried not to think about what this was doing to his blood pressure!

'A word of caution, Mr Aitkens,' he said when the American had finished speaking. 'Do not mention your dinner with his wife to Chief Inspector Maigret. Not ever! Trust me; he will take the news very badly. Especially since at the time you were er... *entertaining* her he was taking care of her grandson in a Potsdam hospital.'

'This matter is more important than Maigret's jealousy or my... *frustration*. I will not let my Government sell our marvellous machine to Saudi Arabia and that's a promise!'

'They'll do it you know: they'll break you, ruin your health and reputation, and destroy your life and your family's. They've done it before – and far worse – and they'll do it again if you cross them. Are you ready for that to happen, Mr Aitkens?'

'Probably not. But I can't walk away from this... this Government *bastardy!*'

'Can you actually do it? Disable it I mean, Mr Aitkens?'

'For God's sake call me Tom! And no, I can't but I'd certainly take an axe to it quite happily! But there's no time for that now and it's under guard in a secure hanger. But Owen could...'

'Owen?'

'Owen Griffiths, my business partner. He designed and developed it. He's the star; I'm only the front of house man – or the ticket seller! He could certainly disable it. Or reprogram it if necessary.'

At the mention of reprogramming a piece of the jigsaw found its place in Clive's brain.

'How do these things actually work?' he asked as casually as he could. 'Is it all done by remote control, involving humans in another location, or is there a computer in the cockpit itself?'

'Either way, or both ways. Owen's genius has simplified the process – given it greater flexibility and far greater range too. And at the same time it weighs considerably less, which means it costs less. Oh God – Owen! It's his company too. If they destroy me, they'll do the same to him. I have to let him know, but not now, tomorrow morning.'

'Is the inventive genius here with you?'

'No, he's in Switzerland.'

'Switzerland?'

'Yes. His wife's been battling cancer for a year and the doctors in the States have finally said there's nothing more they can do for her. Owen's taken her to a clinic in Geneva where they might be able to help.'

'The proverbial last chance saloon,' Clive said quietly.

'Very much so, heaven help them. If Lucy dies… well it doesn't bear thinking about. Owen's not ready for that – none of us is.'

'If you're determined to stop this drone of yours falling into the wrong hands then get him to disable it or blow it up, or something! Can he do it from Switzerland? Or would that be out of range?'

'He could probably do it from the moon! Geneva's little more than five hundred miles away.'

'Where's the test site?'

'The old Gatow airport in the former British section of Berlin. Long since decommissioned and owned by the Germans now.'

'I know it. My father was part of the British Army on the Rhine and I was born in Hanover. That's a populated area and too close to the city for comfort if anything goes wrong. The major train line into Berlin Hauptbahnhof runs close to the airport. Who chose the site?'

'Not us! That's all I know.'

'Er how difficult would it be for a… er… *outside source* to take control of a drone either when it was stationary or while it was in flight?' Clive asked, trying to sound calm.

'Couldn't be done: not unless that source had the coordinates, or the programming details. Why, what do you know, Clive?'

'As of tonight we've a body in the Berlin morgue which resembles a young British man, Jamal Ahmadi, but is not him even though the victim was carrying a wallet with ID in his name. Turns out young Jamal has a degree in Computer Sciences and is on a no fly watch with your Government.'

'Why?'

'My source in London didn't know because your guys won't share.'

'Think he's a hacker? Think he's planning something bad for our test tomorrow?'

'Yes and yes. That's exactly what I think.'

'But if his *doppelgänger* wasn't carrying the suspect's passport then…'

'He's not a suicide bomber. He's too valuable to the brotherhood to be used as cannon fodder like the other poor shmucks that blow themselves to pieces: he needs his passport to escape afterwards. And speaking of which, I'll forward you his passport photo as soon as we've finished our call.'

'Thanks. I'll keep my eyes open for him.'

'If you see him, don't try any heroics. Alert your security, and let me know too.'

'Will do. And I'll call Owen in the morning. What do you want me to do about Quinn? I asked Megan to get him to call me in the morning, too.'

'Tell him everything, and then tell him it's time for him to come in from the cold. He'll know what that means.'

'Hell, Clive, I *know* what that means! *Everyone* knows after Le Carré wrote his spy book. You want him to give himself up.'

'Yes. And tell him I'll protect him, from MI5, or whoever else he's worried about.'

'Will Maigret be so forgiving?'

'Maybe not. It was his wife and grandson that Quinn kidnapped…'

'No, he didn't kidnap them! They left the train willingly after he told them what he knew and what he feared. Megan was adamant about that.'

'Hmm, Philippe Maigret may not be won over by that particular spiel. Quinn's put him through hell with worry and there's the attack he made on Patrick Evremond who was on the train with Megan and Nathaniel. I saw the kid's face this evening and it was quite a mess. And he also attacked a police officer at Pitié-Salpêtrière Hospital in Paris, forced sedatives down his throat, bound and gagged him then stole his wallet, clothes and weapon too.'

'Yes, Megan mentioned that. She said it was clearly self-defence.'

'Self-defence? I doubt Maigret will swallow that line either, even if it does come from his wife!'

'I certainly did. If someone came to a hospital to kill me, after I'd been deliberately run down in the street, I'd certainly want to get out of there fast!'

'Hmm. Maybe that argument might fly after all,' Clive Scott said thoughtfully. 'I presume this gizmo of yours is unarmed, Tom?'

'Then you'd be wrong. It's armed.'

'With what?'

'A couple of small air-to-ground missiles; low grade stuff.'

'Capable of doing how much damage?'

'Er... could knock out a small building or two – maybe an entire block.'

'Isn't it irresponsible to use these weapons in a populated area? Do the Germans know about them?'

'Yes, they know. The missiles will be programmed to hit the targets that have been set up. It's necessary to show speed, impact and accuracy – the drone has to be armed to demonstrate its capability. But no one will get hurt.'

'But what if one of its missiles should suddenly veer off course and hit a crowded commuter train travelling along the line near Gatow? What then? How many casualties would there be?'

'Not going to happen. We have checks, balances and failsafe provisions installed in the program. A disaster like that just couldn't happen. It couldn't.'

'But if it did,' Clive pressed. 'How many dead would there be?'

'Easier to talk about survivors.'

'How many of them, then?'

'Probably none.'

'And that's from *one missile – or both missiles?*'

'One missile.'

'And if both missiles were released at the same time? What would be the effect of that?'

'Nightmare territory; there would be a huge fireball.'

'Then the risk is too great, Tom and you've got to stop the test! We have a hacker on the loose. And if he gets into your program God alone knows what mischief he could do. Can't you see that? Even if the odds are a million to one the risk is still too great!'

'I believe you've convinced me, Clive. I'll call Owen in the morning and tell him everything.'

'Right choice – good man,' Clive said, exhaling deeply. 'I'll sleep much better in my bed now.' But he didn't. Not really. Not for the *entire* night.

★

Wednesday 15th March: The Ides. Berlin

And neither did Tom Aitkens. At 4.30am in the cold grey light of the Berlin morning, he left his bed and sent a long email to Owen Griffiths in Geneva. He spared no detail. He repeated the threats made by his State Department contact at the embassy; he was never exactly sure what agency this man worked for but he suspected it might be the CIA. And he told Owen that he realised they were not idle threats. He spelled out what he knew *the forces of darkness* (which was shorthand for the US security agencies when speaking with Owen) could do to both of them. Murder was top of the list. Of them, or one of their family. Then followed blackmail and/or their labelling as spies, traitors, scoundrels, wife-beaters, paedophiles – the list was almost endless, he said.

Then he finished with these words: *we've been friends for a long time Owen, and you and I are closer than most brothers. I wouldn't blame you if you decide to distance yourself from me now. Protect yourself; you've got Lucy and the kids to consider. It could all get very nasty buddy, so if you have any doubts – any doubts at all – about the course I've taken it is best you bail out now before the brown stuff really does hit the whirring object. Because when it does, it will be at warp speed!*

At 5.30am he received Owen's response.

Hell no, Tom! We won't let those bloody basduns get away with it! We're solid on this. When they threaten you they threaten me. With you all the way! Call in the bloodsuckers as soon as you like. I've checked the program, it all looks good at present – no unauthorised changes made, but I agree: abort. Do you want me to program it to blow up over the sea? I'd choose a very deep part: if they can't find that Boeing 777 that went missing ages ago they won't find our debris. Or is there a safe place we could land it – out of harm's way, I mean? Home base is the first place they'll look so it can't be there. Lucy had a good night. Very good. I think we've maybe turned a corner. Please God say that's so. Hang in there mate, love Owen.

Tom smiled as he read his friend's email. He always referred to lawyers as *bloodsuckers* and he just about always swore in Welsh!

★

The previous night, shortly before midnight in another another part of Berlin, or, more accurately, in a small industrial zone half-way between Berlin and Gatow, a young Muslim man washed himself carefully then donned a freshly laundered white robe in preparation for *Salat al-'isha,* the final prayer of the day, which took place between sunset and midnight.

He had already prayed four times that day. *Sarlat* is the obligatory Muslim prayer cycle performed each day. His first prayer – *Salat al-fair,* had been said just before sunrise. And the prayer ritual had been repeated throughout the day: at midday, after the sun had passed its highest point; again at the late part of the afternoon; and then just after sunset.

It was a prayer pattern that most Muslims tried to

follow believing that prayer sets the pattern of the day for them. This prayer ritual is also a way of connecting them spiritually to other believers around the world. And more than that, to all those who have said the same words, and made the same movements, down through the years of Islamic history.

The young man had tried to ensure that he was in the right frame of mind before he prayed; he put aside all other cares of the day to concentrate exclusively on God. He believed that if a Muslim prayed without the right attitude of mind it was as if he hadn't prayed at all.

He had not missed a single prayer ritual in the time since the terrible acts he had committed in the *10th arrondissement* of Paris. But none of those prayer rituals had helped him.

He knew that the Fifth Greater Sin was Murder. The murder of a person whose execution had not been ordered by Allah and the Holy Prophet. He knew the verses of the Holy Qur'an that clearly prescribed the Divine punishment for murderers.

Five punishments had been ordained for those who killed believers. First, hell; Second, eternal abode in hell; Third, involvement in the Divine wrath; Fourth, being the accursed by Allah; Fifth, the Great Chastisement.

But Jamal's mind was confused. The murder of his uncle, whom he loved, and his associates, *had* been sanctioned by Allah. His friends had proved that to him. Their deaths were necessary so that the will of Allah could be fulfilled. And when, at the last moment, he had drawn back in fear and revulsion of what was expected of him, his friends had given him a small pill. *And that pill had changed everything.*

They had a number of specially developed pills at their disposal, those so-called friends of Jamal. The pill they gave him was different from the ones they gave the brothers as they connected the wires and explosives to their bodies for their final act of obedience: a suicide mission.

Those brothers were given a pill that didn't begin to work until their heartbeat and blood pressure reached certain elevated levels. Then they quickly became euphoric at the thought of the Paradise that awaited them. And when that euphoria kicked in almost nothing could stop them.

But his handlers did not want Jamal to become euphoric. *Euphoria was sometimes difficult to control.* The pill they gave Jamal allowed high functioning without feeling. Without remorse. So the pill they gave him, when his brain rebelled against the outrage he had been asked to commit, *instantly* went to work. It very methodically wiped his mind clean of every last scrap of humanity: first education, then tolerance, then understanding, then compassion and memory. The last emotion that devil pill deleted was *love*. That was always the toughest obstacle for the pill to override. Love. *The mind held out for as long as it could, and its resistance was remarkable.* These new friends of Jamal's knew that. Knew it, but were not impressed. Why would they be? Love, in all its glorious variety, was alien to them.

But after love fell all hope went with it: the mind became as a blackboard from which every strand of civilisation had been erased. That pill transformed him from a sentient human being into a robot. And after that he could do what his new friends had told him Allah wanted him to do.

And he felt nothing. Nothing at all, as he did it.

Yes, that was the pill Jamal had been given – *this time*. The dehumanising effects wore off after four or five hours but a trace of what he had done remained with him. He could still smell the blood that had been spilt, and had therefore eaten no meat since that day. He couldn't: he gagged at the very sight of it. And though he repeatedly washed the clothes he had been wearing, he could, in his broken mind's eye see that they remained covered in blood. And all his faithful Sarlat prayers couldn't free him from that belief. So, in the end, he burnt them. Every last piece of the clothing he had worn that day; yet as he watched flames consume the accursed threads the blood remained. And the screams. The screams were always with him, even as he prayed. *Especially as he prayed.* And so were his Ammi's eyes; the bewildered eyes, and his mouth forming a single word – 'Why'?

That was the pill he had swallowed the day of the bloodbath. However, when he was no longer useful to the cause, or if he should come to the attention of the police or security services, he would be given the euphoria pill and the wires would be strapped to his body too; without hesitation, without regret.

Those who had pushed his buttons and brainwashed him within an inch of insanity had no remorse about what they had done. Jamal was unimportant, even with his computer skills: clever, educated, articulate, Jamal was expendable. He didn't matter in the slightest. All that counted was the Caliphate, and the world domination that would flow from it. And they knew that this had nothing whatsoever to do with faith, or religion, or Allah or the Prophet.

The cause was, and always had been, Power. That was their goal. And that was all that mattered.

THIRTY

Wednesday 15th March:
The Ides. Berlin

After he'd read Owen's email Tom managed to fall asleep again but was disturbed by strange dreams and an annoying idea which kept buzzing around the margins of his brain, just out of reach.

He woke with the memory of that infuriating notion still on his mind. *Was it worker bee or drone,* he wondered. *Nothing more than the by-product of an eventful night and an over wrought brain, or a vital message that needed to be dealt with fast?*

He took a shower and let the water run over his head and body for a long time. Then, as he was drying himself on the rough towels which he always specified, he was given a small hint. *Money,* it was something to do with money. *No, not money,* his brain countered, *the accounts. The play's the thing. No, that's Shakespeare,* he argued. *Not that kind of play, you idiot,* his brain replied in disgust, *concentrate, won't you? The money play is the power play! Don't you get it now?*

And finally he did.

He threw the hotel's bath robe over his naked body and sat down at the desk to write another email. This time to *Scarborough Fair's* finance department in Bridgeport, Connecticut.

Hi folks, he wrote, *if there's anyone still there which I doubt – or whenever someone opens this. It's seven in the morning of March 15 here in Berlin which makes it midnight your time. And today is the day Mighty Mouse finally makes his debut in front of a critical audience. But the weather's set fair so fingers crossed all goes well. Humour me – is Big Brother up-to-date with his progress payments? Let me know chapter and verse by return please, if by some miracle someone's working late! Regards, Tom.*

He hadn't expected an answer for hours but was surprised to hear his MacBook ping not more than twenty minutes later.

Morning boss, Cathy here. Just pilfering the petty cash before jetting off to somewhere warm with no extradition agreement with the US of A, and before anyone discovers that I've been plundering the accounts for years. Hah, hah! But to answer your question, Big Brother's been even naughtier than me. He's considerably in default. Three progress payments received in last three months: total a measly $15 million. Want me to rattle his cage? Happy to do so – my tax dollars finally at work! Good luck with the debut and hurry home – we miss you. All the best from your favourite redhead.

Tom chuckled as he read Cathy's email. She was the Deputy Finance Director and had been with the company since its inception: their most loyal employee and absolutely terrified of flying!

He quickly sent a reply.

No, don't want you to rattle anything at present so definitely don't remind BB that he's in default. This suits my purposes very nicely, thank you ma'am. And I'll bring you something gorgeous from Berlin to prove it. Really gorgeous and expensive! Promise. Love and kisses, Tom.

Next he poured himself a coffee from the newly arrived breakfast trolley and sent another email to Owen in Geneva.

Cathy tells me Big Brother is in default, ergo he doesn't own Mighty Mouse so we can do with it as we please. So far BB has paid us $15 mill, which I figure might have bought him a tiny tip of one wing! But don't destroy MM. I'm looking for a safe harbour in which to shelter him. More ASAP. Keep checking the program; the F.O.E might be leaving it to the last moment to change so you'll discover it too late. Any luck finding culprit? Give my love to Lucy, Tom.

Within thirty minutes he had his reply.

The forces of evil are definitely giving it their best shot but they haven't got in yet. Can't locate the source – their attempts are being bounced all around the world. Anyone you know with access to a satellite? It would be very useful. Lucy definitely better; she's been giving me a hard time this morning and it's great! Love, Owen.

★

Chief Inspector Maigret arrived at the Potsdam guest house at 9am which was precisely the same time as Tom Aitkens' flowers were delivered. Two dozen perfectly formed, long stemmed red roses, with a card that read:

Thank you for last night, it was wonderful. With all my love, Tom xxx

Philippe followed the roses into the entrance hall where the owner immediately engaged the delivery man in excited conversation some of which he understood. The flowers were for *Frau* Maigret and had been sent from the Hotel Adlon in Berlin.

Philippe spoke to the woman in French first but she shook her head. '*Auf Englisch?*' he asked dredging up what school boy German he remembered.

'Okay,' she replied, 'but please to speak slowly for me.' Philippe produced his *Police Nationale* ID which she studied carefully. Then he took a photograph of Megan from his wallet and showed her that too.

'Ah,' she said. '*Polizei?*'

'Yes. But this is not a police matter, Madame. *Frau* Maigret is my wife. Please take me to her now. I will give her the flowers.'

'Of course, of course,' she said, bustling busily around him. 'This way please, she is in our breakfast room.'

'Oh hell!' David Quinn exclaimed as he saw Maigret enter the room carrying the roses. *What are the odds that the husband's delivering the lover's flowers? That's a chump's bet,* his subconscious replied. *No one is going to take that one – we can't even calculate the odds!*

Megan jumped up from her seat and hugged Philippe who remained stiffly formal.

'Want to see the card that came with the roses, Megan?' he said coldly. 'There are, however, no prizes for guessing who sent them.'

'I can explain,' she said.

'I doubt that.'

'I'll do the honours,' Quinn said. 'I set everything up and Megan...'

'No, you won't,' Philippe interrupted angrily. 'I'll deal with you later, Quinn – you can count on that!'

'Then I will,' Patrick Evremond said quietly. 'Because you need to listen, Philippe. Things are not as they may seem.'

'No, I'll do it,' Megan said. 'And keep your voice down, Philippe, people are looking at us.'

And indeed they were. Six other people were also having breakfast. It was obvious that their curiosity had been aroused but they were doing their best not to show it.

'I had dinner with Tom last night and then he gave me a lift home. Quinn can vouch for that, and so can Patrick because we woke him when we came upstairs to our room even though we tried to be quiet.'

'You're all staying in the one room?' Philippe asked incredulously.

'Had to for security reasons,' Quinn volunteered. 'It's a family room and we each have our own bed.'

'I told you before to shut up, Quinn – and I meant it!'

'This is getting us nowhere,' Megan said, looking at her watch. 'Will you take me to the hospital to see Nat now please, David?'

'Of course. And happy to do so.'

'Have you had breakfast yet, Philippe?' Patrick asked, but he was ignored.

'Ready?' Quinn asked.

'Absolutely.'

'Good – let's go.'

As they moved towards the door Quinn whispered, 'Keep walking, he doesn't know what to do. He's so far out of his comfort zone that he can't think straight.'

'How would you know?'

'I've been there a couple of times myself. His heart is telling him one thing and his brain is saying the opposite. He'll come around. I always did!'

Quinn opened the glass-panelled door to the street for Megan and they walked out into the spring sunshine.

'He hasn't followed us yet,' Megan said, looking quickly over her shoulder. 'And we're almost at the car.'

'Perhaps Patrick is filling him in on recent events!'

'Or perhaps you're totally wrong and he's not coming at all.'

'Want to bet?'

'You *know* I don't have any money.'

'I'll stake you. Ten euros says he's here before I start the car.'

'No, this is too important to me for a bet,' Megan said. It proved a wise decision; it was a bet she would have lost.

At the same time as this conversation was taking place, Tom Aitkens dialled the British Embassy again.

'*Morgen*, Chief Inspector Scott,' he said breezily. 'Sleep well?'

'No, I damn well didn't, and I'll call you a liar if you

tell me *you* did!' Clive Scott replied grumpily. 'And you sound far too cheerful for my present mood.'

Tom laughed. 'I slept well, at times,' he said. 'But I have some good news, Clive.'

'What?'

'The people who threatened me last night, the forces of darkness, as Owen calls them, haven't a leg to stand on.'

'How so?'

'They haven't kept their side of the bargain: they've defaulted, and that renders the contract null and void, no ifs or buts about it, it's a done deal. My Berlin lawyers have confirmed that in writing this morning.'

'So? How is that good news?'

'It means we can do whatever we damn well want with Mighty Mouse…'

'What?'

'That's what we call our marvellous new flying machine, mostly abbreviated to MM. But I need something from you, Clive.'

'What exactly?' Clive said, sounding the way he felt: suspicious.

'We have two options for MM. Destroy or deflect.'

'Go on, you have my attention.'

'Naturally I prefer the second option. But where to… *relocate,* that's the problem. Can't be on home ground, for obvious reasons, so where? A neutral safe country clearly – any suggestions?'

Clive chuckled. 'How about somewhere remote and fairly inhospitable as far as the weather's concerned?'

'Has to be kept undercover if possible, it's not a 747.

Nor is it particularly robust which means it can't be exposed to the elements for long periods of time.'

'Have no fear; it will be kept undercover in both senses of the word. I'll get back to you in an hour.'

'Make it quicker – 3pm is looming large now!'

'Okay, ASAP!' Clive replied, cutting the connection.

He was as good as his word. Thirty minutes later Clive phoned Tom Aitkens.

'All fixed,' he boomed down the line. *'Fait accompli,* all systems go!'

'Plain speech now please, Clive.'

'Right you are. My younger brother's son, my nephew Angus – although he has a different name now which I can never remember…'

'Short version please, Clive.'

'Okay. Angus is a Buddhist monk. Well, not a full monk yet, only a novice, or an acolyte, something like that although he's been in the commune for five years. Takes a long time to reach full monkhood, apparently…'

'For God's sake, Clive!'

'Okay listen up now. I've just spoken to Angus on his mobile and…'

'Buddhists are allowed the use of cell phones?'

'Who knows? Angus is, but as I said, he's not a monk yet.'

'Okay – go on.'

'The commune or monastery whatever that Angus joined is on Arran, the largest of a number of islands inside Lamlash Bay in the Firth of Clyde, off the west coast of central Scotland, which collectively go under the name of Holy Island. Arran is only about three kilometres long and around one kilometre wide. Its highest point is the hill Mullach Mòr.'

'Fascinating, but so what?'

'So this! Holy Island has a long history as a sacred site with a spring or holy well believed to have healing properties.'

'Relevance, Clive?'

'It's now owned by the Samyé Ling Buddhist Community which belongs to a school of Tibetan Buddhism. One of the settlements on the island is the *Centre for World Peace and Health* on the north side of the island. It has solar water heating and a reed bed sewage treatment system.'

'Wonderful, good for them!' Tom said drily.

'And they'd be very happy to hide your flying machine in one of their nice dry barns for as long as you want.'

'What?'

'Think, man! They don't want your mobile weapon of destruction unleashed on the world any more than any other sane person does! They're happy to take it off your hands for all eternity, if that's what you wish.'

'And what would they want in return?'

'Five hundred pounds.'

'Well that sounds reasonable. Five hundred pounds a week is really chicken feed...'

'Five hundred pounds *per year*, not week! These are

gentle, unworldly people; they don't place any intrinsic value on money.'

'Then what's the five hundred pounds for?'

'Charitable works, as and when needed.'

'If that's the case let's offer them five thousand a year!'

'You'd insult them if you did. Five hundred is their price but there's something else too.'

'I knew it! What else do they want?'

'They said that they're very sorry but, being a peace loving community they cannot have any weapons on their soil, and they hope you'll understand. You have to get rid of the missiles before they'll accept the drone.'

'That's no problem. Owen can arrange that they're dumped in a very deep part of the North Sea if that's acceptable to the monks.'

'I think it will be, Tom. There's just one remaining problem as far as I can tell.'

'Which is?'

'Avoiding detection when it enters UK air space. The RAF boys are on high alert these days because the Russians keep testing our air defences, both over the Channel and off the north coast of Scotland. Northern Ireland, too. It would be a pity if the Royal Air Force shot down Mighty Mouse before he reached sanctuary.'

'That's not a problem, Clive.'

'Oh no?'

'I can't give you any details but MM is designed for non-detection so...'

'Just like your stealth bombers, is it? Coated with something to make it well-nigh invisible?'

'No comment,' Tom chuckled, 'but you could be in the right zone, Clive. I'll need to send Owen the coordinates so he can change the program of course and…'

'Angus thought of that, they're on my mobile now, I'll send to you as soon as we've finished speaking.'

'That's great, Clive, thanks for everything. Now I've got to get going.'

'To where?'

'Gatow. I've got to somehow get Mighty Mouse out of the hangar ahead of schedule: can't risk the damage if he has to crash through closed doors.'

'Want some help, mate?'

'You bet – as much as you can drum up!'

'Say when.'

'Would 11am at my hotel suit you?'

'Yes, see you then, I'll drive. One more thing; would Philippe Maigret be welcome? You did say the more the merrier.'

There was a pause on the other end of the line. 'If you must, although…'

'He's a good man, Tom. A *very* good man.'

'Not what I wanted to hear, but bring him if you need to, just keep him out of my way!'

As soon as Tom finished the call the coordinates arrived and he forwarded them to Owen in Geneva. Ten minutes later Owen phoned.

'The *basduns* are clever, Tom. They've got in and now they're trying to change the program, but they'll find that considerably more difficult. I haven't done anything yet so they don't know that we know.'

'You can't tell what their target is, Owen?'

'No, but from the coordinates they're trying to put in I can risk an educated guess.'

'Tell me.'

'Very predictable, given what they are: a large chunk of the old Jewish quarter of east Berlin – a school, an elderly people's home and a couple of synagogues. Do you know where the Chancellor is going today?'

'No.'

'Well I do. She's opening a new wing of the old people's home, and she's not going alone; it looks like at least a quarter of the German Cabinet is going too.'

'How do you know, Owen?'

'Checked with… a security source, Tom, and that's all I can say.'

'And the time she'll be there?'

'There's a lunch first, at 1pm. So sometime after that.'

'3pm perhaps?'

'That's my guess, although the *basduns* might intend to move the time forward if they succeed in changing the program. What do you want me to do, Tom?'

'Keep your phone on, and keep checking the program. I'll let you know as soon as MM is on the runway. But don't take any risks, Owen. If they make a move before I'm ready then just bust it out of the hanger and send it on its way.'

'Will do. Godspeed, Tom.'

'And you too, buddy – and you too.'

A few moments after he finished his conversation

with Owen, Tom's mobile rang. It was his contact at the US Embassy and he was far from happy.

'What the hell do you think you're playing at, Aitkens?' he said angrily.

'I assume you've received the Termination of Contract notice from my Berlin lawyers,' Tom said calmly. 'A similar one from my US lawyers will be with you later today.'

'I warned you about making a move like this! If you go through with this nonsense you'll live to regret it and that's…'

'Your political masters are in breach of contract. We had every reason to act as we've done.'

'Look, Tom,' his contact said, sounding more conciliatory, 'so our accounts people were a little slack with their payments – these things happen, and no real harm done. We'll transfer what we owe you by the close of business, New York time, today. How'd that be?'

'Too late, much too late, that's how it would be. And by the way, you should check with the Paris police; I believe they have one of your goons in their morgue.'

'What are you talking about, Aitkens?'

'I'm talking about the gorilla you sent to murder David Quinn the GCHQ defector in Paris last week.'

'Nothing to do with us.'

'Really? Then you have nothing to worry about, do you? However, if he *should* turn out to be one of your thugs it won't be long before the French find out and start making an international incident out of it. And that might happen sooner if someone should whisper in the ear of a journalist working for *Le Canard enchaîné* or some other left-wing newspaper.'

'You wouldn't dare, Aitkens.'

'Wouldn't I? You go anywhere near my family, or my friends and you will find out how dirty I can really play, Reynolds! And that's a fact.'

Then, before the CIA man could answer, Tom Aitkens slammed down his phone. *Mission accomplished,* he thought with satisfaction. *And how good it feels to take the kid gloves off at long last!*

THIRTY-ONE

The Ides of March – afternoon

Years later Clive Scott would still remember almost every detail of that day in Berlin: the Ides of March. He would relate the story, frame by frame, to his grandchildren who, no matter how many times they'd heard it before, never tired of it being told again. And not only Clive remembered: Georges Martin also told and retold the day's events to his twin sons, who were not even alive on that 15th March. How could they have been when Georges had not yet met their mother? But he would very soon.

This was how history was recorded and recounted in past times: stories told around the camp fires at night. Significant experiences were passed down from generation to generation long before the written word came into being. It was how the Australian aborigines passed on their stories of *the dream time* for thousands of years. And not only them; all peoples, all cultures, have done the same thing in one form or another.

And the curious thing was that no matter how many

times Clive and Georges repeated the deeds of that day, the story was never diminished, never diluted or lessened in any way.

Perhaps the air around Gatow airport, or the light from the sun *recorded* the events of that day on the brain; made an imprint on the psyche, or the innermost part of those who witnessed it. Was such a thing possible? Who knows? But maybe it is not entirely impossible.

In 1988, Jacques Benveniste, a French immunologist, born in Paris on 12th March 1935, published a paper in the prestigious scientific journal *Nature* describing the action of very high dilutions of an antibody which seemed to support the belief of homeopathy. Biologists were puzzled by Benveniste's results as only molecules of water, and no molecules of the original antibody, remained in these high dilutions, and immediately he was at the centre of a major international controversy. Benveniste concluded that the formation of molecules in water was *biologically active*. A journalist used the term *water memory* for this theory. Much later, in the 1990s, Benveniste also asserted that this *memory* could be digitised, transmitted, and reinserted into another sample of water which would then contain the same active qualities as the first. *The water would remember!*

In the years following the publication of Benveniste's paper multiple supervised experiments were run by his team, the United States Department of Defense, the BBC's *Horizon* program and other researchers, but none was able to reproduce Benveniste's results under controlled conditions.

And yet the idea of the memory of water has never quite died.

New research at the University of Stuttgart appears to support the theory that water has a memory – a claim that if true, could change our whole way of looking at the world. *Does water really have memory?* If it does, and Benveniste was right, then the implications are beyond our imagining. More than 70% of the earth is covered in water, and the human body is made of 60% water; the brain, 70%; the lungs, nearly 90%. Our energy might be travelling from our brains and bodies into those of living beings of all kinds, through imprints on this amazing element – water. Perhaps the rivers and oceans and rains have been carrying arcane information throughout the world for eons without our knowledge.

Be that as it may, for one of those involved in what happened at Gatow on that Ides of March the impact would be far greater than any of the others, with one possible exception, because it would change his world forever. That person was Philippe Maigret.

He had received Clive Scott's text while visiting Nathaniel at the hospital with Megan; Nat's mother and stepfather had arrived early that morning. As soon as he could he left them and hurried outside. Georges Martin was standing next to a French Embassy car at the main entrance. 'Where to now, Chief?' he asked as soon as Philippe appeared.

'The Hotel Adlon in Berlin and as fast as you can please, Georges,' he replied, deciding to relate the morning's events on the way.

★

They drove from the hotel in convey to Gatow airport. Clive Scott and Tom Aitkens were in the front car, the two French detectives in the car behind them; David Quinn and two of his colleagues followed in the rear.

On the way there Tom Aitkens took a call from Owen Griffiths in Geneva. He listened intently but said nothing, much to Clive Scott's frustration.

'But surely that's good news, Owen?' he said eventually. 'Oh, I get it now. I guess I was looking through an optimistic lens – my mistake!' Then he sighed deeply and ended with, 'Stay in touch, buddy, with regular updates when you can and keep watching the program for any last minute changes.'

'What's up?' Clive said as soon as the call was over.

'The forces of evil appear to have given up attempting to change the program – seems they've finally realised they can't do it despite being able to hack into our system.'

'But why isn't that good news? It has to be, doesn't it?'

'Yes, it would be, if there wasn't another option – Plan B – Owen called it, and I'm afraid he might be right.'

'Plan B?'

'Direct action. The old blood and guts routine that the butchering barbarians seem to relish!'

As they drew closer to the airport it became apparent that this part of Gatow was a flat windswept plain devoid of any memorable features. Drab, dreary, desolate and deserted was their unspoken evaluation. And the former

BAOR airport was quiet, too quiet, the detectives thought. It seemed eerily so.

'Where's the security?' Aitkens said. 'I'd expected to find some of our marines on duty but I can't even see any local police or civilian security.'

'That's because there *is* none,' Clive Scott replied. 'Not in the guardhouse or anywhere else, as far as I can tell.'

He got out of the car and walked towards Philippe Maigret and Georges Martin. Aitkens hesitated briefly then did the same.

'Something's up, Philippe,' Clive said, 'and the hairs on the back of my neck know it! This place makes the *Mary Celeste* look like a blasted tourist cruise! I don't like it.' Then he told them about Tom's conversation with Owen Griffiths.

'I think we're walking into a trap,' Tom Aitkens volunteered. Philippe Maigret shot him a contemptuous look but said nothing.

'What's up?' Quinn said, joining them. 'Where's the welcoming party?'

'That's just it,' Clive said, 'there is none and this whole setup feels very suspect to me.'

'I agree, especially following the phone call from Geneva,' Maigret said. 'I suggest that we – you, Georges and I proceed cautiously on foot towards the main buildings while the others wait at the gates.'

'You armed, Philippe?'

'*Oui,* and so is Georges.'

'I'm not talking about that revolver you wear

strapped above your ankle, the one that's hardly ever loaded, much less actually fired! I'm talking about *real firepower* not *pantomimes* for frightening unruly school boys or cantankerous old women!'

Despite himself, Philippe laughed. 'Both of my revolvers are loaded, *mon ami,* and so are those that Georges is carrying!'

'I'm also armed,' Aitkens volunteered.

'Americans usually are,' Maigret said pointedly. Tom, bearing in mind Clive's warning, wisely kept quiet.

'Want to come with us, Tom?' Scott asked, darting an exasperated *pull yourself together man* look at Philippe.

'Yes, of course I do! This is my company's project, something we've worked on for years, and I'm not turning my back on it now! I can see from here that the hangar doors are closed which should mean that all's well, but I agree; there's something very weird about this scene and I don't think we should take any risks.'

Quinn and his mates walked over to the robust steel gates, firmly padlocked against intruders, and inspected them carefully. 'Want us to do the honours?' he called back over his shoulder after they'd conferred for a time.

'Can you?' Clive Scott asked.

'You bet,' one of Quinn's colleagues said cheekily. 'It's safecracking for beginners!'

'Aren't you grateful they're on our side?' Clive remarked to Philippe.

'I would be – if only I could be absolutely sure that they were!'

'Any of you who are... er... of a *squeamish* disposition should look away now,' Quinn advised.

'Hell no! I want to see how it's done!' Aitkens said, wandering over to them to observe the procedure more closely.

'He's behaving like an immature clown,' Maigret hissed out of the corner of his mouth to Clive Scott.

'Give him a break, Philippe! This is his big day. There's millions of dollars riding on the success of this drone of his and he's trying not to show how anxious he is about everything. Besides, he can't help the way he feels about...'

'Stop now, Clive, and say nothing more – you've made your point. I apologise for my earlier bad manners but this... *situation* is not easy for me either.'

Within a few moments the padlock on the gate had been expertly picked with no visible damage done to it.

'Now what, boss?' Quinn asked, directing his question to Chief Inspector Scott. 'Do we all march straight up to the front door and knock?'

'No, we don't. I told you – you and your... buddies – and please note that I do not want to be *formally* introduced to either of them, nor do I want to know from whence they came or for whom they work – stay here and take cover in the guardhouse. Anyone approaches call either me or Chief Inspector Maigret. Is that clear? I assume at least *you* are armed, if not the others, Quinn.'

'Yes, I've got a nice Sig Sauer that I... er *picked up* in Paris.' Quinn replied, with a sideways glance at Philippe Maigret.

'That's property belonging to the French Republic, Quinn, and you know it,' Maigret said. 'Hand it over now!'

'No! Not until this present… *ruckus* is over. Then I'll return it.'

'Let him keep it for now, Philippe,' Clive Scott advised. 'It's probably wise anyway since we don't know what we might be facing.'

'Fine. Shall we go?' Maigret said curtly.

'Chief, there's no cover for us; if there are hostiles inside already we'll be like sitting ducks walking across that open ground,' Inspector Martin said.

'Georges is right,' Clive agreed before Maigret could answer. 'And this setup reminds me of a story my old dad told me about a smallholder he knew in the north of England somewhere.'

'Tell it later, Clive,' Tom Aitkens said, 'it's almost 12.30 and the official guests are due to start arriving at around 2pm.'

'No, tell it now, Clive, if it's pertinent,' Maigret said, chiefly to put Aitkens in his place. He knew he was being childish but he couldn't manage to change his attitude.

'It's very pertinent. This smallholder – he farmed about twenty acres or so – was a man of about seventy. One morning his wife said she wasn't feeling very well, so he told her to stay in bed, brought her some breakfast, then left to go about his chores. 'I'll be back in time to get your lunch, dearie,' he said, as he kissed her goodbye.

Outside, in the courtyard in front of the farmhouse, he greeted their pet animals: three dogs – one of which he always took with him; four or five cats; and a couple of ducks who fussed around his feet as he left.

When he returned home just after noon, there was not an animal to be seen anywhere. *That's strange,* he thought, *what's happened to them – where have they scarpered off to now?* Then he went upstairs and found his wife lying dead in their bed having suffered a massive heart attack.

And the extraordinary thing is that the animals instinctively *knew* that she had died, even though they could not get inside the house. *They had sensed it.* And the…'

'A poignant story, Clive – but what's your point?' Tom Aitkens interrupted.

'The point is that the animals could not *bear* to be anywhere in the vicinity when the loving husband found his dead wife, the kind woman who had been their carer and mistress. It was so painful for them that they'd each scurried away to deal with their grief alone. In time they would come back of course, but it would be many hours later, after they could be sure that the Grim Reaper had left the farm.'

'So? I still don't get it.'

'Ask yourself this, my American friend. What would make the entire security staff make such a hasty retreat from this place?' Clive said.

'*They knew what was coming,*' Philippe said thoughtfully. 'And what it was scared the life out of them.'

'Exactly. And that's the way we should feel too.'

'There must be another way in,' Tom Aitkens said. 'One for emergency vehicles that's not quite so obvious and exposed.'

'Of course there will be; we need to drive around the perimeter to find it.'

'Should we take the safecrackers with us? They might be useful.'

'No, leave them on guard,' Maigret said before Clive could answer. And again he was playing devil's advocate for no other reason than to spite the American. *You are behaving like a spoilt child who has lost his favourite toy,* his conscience reproached. *Stop it now! I can't,* he replied. *And I haven't lost her yet.*

'I've had some… limited *experience* in that field,' Georges Martin said. 'I might be able to do the trick with any locks.'

'Heck, I'm willing to shoot the damn lock off if we can't pick it,' Clive Scott said in his usual candid way of reducing tension. And that particular trick *did* actually work – without fail!

The four of them; Aitkens, Scott who was driving, and the two French detectives, piled into the Paris Embassy's car and drove around the perimeter. They found the emergency entrance which was padlocked but the lock was ancient, rusted, and easy to open.

They drove in cautiously with their eyes and ears on the alert, past the hangars and control tower, then towards the other main buildings. They saw no one and everything remained unnaturally quiet.

'This place is beginning to give me the creeps,' Clive

Scott said, expressing what they were all feeling. 'I think we should leave the car here and make our final approach on foot.'

'Go a little further, Clive,' Philippe Maigret urged. 'If we're challenged we'll stop, but the car does provide some cover.'

'Okay.'

'We need backup, don't we?' Aitkens said. 'We need to get the German police to send reinforcements.'

'Does anyone have a signal?' Georges Martin asked, fiddling with his phone, 'because I don't.'

'Not really, it's intermittent at best,' his chief replied.

'Same here,' Clive Scott added. 'It looks like we're it, and likely to remain that way for the duration.'

The first hangar they came to was open and empty. So, it transpired, were the rest of them.

'Where's the drone, Mr Aitkens?' Philippe Maigret asked, making a determined effort to be polite in the hope of silencing the critical chatter coming from his subconscious.

'Wait!' Tom Aitkens said in an authoritative voice which took everyone by surprise. 'I'm thinking!'

No one said anything for what seemed like a long time. Then the American spoke again. 'There is actually a Plan C,' he said finally, 'or there might be. Could well be.'

'Which is?'

'Changing the program from the cockpit, rather than by remote control.'

'Is that possible?' Clive Scott asked.

'I told you it was last night – don't you remember?'

'And would it be easier to do it that way?' Georges Martin queried.

'I don't know, I'm only the salesman. Owen's the genius but it might be – probably is, in fact. We need to get to the drone's hangar now. Follow me, everyone!'

By a process of elimination they found the drone's hangar and broke into it through a window: they couldn't pick the lock and they didn't want the sound of gunfire to reverberate around the site. Breaking the glass made some noise but it wasn't excessive, and no one came to challenge them. In fact there was still no sign of life anywhere.

'It's not very big, is it?' Scotland Yard's finest said, walking around Mighty Mouse and inspecting it carefully.

'That's our company's main selling point,' Aitkens said. 'It's fast, light, and yet it can carry up to four missiles.'

'Where are they?' Georges and Clive asked at the same time.

'Embedded in separate chambers towards the rear, underneath the fuselage; you can't even see where the opening is from the outside. They can be fired independently or together, depending on the circumstances and the programming. But only two missiles were loaded for the purpose of today's demonstration.'

'Thank the Lord for that,' Maigret whispered to Georges.

Loud knocking on the outside of the hangar's door made them all jump.

'It's only us.' It was Quinn's voice. 'We saw you go round the back and figured you might need some help with the padlock. Do you?'

'Of course we damn well do,' Clive roared. 'How else can we push the drone out? Get a move on!'

It took a little longer for the safecrackers to open that padlock than it had with the one on the front gates but Quinn's mates eventually did the trick.

'What a little beauty!' Quinn said admiringly when he saw the drone. 'These will sell like hotcakes.'

'Or maybe not,' Clive said, winking at Tom.

'Want a hand to push it outside?' the taller of Quinn's mates asked.

'Not yet – let's see if I can get a signal first,' Aitkens said, walking through the open door. He could.

Speaking very rapidly to Owen Griffiths in Geneva he related what they had found. 'Time for Mighty Mouse to fly now, buddy,' he said, 'get it out of here as fast as you can. You have the coordinates and all the other info I sent you?'

'Yes, good ole Mighty Mouse will be on its way in less than ten minutes. But so should you be, Tom, you know they're coming – they must be! Time to get out of there as quick as you can.'

'We will, just as soon as MM is on the tarmac.'

It only took four of them – Quinn, his two mysterious colleagues, and Georges Martin – to push the drone out of the hangar; that was how light it was even with the missiles.

'Here they come!' Maigret said, looking towards the now unguarded front gates where the black-clothed, black-masked Jihads were marshalling. 'I suggest we fan out around the drone to protect it as long as we can!'

'Oh my God!' Quinn exclaimed. 'Is that a rocket launcher on the back of their truck?'

His question went unanswered but they all knew he might be right.

'What kind of take-off does this little baby have?' Quinn's other colleague asked nonchalantly.

'Pretty much straight vertical,' Aitkens replied.

'With rapid ascent?'

'You'd better believe it, pal! A $320 million hypersonic drone developed by the Pentagon tore itself apart in 2012 *after flying for just three minutes* when it blasted through the atmosphere at twenty times the speed of sound. Of course it was fired from a rocket launcher, not a standing start as Mighty Mouse will be, and he's not *quite* hypersonic, but he is very much *supersonic,* so he'll be the fastest thing you've ever seen – and that goes for all of us! And that's another part of our spiel that goes down well with potential customers.'

'Noisy too, I guess.'

'Not as noisy as you might expect,' Tom said, 'and that's yet another aspect of our marketing pitch – *stealth*!'

'It's not a rocket launcher,' Quinn said, peering into the distance. 'It's *only* a grenade launcher.'

'Oh, well that's alright then, no worries,' Clive Scott said ironically.

The soft purring of Mighty Mouse coming to life was accompanied by a shout from Georges. 'Look out! Incoming grenade!'

The grenade exploded a safe distance from them. They knew that it was only meant to intimidate: the Jihads would not risk damaging the drone.

The purring grew louder and louder. 'Step back now, everyone – Mighty Mouse is about to take to the skies!' Tom Aitkens shouted.

'Keep firing at the *dratsabs,*' Quinn said. 'Keep them busy until the drone has flown out of range.'

They watched in something approaching awe as the drone sped upwards towards the heavens, gathering speed as it effortlessly climbed. It was a beautiful sight: elegant, graceful, sophisticated – *deadly, destructive, devastating.* Within seconds it had disappeared from their sight.

But the forces of evil had not disappeared. And once they realised that the drone was beyond their reach they vented their fury on those who had thwarted them, running forward with shouts of *Allahu Akbar – God is greater, God is the greatest.*

'*Right back at you freaks!*' Clive Scott responded, picking off the two front runners with his semi-automatic pistol.

Simultaneously they heard the sound of the approaching sirens and the whistle of the incoming grenades. Without the protection of the drone they were like rabbits caught in the headlights of a tank. *Or David, facing down Goliath.* Nor did they suspect that a second attack was coming from behind – the same direction they had recently covered themselves.

From the corner of his eye, Tom Aikens saw the momentary flash of light from the barrel of a rifle aimed directly at Philippe Maigret's head and, with a warning shout, shoved him out of the way. Aitkens was hit twice in the spine. Once in the region of the sacrum, the triangular-shaped bone at the base of the spine, and again in the same area but two or three centimetres higher. He dropped to the ground like a stone but remained conscious. Clive Scott killed his attacker with a single shot to the heart.

Philippe Maigret bent over Tom Aitkens, trying to decide how best to help. 'Why?' he asked before the others came to offer assistance.

'She loves you,' Aitkens whispered, then lapsed into the pain free void.

After a brief shoot-out the heavily armed German police despatched the rest of the Jihads to their Maker's judgement without too much difficulty.

'He's won, hasn't he?' Maigret asked Clive as they watched the ambulance speeding Tom Aitkens towards Berlin.

'What?'

'Aitkens. Even if he dies, he's won!'

AFTERMATH

Thomas Jefferson Aitkens didn't die that day. Nor did Jamal Ahmadi.

When clever, *educated* Jamal had failed in his attempts to change the drone's program, he was ruthlessly assessed as expendable. Then he was chosen for another Jihad mission: that of a suicide bomber.

He sat silently while the vest packed with explosives was firmly strapped on his body, and listened intently to his instructions, repeated many times, to ensure that he made no mistakes.

'As Allah wills, it shall be done,' he said submissively. But clever, *precise* Jamal no longer believed what his new friends said. *He believed none of it*. Not the part about the seventy-two virgins who would be his reward for murdering innocent unarmed civilians, and especially not that this was the will of Allah.

And he remembered every detail of what these erstwhile friends had made him do in Paris. He especially remembered his beloved uncle's eyes and the question in them – *Why?* Yes, why, that was the question he had asked himself over and over in those intense days since the Paris massacre. He *knew* this had not been the will of Allah because as he prayed Allah had spoken to him. He told him that only the holy martyrs, slaughtered for their faith, were worthy of unique blessings after death. And Allah had also said that no venal gratification of the flesh, or any number of virgins, had ever been involved, nor ever would be. Those who deliberately chose to spill innocent blood would feel the full force of his wrath. And as for those craven cowards who violated children or seduced simple-minded adults into becoming suicide bombers, a special punishment was reserved.

And, said Allah, *though their tears flow for a thousand, thousand, thousand years, yet will their penance not end. They are repugnant to me – an abomination – and so is their cause. It will not succeed: I, Allah, have spoken. And as for you, my faithful servant Jamal; be at peace now. I do not hold you responsible for what happened in Paris. The drugs the wicked ones gave you made you do what was abhorrent. Those who developed them and gave them to you are guilty. Now do what you must, with my blessing.*

That night, after Allah had spoken to him, Jamal looked down at his hands and they were spotless. The blood of those he had slain in Paris had been expunged and he knew he had been forgiven. He slept like an infant that night, mind untroubled, and he never saw his uncle's questioning eyes again.

'Take him to the car now,' the Jihad commander ordered. 'And leave him on the steps of the Reichstag. He knows what to do after that, but remember, the pill comes near the end. Wait to see how everything goes, then join us back here later. After you leave we'll go to Gatow to get the drone problem sorted.'

Jamal walked obediently towards the car, but already his plan was fixed in his mind.

Before they reached the main highway into Berlin he told the driver that he felt ill. 'It's my nerves, I suppose and I'm ashamed, but I'm about to throw up. Stop the car.' The driver immediately pulled off the road and hit the brakes.

Jamal made a hurried exit from the car and walked a little way into the grassy verge on the side of the road. There he pretended to dry retch many times before sinking gingerly down to the ground: he knew the vest would not explode until he activated the detonator, but he wasn't taking any chances. He lay quite still on the ground and waited as a predatory animal anticipates the appearance of his prey. He did not have to wait very long.

Inside the car the Jihadi glanced anxiously at his watch. He knew the timetable was tight and delay totally unacceptable. There would be questions asked later if events did not go according to the commander's plan.

He left the car and walked over to Jamal, who was still lying on the ground.

'Come on,' he said gruffly, yanking Jamal up by his arm, 'time to go, we must not be late. Our orders must be followed!'

At the moment that Jamal stood on his feet again he delivered what is sometimes known as a Glasgow kiss: a forceful, unexpected head-butt directly to the driver's forehead. He fell backwards, bleeding from the impact, and promptly passed out. *So far, so good,* Jamal thought, removing the man's phone.

He adjusted the driving seat and headed towards Berlin. When he felt that he had put enough distance between himself and the former driver he pulled into a lay-by and made a series of phone calls.

The first was to the British Embassy in Berlin. The second was to the Berlin *Polizei*. And the third was to Akram Momani in Paris. And in each phone call he had said almost the same thing.

'My name is Jamal Ahmadi, and I am a British citizen by birth. I was seduced into a Jihadi cell and programmed by chemical means to commit the murder of my uncle and his friends in the 10th arrondissement of Paris a few days ago.

'I have a suicide vest strapped to my body which I am meant to detonate on the steps of the Reichstag. I will not, repeat not, do this. But if I try to remove it myself it will detonate. I want to give myself up and I don't want to be shot while doing it.

'But there's something else: the demonstration of a new American drone at Gatow airport this afternoon must be cancelled because it is a trap. The Jihadi cell of which I was a part is attempting to divert the drone to a Jewish target in East Berlin, where the German Chancellor and some of her Cabinet will be attending an official function. The drone carries two missiles – need I say any more?

'What shall I do?'

The startled phone operator at the British Embassy pressed the panic button after hearing the first few words Jamal uttered and put his call on speaker phone.

'Give us your car details – make, colour, registration number – and drive *very slowly* into the compound. Stop immediately when challenged. Do you know location of the embassy?' Jamal said he did.

The panic button was also pressed at the HQ of the Berlin *Polizei* and members of the elite counter-terrorism squad were scrambled, sirens screaming, off to Gatow. An equally well-armed explosives squad was immediately despatched to the British Embassy.

For his part, Akram Momani did nothing other than sink to his knees and give thanks his Maker again and again for this miracle. Then he whispered 'Allah be with you, Jamal. Go in peace – Salaam and Shalom.'

The German terrorism squad found the still dazed Jihadi trudging his way back towards the Jihad headquarters near Gatow. He offered little resistance for two reasons: firstly he was physically unable, and secondly he realised that their campaign was lost. And then he decided to become co-operative – *über* co-operative in fact, in the hope of saving his own miserable skin. He directed the officers to the cell's HQ, and pointed out the stock of variously-coloured pills: yellow, green, red and black. He did not know what all of them were for, or what effect they had on the human brain, but the German forensic Lab would spend a very satisfying time determining that information.

Some of the drugs were actually Class A, run-of-the-mill drugs like ecstasy or ice, while others were more exotic, more dangerous such as Methylphenidate, a central nervous system stimulant, commonly sold as

Ritalin, and GHB, short for Gamma Hydroxybutyrate, a powerful central nervous system depressant, usually known as the date rape drug, and Khat, an amphetamine-like stimulant. All of these drugs had either been produced by Jihad members, or bought from other Jihadi groups and were used not only to serve their purposes, but to sell on the streets to raise money to fund their atrocities.

★

Later on that memorable day in Berlin, Chief Inspector Scott was summoned to the British Embassy to participate in the interrogation of Jamal Ahmadi: he insisted that Chief Inspector Maigret also be present.

'Why did the Jihad commander want your uncle and the other men killed?' Clive Scott asked early in the interview.

'Because they had set up the new peace organisation and increasing numbers of Muslims were joining it.'

'The *Hailemariam* group?'

'Yes. But how did you know about it?'

'Not all my friends are Christian,' Clive Scott replied, with a nod in Philippe's direction. 'I know *that Hailemariam* means the Power of Mary; the Blessed Virgin Mary, as we refer to her.'

'Yes. And the Blessed One's power brought success to our group and that's why my *infidel* associates decided they must die.'

At the use of the word *infidel* both chief inspectors

looked surprised: that word was more commonly used by Islamists to describe people of other faiths.

'Don't be amazed that I use such a pejorative word for the people with whom I have recently been connected. They are perverters of my faith, *no better than dogs*, and I curse them now before Allah.'

'Dogs don't send people out to commit beheadings or mass murder,' Clive Scott said firmly. 'You insult all animals when you link them with those low life parasites.'

'You're right, Chief Inspector. I apologise to those of the canine species. Now what else do you want to know about the *low life* parasites?'

After almost two hours' debriefing Chief Inspector Scott glanced at his watch. 'Time to call it a day now, gents – don't you think? Jamal needs food and a rest.'

'Where?' Philippe Maigret asked.

'Well here, under the embassy's roof, of course,' Clive replied.

'Not so fast, *mon ami*, Monsieur Ahmadi is wanted in Paris in connection with the… *unpleasantness* in the 10th. I have been instructed to offer him the comfort of my embassy's guest quarters until his extradition to France can be arranged.'

'Not possible, Chief Inspector Maigret. Mr Ahmadi is a British citizen and he will be kept on our embassy's sovereign soil until his… *repatriation* to the United Kingdom can be arranged,' the First Secretary of the British Embassy in Berlin said, choosing his words carefully.

'Now hang on a moment, chum,' Clive Scott said.

'I'm here to tell you that if you're planning to turn him over to MI5 or MI6 it will be over my dead body!'

'Watch what you're saying, Chief Inspector Scott,' the First Secretary warned, with a sideways glance at Philippe Maigret, 'I'm sure *satisfactory* arrangements can be made to accommodate all points of view.'

'Don't try to con me with diplomatic-speak my friend, because my natural radar could spot that from outer space! And don't even *think* of locking him up in Belmarsh because he wouldn't survive half a day before the butchers there got to him,' Clive Scott said, turning puce with anger.

Then he calmed down a little and asked, 'Still armed, Chief Inspector Maigret?'

'Yes.'

'Then let's get out of here, and Jamal goes with us – agreed!'

'If Chief Inspector Maigret even *displays* a weapon inside this embassy he will be violation of Article 22 of the Vienna Convention,' another embassy official said, reaching for the security button.

'Touch it and risk your hand,' Clive Scott warned noticing his action.

'Wait! Am I under arrest, or am I free to leave at any time?' Jamal asked.

The embassy officials looked to Clive Scott for guidance and he stared back without flinching.

'You are *not* under arrest Jamal. Agreed Chief Inspector Maigret?'

'Agreed, Chief Inspector Scott. In the eyes of the

French Republic this man is an important *witness, not a... criminal*. He has also, at considerable risk to himself, prevented a terrorist outrage of immense proportions today. He is a hero, and I expect that he will be the recipient of many honours from a grateful Germany in due course.'

And he will probably also have to spend the rest of his life looking over his shoulder, even if the British give him a new identity, as I expect they will, Philippe Maigret thought.

The embassy people went into a huddle for a few moments then left the room. When they returned ten minutes later, they were full of smiles and a false bonhomie which fooled no one.

'Members of our... er... *security service* are on their way to Berlin now with an interesting... proposal for Mr Ahmadi's consideration: future employment, at a suitably *indulgent* rate of remuneration. They ask that he remains within the embassy compound for the time-being. However, and I do stress this aspect of their communication, they accept that Mr Ahmadi is free to leave whenever he wishes,' the Second Secretary said.

'Well, well, well, Jamal old son, you appear to have landed on your feet,' Clive Scott chuckled. 'Want me to translate what you just heard?'

Jamal nodded, 'I'd be grateful if you would, Chief Inspector Scott. I think I've caught the gist of it but it all seems too far-fetched to be true.'

'Then let me explain the facts of life to you. MI5 or MI6 – probably MI6 – wishes to offer you a job with them at whatever price you stipulate, no questions asked. They know that we can't put you on trial – you have too much sensitive information to give evidence in an open court, and the French have the same problem. So name your price. And if, in the fullness of time, you'd like a knighthood you could probably have that thrown in too.'

'Is that all true?' Jamal asked, looking towards the First Secretary.

'Crudely put – *very crudely put in fact* – but yes, what Chief Inspector Scott said is correct.'

'And the French really won't put me on trial either?'

'*Non,* monsieur. France would not expect a mentally ill person to stand trial for what they had done, nor someone acting under duress – both of which altered states of mind I believe apply to you and your actions in Paris. And I will ask my Government to put that… *indemnity* in writing and deliver it to you before you choose to leave this embassy.'

★

While this interview was taking place in Berlin, Mighty Mouse, having been programmed by Owen Griffiths to fly low over the deepest, most solitary area of the North Sea, to the east of the Shetland Islands, safely discharged the missiles.

After that release the drone flew around the coast of Scotland in a westerly direction to land on Holy Island.

The gentle Buddhist community, which had been on high alert for hours, was enraptured by the sight of it. They thought it beautiful: a new exotic bird. They encircled the drone, chanting and singing while some scattered rose petals over it and others splashed it with water from the holy well.

The euphoric celebrations continued for a considerable time before they gently guided Mighty Mouse into their sequestered barn and surrounded it with sweet-smelling candles. And in that place of sanctuary they kept their vigil all through that first night rejoicing that a weapon of warfare was now under their roof and would therefore harm no one and destroy nothing.

★

When Quinn informed Megan that Tom Aitkens had been seriously injured while saving her husband's life, she insisted that he drive her to the Charité-Universitätsmedizin Hospital in Berlin where he'd been taken. And there she would stay for the next 48 hours, barely sleeping, hardly eating or drinking. And nothing Philippe Maigret could do or say would persuade her to budge, not even the arrival of Tom's children from the US.

'What can I do, *mon ami,*' he asked Georges Martin dejectedly. 'She says she can't – *won't* – return to Paris with me. She believes she should stay here until Aitkens is well enough to be transferred either to the American Hospital in Paris, or back to the States.'

'She needs time to adjust, Chief. The doctors have told her that he's unlikely to walk again and she thinks it's her fault.'

'How could it be?'

'She is convinced that it is only because of her... and their former... er association that Aitkens became embroiled in what happened at Gatow.'

'But it was his bloody drone! How could he not be involved?'

'I know, boss, but Madame is not thinking logically at present.'

'No, she's not. I *knew* he'd win. And he has.'

'He might *seem* to have gained some kind of... advantage because of his present circumstances, but if he has I'm sure it is only temporary.' Georges said quietly. 'You just need to be patient for a while, Chief. She loves you; we all *know* that she does. She'll come home soon. And besides, she's not likely to trust you with the feisty little tabby's care for too long – now is she?'

Philippe Maigret smiled. 'That's true, Georges. She might desert me but she'd never leave the cat! How did you become so wise, *mon ami?*' he said, patting him on the shoulder.

'It happened gradually, sir, over quite a long time, after I had the good fortune to acquire an excellent mentor – although I'm sure he'd say I still have a lot more to learn!'

★

When the international media heard the news of the near-disaster in Berlin, pandemonium ensued. Tom Aitkens and his partner, Owen Griffiths, were hailed as heroes. And Tom Aitkens narrowly escaped *veneration* for saving Chief Inspector Philippe Maigret's life at great personal cost.

'You know what this means, folks,' the CIA man at the US Embassy in Berlin said to his superiors in Washington. 'We're *screwed! Totally and utterly screwed.* Aitkens is now like Teflon – no matter how we might try to smear him nothing will stick. We really can't touch him or Griffiths either. He's now Teflon by association and he also has a wife battling cancer in a clinic in Geneva. We've had it folks; time to cut our losses and up sticks.'

But what about the drone, they asked. *We want it. Where is it?*

'God knows, could be anywhere; probably squirreled away in some third-world hell-hole.'

Aitkens is in breach of contract, get our lawyers on to it – and make it snappy!

'No can do. I told you, he's untouchable. If you klutzes want to sue a man who will probably never walk again and a hero as well, go right ahead. *But do it without me!* Hell, any day now I expect to read in the Berlin papers that before he was shot bloody Thomas Jefferson Aitkens could walk on water!'

★

David Quinn and his enigmatic friends melted quietly away from Berlin before they could be asked any awkward questions. He never did resume his position with GCHQ, the British Government's listening post in Cheltenham. Rumour has it that he's either writing a book, or planning to stand for parliament – or both.

Patrick Evremond flew back to London the next day, also without answering any difficult questions, although he went with Philippe Maigret's blessing. But Nat, fresh from hospital and fully recovered, stayed on in Berlin with his family for a few more days.

Early on the Saturday morning the three detectives also left Berlin travelling once again in the British Embassy's Jaguar with Georges Martin, in his element, driving all the way to Paris.

On his first night home, Philippe Maigret collected the feisty furry one from his mother's apartment on Avenue Foch, and walked her in the neighbourhood park. She seemed happy to see him; she purred occasionally and only scratched him once. When they returned to their Rive Gauche apartment Philippe was barely inside the door before the phone rang. It was Megan.

'I'll be home soon, darling,' she said. 'Tom's consultant believes a medivac flight to to Paris around the middle of next week, should be possible, and his children have asked me to accompany them.'

'And what then for us, my love?'

'What do you mean?'

'You *know* what I mean, Megan.'

'Not now, Philippe. We'll talk about *everything* when I'm home.'

'Our life together, Megan. Can it ever be the same as it was before Berlin?' he asked.

There was a significant pause on the other end of the line.

'Maybe not *quite* the same,' she said carefully.